THE DARKNESS BEYOND THE STARS

An Anthology of
Space Horror

Published in the United States by Salt Heart Press.
www.saltheartpress.com

All rights reserved. No part of this publication may be reproduced, distributed, or transmitted in any form or by any means, including photocopying, recording, or other electronic or mechanical methods, without the prior written permission of the author, except in the case of brief quotations embodied in critical reviews and certain other noncommercial uses permitted by copyright law.

Any references to historical events, real people, or real places are used fictitiously. Names, characters, and places are products of the author's imagination.

Front & back cover image by Stefan Koidl.
Book design by M. Halstead.
Formatting by M. Halstead.
Interior illustrations by P.L. McMillan.

First printing edition 2023.

979-8-9858713-7-1

Praise for The Darkness Beyond The Stars

"The old tagline claims that in space, no one can hear you scream. The stories here offer plenty of far-flung screams in a chorus of voices and cadences. Exploration, the future, the stars, the cold of the cosmos — these are all lonely concepts that are wide open to the power of horror, and this selection of familiar indie horror names and new favorites sets the coordinates of the genre to new frontiers."
★ *Michael Wehunt, author of* Greener Pastures *and* The Inconsolables

"The Darkness Beyond The Stars *forces us to confront the lull of the unknown, emphasizing both its dangers and allure—of wanting to know yet being afraid to know. The stories are at times claustrophobic and suffocating, yet they can also bring comfort through unease in the unfamiliar. The anthology holds tales of isolation that fester darkness within the mind and take you on journeys of which you are unsure if you might return—if you even desire return upon its conclusion."*
★ *Ai Jiang, Nebula finalist and author of* LINGHUN *and* I AM AI

"Horror stories set in space possess a special sense of claustrophobic dread and desperation—help is not on the way, or not soon. The Darkness Beyond The Stars *offers fifteen tales of horror—cosmic, botanical, body horror, and more—all set in the darkest reaches of the cosmos. You will be disturbed."*
★ *Christi Nogle, author of the Bram Stoker Award® winning first novel,* Beulah

Praise for The Darkness Beyond The Stars

"*The void beckons and these authors have answered forcefully, their volatile transmissions filtered through the cold unknown, burning right through the page before impact.*"
★ *Andrew F. Sullivan, author of* The Marigold *and* The Handyman Method

"*Eerie, thought-provoking, and dynamically sequenced, this anthology of space horror travels light-years ahead of its time. From investigations of the liminal to the limitless, from near-Earth orbit to far-flung exoplanets, these stories chart new courses in terror for those bold enough to go not only to the stars, but also beyond—where the edge of sanity lies.*"
★ *TJ Price, author of* The Disappearance of Tom Nero

"*Killer aliens, strange frequencies, and murderous space plants, oh my! This anthology is packed with unique, skin-crawly horror that'll make you yearn for solid ground and open air.* The Darkness Beyond The Stars *is a brilliant rendering of the lonely unknown waiting in the black vacuum outside our world. But it's also an exploration inward, toward the even colder, darker unknown waiting in all of our hearts. Don't miss it! It's out of this world (sorry not sorry).*"
★ *Sam Rebelein, author of* Edenville

CONTENTS

Foreword by David Wellington..11
Interstellar Transmission From [CLASSIFIED]..16
Space Walk by Bob Warlock..21
A Voice from the Dark by Lindsey Ragsdale..29
Red Rovers by Patrick Barb...37
Son of Demeter by Bryan Young..53
The Scream by Timothy Lanz..67
The Weight of Faith by Carson Winter...83
The Faceless by Ryan Marie Ketterer..95
Planted in the Soil of Another World by Dana Vickerson......................107
The Vela Remnant by David Worn..125
The Wreckage of Hestia by Jessica Peter...155
The Trocophore by Rachel Searcey..165
Locked Out by Joseph Andre Thomas..179
Tempest by Emma Louise Gill..197
Last Transmission from the FedComm Sargasso by Bridget D. Brave....215
Authors..228
Acknowledgements 233
Salt Heart Press..234

FOREWORD
The Non-Zero Chance

For writers of science fiction, the Fermi Paradox is the one question we can't stop asking. Our galaxy is immense, filled with billions of stars, potentially millions of planets where life may have developed. Life that might have evolved sentience, curiosity, the desire to communicate with other beings. After all, that's our story. It should have happened over and over again in the fourteen billion years since the Big Bang. So where are the aliens? Why, when we look outward, do we hear only silence? Why do we detect only dead worlds? Worse that dead worlds, actually, because dead suggests something lived there, once. We look out at the sky and we see: sterility. Worlds where life never had a chance. Choking skies. Dry deserts so cold they would freeze your bones. Unsolid worlds made of superhot poison gas.

Where are the others like us?

Why aren't they talking?

There are many suggested solutions to the Paradox. A lot of the stories in this volume wrestle with one possible answer or another, answers that resound in the imagination like the faces of evil gods: the Dark Forest, the Great Filter, the horrible secrets of Deep Time.

But all those answers are optimistic, compared to the possibility that keeps me awake at night, the one I call the Non-Zero Chance. They all assume that there are aliens out there, aliens we might one day communicate with, even if that's a bad idea. Even if that would mean the end of us.

The Non-Zero Chance is, to me, worse.

Given the enormous size of our galaxy, given the potential number of habitable worlds, it is nearly impossible, extraordinarily unlikely that, given enough chemicals and enough time, life would have emerged on just one single planet out of countless worlds.

Extraordinarily unlikely. Nearly impossible. But the equation doesn't actually rule out the negative result. Imagine it:

We are alone.

Of all the planets whirling through the great galactic gyre, all the bits of rock and dust in an unfathomably big volume of space, life, you and me and everyone we know, every animal you've ever seen in a petting zoo, all the tiny little transparent bits of goo writhing on your face right now, all that bio-diverse panoply only happened once. Right here. Four billion years ago a stray cosmic ray hit a phosphorous molecule in a way it shouldn't have, by complete accident, and it never happened again. Nowhere else.

We are alone.

Let this one sink in. The thing about horror is that it requires an open mind. Horror is the penalty—or, for some us, the reward—for chasing a thought too far. So if you want a good chill, really sit down and think about what the Non-Zero Chance means.

The galaxy, and all the galaxies beyond, reaching out into infinity, are empty. All of those planets are silent under empty skies. Out of all those craters dotting alien landscapes, not a single one has footprints crossing its dusty floor. No eye has ever opened blearily at the bottom of an icy sea and looked up to see the light of a red star. The voiceless winds blowing through all those alien canyons can't even be called haunted, can't be called spooky, because without life there are no ghosts.

Life only happened here. Nowhere else.

And life, as we know all too well, is finite.

Humanity won't last forever. The Earth only has a few billion years left, and the chance that we will find a way to colonize other stars before then is starting to seem like a longshot. There will come a time when the last organism on this planet draws its last breath and then…

In every direction, there will be nothing alive. Nothing moving under its own volition. The universe will once again be unseen. Unknown. Unremembered. Unmourned.

Scary enough to contemplate, but now, the kicker: there is a non-zero chance that what I just described is an accurate picture of the cosmos.

Just keep telling yourself it's extraordinarily unlikely.

Of course even if we were alone, we would still want to tell each other stories about bug-eyed monsters and little green men. Science fiction does not often trouble itself with empty skies. Thus the variety of tales in the present volume. There are aliens in this book—a lot of them! Rachel Searcey's "The Trocophore" gives us a new take on that most beloved classic, the tentacled murderbeast. Bridget D. Brave's "Last Transmission from the FedComm Sargasso" gives us something far weirder but very much alive, breathing and waiting just beyond the corner of your eye. The monster at the heart of David Worn's "The Vela Remnant" is… no. You know what? I'm not going to spoil that one, not one bit. Go read it for yourself. You won't regret it.

Other stories in this collection look at the Fermi Paradox from the opposite end of the telescope. What will it take for us to explore the galaxy, to find others like us? Some of them examine the interface between human life and the technology we will need to reach other stars. "Son of Demeter," Bryan Young's take on the generation ship, is downright horrifying in its implications. "Red Rovers", Patrick Barb's contribution, turns some of the cutest machines we've ever built into terrifying monsters.

My non-zero chance scares me, but it's not the only possibility that does. Which is a good thing for us writers. A future with people in it, aliens and humans distorted by technology beyond comprehension, just makes for better stories. Before you lies a wonderful assortment of futures that explore their own non-zero chances. Because if there is a question more deeply rooted in the genre than the Fermi Paradox, it is the much simpler, but even more evocative: What if…?

It is the duty of a writer to ask questions. To go *there*. To look at all the myriad possibilities that exist and not to flinch away from what you find. Like the scientists whose ideas we borrow, we would rather have answers than ignorance.

Even if the things we discover are uncomfortable. Dangerous. Terrifying. Because there is some part of us that loves the tingling dread, the way the hair stands up on the back of our necks when we realize the universe is bigger—and darker—than previously suspected. That's what this book is for, that deliciously awful feeling.

P.L. McMillan has put together a great assortment of frights for you. I hope you will enjoy the stories here collected, just as I have. And I hope, for your sake, for all of our sakes, that we are not alone.

But you never know.

—*David Wellington, author of* The Last Astronaut *and* Paradise-1

New York City, 2023

INTERSTELLAR TRANSMISSION FROM [CLASSIFIED]

[star static]

I can feel your eyes seeking, looking up, straining as you gaze hungrily at the stars, the planets, the voids between.

I share your passion. To fall into the infinite galaxies and the darkness. I feel its pull, the same delicious shiver as it makes you feel oh so small.

The possibilities are endless. What lurks on those unknown planets, what hides in the dead light of stars now burned to dust?

Are you like me? Wishing to drown in interstellar terror, yearn to behold things larger than yourself, of things beyond belief and imagination?

Space, where beyond the thin walls of your spaceship, of your space suit, lies death. Where every planet could hold pain.

[screechy whispers]

What could thrill more than to discover life elsewhere, even if hostile? It may be plant or animal or spectral being, or perhaps something else.

Something incomprehensible.

What of the dangers of travelling through the stars, of complications or sickness, of isolation or betrayal of friends?

The horrors are bountiful, they are beautiful and terrible in turn, and they will sate your desperate hunger for that next discovery.

For the darkness beyond the stars is decadent in its brutality.

[strange clicking and howls]

Strive for the darkness. Scream for the stars. They are gone and only echoes remain. The planets you will discover will fight you, lay you low. Your companions cannot be trusted.

Perhaps worst of all will be your own mind, your paranoia, your failing strength.

You won't be able to resist the pull. I know you're as curious as I am. Nothing will stop you from reaching out and searching.

[star static]

Take this, my offering to you. A gift, let's say. A promise.

A declaration of war, even, on your sense of well-being and safety in your place in this cold, unfeeling universe.

I hope you enjoy each story, I hope in them you hear those cosmic whispers and galaxial cries. Feel each author's howl of fear in the inked words, feast your eyes on the ominous visions. May every page pull you deeper, towards a literary event horizon.

Be seeing you soon.
Until then, look to the stars.

x P.L. McMillan

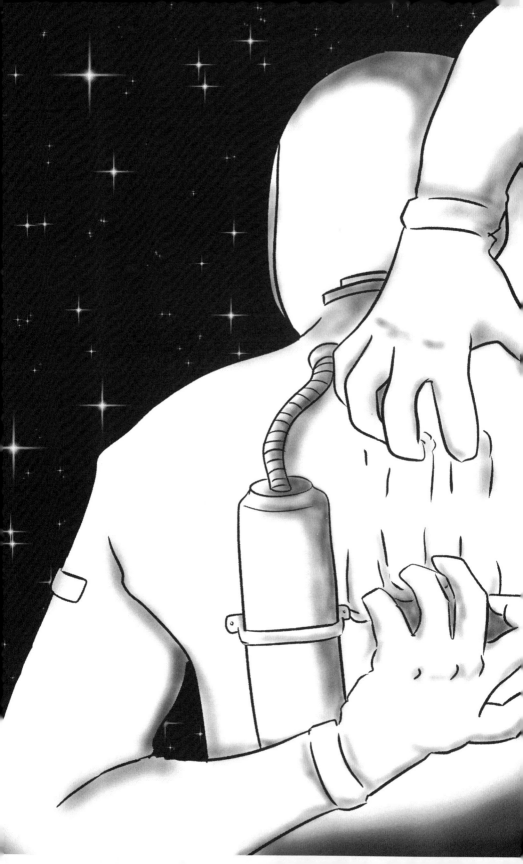

SPACE WALK

Bob Warlock

Everyone hates space walks.

That's not quite right. I should say, of the vanishingly small number of humans who have experienced extra-vehicular activity in space, almost all come to hate it. Most of us think we will be the exception—when old hands tell us about how frankly unpleasant it is, we all nod respectfully and secretly think 'yes, but *I'm* different.' We're adventurous types after all, we have to be. Only the cleverest, bravest, and most physically fit human specimens are ever offered the privilege of riding a hydrogen explosion out of Earth's clinging atmosphere.

I was one of the happy few, and I am not the exception.

The date is June 13th, 2025. A quarter-mile below the ISS, a satellite owned by the Chinese government has collided with one owned by an American billionaire. Both are sent spinning out of orbit and into the atmosphere; an expensive but largely harmless mistake for which both parties refuse culpability. Meanwhile, in higher orbit, a solar panel is damaged by a shard of debris as it hurtles past, and two solar cells need to be replaced. A simple job for any electrical engineer, and it's my shift in the rotation.

Here's something we don't tell wide-eyed schoolkids with dreams of flying through space. Putting on a space suit is a huge pain in the ass, second only to walking in one. Getting dressed starts with an adult diaper, followed by a cooling garment which looks like thick Lycra but is really 300 feet of water tubing in a synthetic matrix. Next is the pressure layer, and the oxygen layer, and the micro-meteor shield layer. On and on, until I'm safely encased in sixteen layers of clean, plastic-smelling extravehicular mobility unit. My own personal spaceship. And of course, *of course,* as soon as the life support system is strapped to my back and the door to the airlock closes, I realize I have an itch right between my shoulder blades, right under the backpack where I can't reach with my bulky padded gloves. There's no helping it now, and I push the sensation out of my awareness. Nguyen, coordinator for this EVA, gives me an 'OK' signal through the porthole and, when I respond, opens the airlock.

This is not my first spacewalk, but still when I step out of the airlock I make sure to keep my eyes anchored to the comfortingly ugly, man-made bulk of the station. Earth is an enormous blue beach ball behind me, and the other half of the sky cups me in a vast black fist. For a moment the awareness of being *in space* rises like nausea in my gullet, and I cling to the ladder, frozen. In just a few seconds the training kicks in, and I can bring my pulse to a more normal tempo. The terror is not *gone* exactly, just pushed to the side. A tiny, locked-out part of my mind is screaming at me that this is *insane*, but my body is an instrument of my will. I let the adrenaline buoy me up, not overwhelm me. I do not shiver. I can do the task before me, and I can ignore the environment.

"Mason confirmcommunicationover." Nguyen's voice in my earpiece, his words blurred together from habit.

"Confirmed. I'm outside. Suit function normal. Making my way to the panel now. Stand by for visual status update, over."

Each step on the surface of the station is a tortuously slow process. I take a step, place my foot, engage an electromagnet, release my other foot, take another step. I'm tethered, of course, and my suit is fitted with air canisters which I can use in an emergency to pilot my body back to the safety of the airlock. But the first line of safety is iron, itself forged in dying stars and flung across the galaxy. Step, engage, release, step.

By the time I reach the outstretched arm of the solar panel, I'm sweating. The suit does its job, cooling my skin with tubes of flowing water and wicking away moisture into aquifers. Except for that one spot right between my shoulder blades, which still prickles infuriatingly. I picture tiny beads of sweat pressed against the fine hair follicles and the instinct to scratch is almost overwhelming. I breathe through it.

"Nguyen, are you receiving? Over."

"Ten-four Mason, whatsyourstatus?"

"Visuals confirmed, surface shattering on modules 248 and 249. Definitely looks like collision damage. I'll need to check the electronics, but it doesn't look too bad. The cells should be ok." Nguyen knows this already, of course; he can see what's in front of me through the camera mounted on my helmet. But speaking aloud is comforting, makes me feel less alone.

I reach for the toolkit attached to my backpack and begin the painstaking process of replacing the tempered glass surface of the solar cells. It's not difficult, but it is slow. First, I detach the frame of module 248 and lift it away, clipping it to my belt to make sure it doesn't float away. Then I remove the cracked six-inch pane of glass and peer at the voltaic cells below. The steel microfibres laced through the glass have done their job and I breathe a sigh of relief.

"Good news Nguyen, no appearance of damage to the cells on 248. Commencing surface replacement, over."

"Glad to hear it Mason, we'll have you back on board in no time."

I place the cracked pane into a disposal baggie and remove a fresh pane from its sterile container, working with gentle, deliberate movements in my insulated gloves. Just as I lower the clean square of new glass into position, the itching prickle on my back *moves*. Barely an inch, straight up my spine. The animal instinct battering at my conscious mind rises from a whine to a shriek.

I freeze. The glass in my hands is strong and highly resistant to surface damage, but it can still be snapped by pressure at the edges. I struggle to keep my hands steady and gentle. Cold sweat stands out on my forehead.

"Whoa, Mason! What happened there? Your heart-rate's spiking."

"Nuh—nothing." I force myself to breathe. Slowly, in and out. I force a chuckle. "Thought I was gonna drop the new pane."

Nguyen laughs, "Good thing there's no gravity to worry about, huh?"

"Hah. Yeah."

The itching sensation is still there, but it is not moving. It must be a fault in the suit, maybe an exposed tube rubbing at my skin, possibly even trickling droplets of water. I take a deep breath. I can do this.

It happens again just as I'm unclipping the frame from my belt, and I twitch so violently that I almost fling the frame into space. I keep working, but my breath is coming faster now despite my effort to slow it. Place the frame, secure it, move onto the next module.

"Mason, you sure you're OK out there?"

I can't trust my voice, so I don't answer. All my energy is focused on two things: repairing the solar panel, and keeping my conscious mind from the thought that *there is something in the suit.*

At the moment I release the second frame from 249, the tickling moves to the nape of my neck, and I realize I've made a terrible mistake, because now it is *inside* the helmet. I barely manage to clip the frame to my belt before instinct takes over and I can't stop myself from reaching up, batting at the back of the helmet. It's useless of course, and I have the sudden mad impulse to release the helmet—just for a second—so that I can scrub my fingers through my hair, swat away whatever *thing* is slowly tickling its way up to the crown of my head. Instead I shake my head inside the helmet, trying to dislodge whatever it is against the padding that supports my neck. It has no effect but that the maddening tickle sharpens, turns into dots of pain on my scalp as sharp points (*pincers? claws?*) dig into the skin.

From far away I hear Nguyen, "Mason. Do you copy? Please respond. Over."

The flat military tone manages to pull a response from me.

"Receiving," comes out with a gasp. Is that my voice?

"Status report. Now."

"Something is…wrong. Over."

What else can I say? I want to scream that there is something in my helmet, something *living,* but that is simply not possible. I am in a sterile plastic boilersuit. No crawling, biting thing could have stowed away inside it and survived the journey to space, no spider or scorpion or…

It's moving again. I can feel each tiny digging claw now, pinpricks tracking over my scalp. My skin is alive with revulsion, waves of goosebumps making every hair stand on end.

"Mason, return to the airlock, now. Do you copy?"

Nguyen's voice is still clipped, but I can hear the urgency in it. Poor guy must think I've lost my mind, it's not as though he can see *inside* the helmet. I want to say no, tell him that I can finish the job, but the tracking claws are jabbing needles at my right temple, moving down towards my face. I don't even reattach the frame that I've clipped to my belt, I just turn and begin to walk. My whole body is consumed with the need to get back inside, to escape this suit. The animal hindbrain is *screaming* at me to run but I am locked into the slow march dictated by the suit. I realize that my lips are wet and I lick them, tasting sweat and iron. I am bleeding from tiny wounds at my hairline, and it is still such a long, long way back to the airlock.

Step. Engage. Release. Step. Each second lasts a thousand years and I am in an aeon-long battle against rising panic. In the next frozen moment, I reach the ladder to the airlock. I am sobbing, Nguyen's voice is barking something unintelligible through my earpiece. The stabbing claws reach my right cheek at the same time as I step onto the ladder, and I can't take it anymore. I shake my head like a maddened dog, mash my right cheek against the padded neck support, hoping to crush or dislodge or at least damage the crawling thing that is digging into my flesh. It responds to my panic in kind, skittering back and forth over my face. I feel it on my mouth and nostrils and I see *something* in the brief second before one of its jabbing claws tears into my right eye and I jerk backward, a single scream of pain filling the plastic dome before being swallowed by the vacuum of space. For an instant I am certain that I will keep flying backward forever, tumbling into the starless void.

The tether caught me, of course, but I was not conscious of it. What happened next is a dark blur to me, and I rely on what I have been told by Nguyen after the fact. Despite continuous attempts to communicate, he could get no response from me and assumed I had passed out or even had some kind of fit. He reeled me in and sent Volkov, the medic, to bring me into the airlock and issue whatever first-aid she could. When Volkov removed my helmet she found my face gouged with bloody scratches, my eye a swollen pulpy mess. A stoic and world-weary Ukrainian surgeon, she was less horrified than baffled, as she could find no obvious cause for my wounds. Whatever *thing* I had felt in the suit with me was gone.

A VOICE FROM THE DARK
Lindsey Ragsdale

A long time ago, the universe was actually expanding more slowly than it is today. So the expansion of the universe has not been slowing due to gravity, as everyone thought, it has been accelerating. No one expected this, no one knew how to explain it. But something was causing it.
—NASA and the Space Telescope Science Institute

0100 hours.

Whispering leaked through the bulkhead. It began the first night as a suggestion of a sound, almost as if the air circulation system was resetting itself. Nothing that aroused Lena's attention at first. It was only on the second and third nights that the sounds kept her awake in her sleeping sack anchored to the International Space Station's wall. It had begun as a monotonous, dull humming, but by the fourth night, the sound was broken up into sharp whispers, just low enough that Lena couldn't make out what they might be saying. She pressed one ear hard against the curved metal bulkhead, only the fractional inch of aluminum separating her from the frozen, endless depths of outer space.

Static, or background noise? No, definitely voices. A jumbled conversation, the chatter overlapping in a frenzied free-for-all. Lena concentrated and counted five separate murmuring voices, one sounding like garbled English, and the other four in languages she didn't quite recognize. She tried to separate the English from the rest, but the words were muffled, as if underwater.

The babbling carried on at the same volume and tempo until it shut off like a switch had been flipped. Lena checked the time: 0136. Thirty-six minutes of nonsense and lost sleep.

She raised her head from her sleeping sack to glance up and down the length of the living module. Reyes slept anchored to the starboard bulkhead directly across from Lena, jaw slack, small droplets of spittle floating around his head. Bates, also sound asleep, shifted in her sack nearby, throwing one arm over her head where it hung motionless in the lack of gravity. Light and sensors studded the cabin walls, glowing and blinking softly. The normal humming sounds of the ship's machinery carried on in the background, comforting in their familiarity.

Lena wondered if the others heard the voices too, or if she was alone.

Theorists still don't know what the correct explanation is, but they have given the solution a name. It is called dark energy.
— *NASA and the Space Telescope Science Institute*

Not a single astronaut aboard the shuttle reported any strange noises or hallucinations over breakfast. Reyes and Bates chatted amicably, and Lena sucked from her nutrient tube, listening with one ear to their conversation, mulling over the previous nights.

She considered saying something about the whispers to her coworkers. Each person filled a role in their motley maintenance crew: Reyes was the loudmouth comedian, Bates the intense conversationalist, and Lena the quiet thinker. Surely, if one of them had heard something odd, they would've spoken up without a second thought. The last thing Lena needed was to be sent down the gravity well for a mental evaluation. Not on her first tour of the ISS; she'd never get a second chance. Lena had passed her astronaut and maintenance training with flying colors, and she'd only been on tour two weeks. It was too soon to throw a wrench in the works.

"Are the air vents operating within normal parameters?" asked Lena, during a lull in the chatter. She wanted to rule out hypoxia-induced hallucinations. Every crewmember had their sleeping bags tethered near air vents to avoid CO_2 buildup around their heads, a real danger of sleeping in space.

Reyes turned to scan a panel and nodded. "All systems are green." His expression grew concerned as he gazed at Lena, perhaps sensing her unease. "You feeling okay, Johnson?"

"Oh, sure." Lena dismissed the other astronaut's concerns with a wave of her hand. "Just had a weird dream. I feel fine."

"Speaking of systems," said Bates, "we might want to run a visual hull check. I'm getting some weird feedback from the port side. Probably just radiation or a stray micrometeoroid, too small to do anything, but you can't be too careful."

"Sure thing," said Reyes, disposing of his breakfast tube. "Johnson, can you add that to the top of your duty list?"

"Yes," whispered Lena, a chill running down her spine.

Her sleeping bag was tethered against that same port hull.

It turns out that roughly 68% of the universe is dark energy. Dark matter makes up about 27%. The rest - everything on Earth, everything ever observed with all of our instruments, all normal matter - adds up to less than 5% of the universe.
— NASA and the Space Telescope Science Institute

Six nights now the voices continued their chatter. Always at 0100, lasting between thirty and forty minutes. Lena couldn't stop herself from listening to them, pressing her ear as hard as she could against the cabin wall. Was it her imagination, or did the pitch of the voices rise slightly on the sixth night?

Every shift Lena began with checking the external sensors and video feeds to see if there was any presence lurking on the port bulkhead. Her hull check from days earlier had returned inconclusive results, but still within normal system parameters. Lena's imagination conjured up an alien form pressing its lips to the cold metal, trying to communicate with her, the two of them hurtling around Earth at seventeen thousand miles per hour. Lena comfortably ensconced inside the temperature-controlled, brightly lit cabin, her alien communique clinging to the frozen metal as the stars hurtled silently past. Was it asking for help? For guidance?

None of her crewmates seemed affected by the whispers. They went along their duties, making small talk, cracking jokes, telling stories. If Lena was more reserved than normal, no one commented; she'd always been the quiet one, the observant crew member who preferred listening to speaking. Input to output.

Perhaps that's why the whispers had targeted her– they knew she'd be the best listener of the bunch.

Another explanation for dark energy is that it is a new kind of dynamical energy fluid or field, something that fills all of space but something whose effect on the expansion of the universe is the opposite of that of matter and normal energy. But…we still don't know what it is like, what it interacts with, or why it exists. So the mystery continues.
— *NASA and the Space Telescope Science Institute*

Day seven presented an extravehicular activity, or EVA, opportunity. One of the video feeds off the bow had malfunctioned and sent back crackly snowy static rather than a clear visual. "I'll fix it," Lena spoke up, surprising her peers. Bates nodded and said, "I'll be your partner."

The women suited up in the small airlock, connecting boots to pants, helmets to shoulders, and, above all, their tethers to each other. "Ready to cycle," Bates' voice crackled through the radio, tinny in Lena's helmet. The airlock light shifted from green, to amber, to red. With a muffled clanking, the outer hatch opened, and they were through, floating in the void. Earth hung below them, a breathtaking blue and green jewel against a dark backdrop.

Lena took a deep breath to calm the inevitable vertigo that came with pitching oneself into the dark chasm of space. She concentrated on the hull, keeping one hand pressed there to steady herself. Bit by bit, she and Bates crept down the starboard side, clamping their tethers in turns onto the metal handholds that studded the hull. They reached the defective camera and Bates passed tools to Lena from a pouch on her spacesuit. It was a simple repair job. Lena checked in with the cockpit. "How's your feed now?"

"Crystal clear. Thanks, Johnson. Return to the airlock."

This was her moment. Lena paused. "Um, I wanted to check something out on the port side, if that's possible."

Silence for a beat, then Bates' voice. "That wasn't in the EVA plan. What's up?"

"I suspect there's an anomaly on the hull." Lena licked her dry lips. "It'll just take a moment."

"Well…" It was Reyes on the comm, who tended to be a little looser with guidelines than the others. "Bates, are you okay with that?"

"I guess." Bates didn't sound happy. "It should've been figured into the plan."

"Next time," Lena said, closing her eyes in relief. "Sorry about that."

She waited until Bates had secured the last tool, then pointed in the direction she wanted to go. The women leap-frogged over to the port side hull in a matter of minutes. Lena cast her eyes along the pitted metal surface. She placed a gloved palm against the hull and the voice surged into her head. Just one this time, in English, crystal clear. And it was actually making sense, but the words caused her pulse to race.

Lena, come to us. Lena, join us. Don't be frightened.

"Do you hear that?" The words tumbled out of Lena's mouth before she could stop them.

"What?" Bates said.

"A voice," stammered Lena. "Calling to me." She felt a wave of calm comfort envelop her, right through her bulky suit, the last thing she thought she'd feel in the cold vacuum of space. Lena was overcome with the desire to float away, cradled and comforted by the voice that had finally figured out how to communicate. She'd never felt anything like it before, priding herself on being so level-headed, normal, and boring; ideal qualities for working in the danger of orbit. It was an otherworldly, intoxicating rush that filled Lena with an impulsive yearning to go wherever the voice told her to. Wherever those voices had come from, whatever they were, they'd broken through the barrier, at last.

"No…" Bates said slowly. Her voice in Lena's helmet was drowned out by the chorus calling Lena's name. "Johnson, I'm terminating this EVA. Back to the airlock, stat." Urgency took over her tone. "Reyes, prepare the airlock for immediate cycling. Something weird's going on out here."

Bates turned back the way they'd come. Lena stayed motionless, both palms pressed against the hull. "Johnson, that's an order!"

"No," said Lena.

Quick as a flash she reached down and unclipped the tether that connected her to Bates. Bates lunged for Lena's arm, but Lena pushed against the ship and floated backwards out of reach, while severing the second tether that anchored her to the hull. She began to drift up and away from the ship into the inky void.

"Stop!" Bates lunged for Lena, but Lena kicked with her feet, picking up speed as she floated away. All she heard was the voice in her helmet, luring her like a siren into the dark reaches of the unknown.

Bates clung to the hull and watched Lena's suited figure drift further and further out, screaming over the comms to Reyes, who watched helplessly over the cameras, lost for words. Once Lena was a dozen meters away from the ISS, gyrating slowly against the velvet, spangled backdrop of space, her body spasmed in place as the dark enveloped her like an ominous black shroud. She twisted into nothingness, undulating and folding into the depths around her, and was gone. Nothing of Lena remained.

The curious dark had reached out and claimed what it sought.

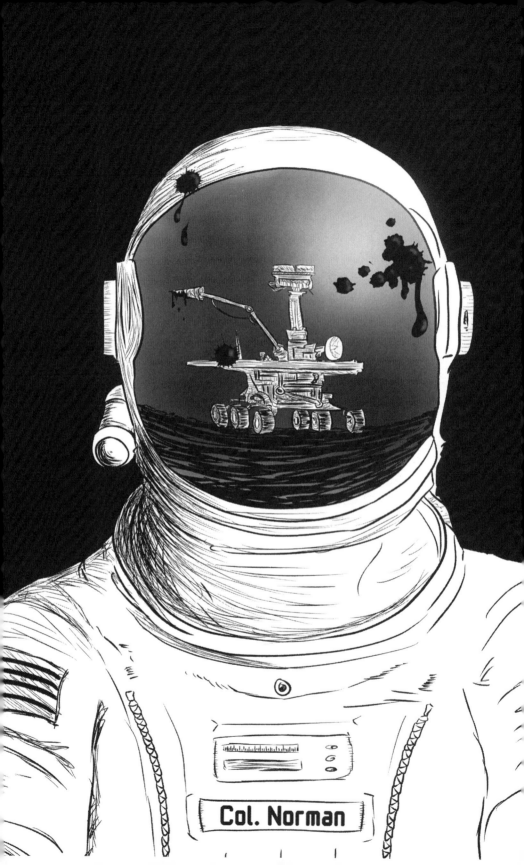

RED ROVERS
Patrick Barb

Children. They sent me to Mars with their children.

With oxygen running low and the sealant she'd smeared across the jagged tears in her spacesuit already disintegrating, Miranda hid behind a blast-damaged column in the underground Martian bunker. In a few moments, she'd die. Like all the others.

The whirring whine of the drill against the door made Miranda's teeth ache. Her helmet—covered in blood, dried and thick like licorice pieces—prevented her from seeing well. Her gloves proved no better than woolen winter mittens when it came to dislodging the gunk from her face mask.

The crash of metal echoed through the tunnels. The rumbling approach of wheels driving over thick layers of radiation-proof tunnel flooring followed.

Miranda had spent too much time thinking about children. And in her final moments, she recalled an old children's playground song. One she never got to share with *her* daughter.

"Red Rover, Red Rover, send Miranda on over…"

Of course, Devon Sachs claimed to know the best way to the bunker. "I don't need your silly holomaps," he insisted.

Colonel Miranda Norman didn't want to fight with the primary investor in the Mars mission, so she took the front passenger seat in their All-Terrain Transport Vehicle. She left as much space between her and the handsy trillionaire as possible. Trying her damnedest not to grind her teeth, she gripped the rumble bar next to her seat and held on as the vehicle took hard bounces along the dry, rocky ground.

Miranda hated being planetside. Whether on Earth or Mars, she felt lost when she abandoned the expansiveness of space.

Orange and brown rocks sprayed behind the back wheels, as Sachs cut figure eights like a stunt car driver. Then, he punched his foot down on the pedal when they went up and over a hill. The vehicle's wheels lifted off the ground. The transport soared higher than it would have done performing the same jump back on Earth.

Miranda closed her eyes, enjoying the temporary feeling of lift-off.

"Hey, watch it, Devon!"

From the back of the transport, Ariyah, one of the four young elites whose parents' investments in the Mars colonization push had secured them a seat on the first manned mission, screeched her discontent. Seconds later, the front wheels returned to the ground. Miranda snapped back to reality in time to avoid biting through her lip.

"What's the matter, Ariyah? Don't like how Daddy hot-rods?" Sachs asked in his non-ironic Eurotrash accent.

The cringe factor of Sachs's attempts at flirtation increased as the expedition proceeded. Miranda shuddered, thinking about how much of a creep she'd learned Great and Grand Devon Sachs could be while on the 140 million mile trip to the Red Planet.

Pathetic, too.

"Please pay attention to where we're going, Mr. Sachs."

Despite her disgust, Miranda couldn't escape the reality Devon Sachs was still a *trillionaire*. As such, she understood what being in his favor might yield.

He didn't slow down.

Then, a rolling mystery object's metallic plating appeared as a sudden glimmer, reflecting off Miranda's face shield, blinding her temporarily.

She didn't know what was coming. She only knew it was moving fast. Faster even than they were.

"Stop!"

Questions raced through her head.

Where'd it come from? Behind us? In front? To the side? Where'd it go?

Sachs must've seen whatever-the-hell it was too, and, like Miranda, had no idea where it went. The steering wheel jerked from side to side in his trembling hands. His grav-boots tap-danced under the steering column. Reaching for…reaching for…

His foot smashed down hard on the brake. Miranda gripped the rumble bar so tight she worried she'd crush it. Her helmet receiver roared with the static of everyone's screams.

The shouting stopped, punctuated by the gasp of the brake's pneumatics. Miranda looked to her left and watched Sachs's spacesuit-covered ass come off the driver's seat. His body thrust forward to resemble a question mark.

The transport rocked from side to side. Dust clouds spun into miniature cyclones. Poison air, poison dust swirling all around them.

"I've got you," Miranda said, grabbing Sachs by his pack and pulling him back onto the seat.

She looked at his feet under the steering column. He'd compressed the brakes, and they rested on level ground.

So, why can I still hear wheels turning, grinding against the rocks?

A shadow fell across the front of the transport, blanketing Sachs and Miranda in a velvet shade. Seconds later, the Rover rolled down off a slight ridge on the inclined path ahead. Moving past his near brush with death, Sachs appeared comforted by the Rover's arrival. With a press of a button on the dash, he shut down the transport. Sliding from his seat, he bounced slightly as his grav-boots touched the rust-colored ground. "Wowie, a real-life Rover!"

Before Miranda got a "Wait!" out, the would-be Prince of Mars closed the gap between transport and Rover. The roaming machine extended a camera down from its topmost point, moving its metal appendage with what looked like insectoid, alien curiosity. Another mechanical arm with a secondary camera on the end stretched from the Rover's side. The camera's lens narrowed as the Rover zoomed in on their transport. Miranda hated the feeling of being watched, of being judged.

One more camera "head" and we'll have robotic Cerberus on our hands.

"Yo, Astronaut Lady, should we get out too or—"

"Stay in the transport."

Her words came at a clipped cadence, a speech pattern retained from her days in Space Force. They shut the speaker, whichever teen from the back of the transport it was, up.

Meanwhile, Sachs placed his hands on the Rover's shielding, solar sails, wheels. Like he needed to ensure the machine was real and not some Martian mirage. Miranda watched from a distance, unsure about what to do next. When faced with any unexpected development—a Mars Rover appearing where no Mars Rover should be, getting saddled with a space crew with little experience who didn't give a damn about any "mission," a dead child meant to live and wait for her back on Earth, any of those things—Miranda shut it all out and turned to data, statistics, and cold hard facts.

NASA announced the last Rover's decommissioning nearly ten years ago.

"Mr. Sachs, please step away from the…Rover. It isn't a part of our mission param…"

"Screw off to parameters I say. Look at this!" Sachs caressed the Rover.

That's strange though. How's it in such good shape? Not a dent or scratch, not a nick. Nothing. Even if it'd lasted this long, wouldn't it show some wear and tear?

Miranda slid out of the transport and onto the planet's surface. She kept her eyes on Sachs and the Rover.

Then, a second glimmer caught her eye. The smooth metal of the Rover facing Sachs appeared to ripple. Concentric circles grew wider and wider across the plating, like the Rover peeled back its "skin" to show Miranda its beating heart.

At this glimpse of the impossible, salty tears fell from her eyes. The immediate hum of her suit's internal regulators converting the water and storing it for later distracted Miranda. She missed the emergence of the Rover's third arm—the one with the diamond-tipped drill bit at the end.

The drill whined and its head spun. The high-pitched sounds reminded Miranda of a dog in heat, desperate, but unsure of what it needed to satisfy a sudden urge with the potential to become an all-encompassing concern.

"Hey you guys, check it out…this Rover, it's moving, changing. Ms. Miranda, you never told us NASA employed nanotech in the old Rover program," Sachs said.

"They didn't."

"What?"

The Rover shoved Sachs down and the whooshing sound of his breath knocked from his body echoed inside everyone else's helmets.

"Oh…she wants to play."

Sachs didn't sound so confident though.

"Sir. Stand up. Step away from the Rover and back up. Come toward us and the transport."

As she spoke, Miranda moved in front of the vehicle. She kept watching the Rover as it towered over her trillionaire employer. She backed into the driver's seat, still watching. "Come on, Mr. Sachs, you've got this," she said, like a parent coaching a toddler, encouraging them to take their first circus-clown steps.

Sachs said, "Yeah, okay, sure. Let me—"

Whatever he meant to say next got drowned out by the cresting whine of the Rover's diamond-tipped drill. Designed for coring out rock samples from the mountains of Mars, the drill pressed down against Sachs's faceplate instead. Down, down, down. Harder and harder.

"Um, is someone going to help me?" It wasn't even a cry for help. Sachs had gone so long having everything just work out in his favor, that he didn't even recognize that he'd reached a moment when he should scream.

By the time he did, it was too late.

Everyone in the expedition wore state-of-the-art spacesuits. "Unbreakable, impenetrable." Claims begging to be proven wrong.

The whine and howl of the unrelenting drill reached a point where Miranda considered taking off her helmet and shoving gloved fingers into her ears.

Then, something popped.

A loud shriek followed, like a radio turned up full-blast. Everyone's comms shorted out. Then, the drill broke through Sachs's reinforced face shield. The curved grooves of the drill-bit went around and around and around, grinding polymer-blend plastic and glass down into Sachs's face. Shattering his paid-for-perfect, white-capped teeth. Pureeing the fat pink slug of his tongue. Blood droplets fell upward into the sky. The hellish atmosphere of the red planet did the rest of the work, producing a cloud of blood steam to envelope the gory tableau, hiding the worst of it from sight.

Once the initial shock of the Rover's attack passed, Miranda offered a quick thanks to whatever higher power reigned on Mars for wrecking her comms and causing her to miss out on hearing what a trillionaire tech wunderkind sounded like as he died bloody-faced and helpless.

She looked away from the blood cloud and turned to the distraught, panicked faces searching for answers at the back of the transport. *Children.* Still strapped into the bench seats, the four remaining civilians seemed to move their mouths together, as one. Miranda knew how to read lips so she made out a few words in piecemeal fashion: "Die…help…what…God…"

Like she expected.

Someone screamed. No words, only a silent pantomimed primal exclamation, reminding Miranda of old terrors she believed were left behind on her home planet.

Didn't I see enough of what someone making those screams looks like, while staring into the mirrors of those children's hospital bathrooms back on Earth?

She signaled for the others to stay seated and buckled in. She motioned for them to hold onto something. *Hold on and don't let go.* She didn't have time to wait and see if they'd understood. Even as the Rover's drill continued pinning Sachs to the ground like a butterfly on display, two new shadows, tall towering forms with spider-like attachments already out, appeared on either side of the transport.

Miranda switched the vehicle back on and activated its nav-system—the one Sachs refused to use. She threw the vehicle into reverse.

Back up. Back up. Back up.

A blinking orange beacon on the dash showed her target: the machine-built, reinforced, climatized bunker.

First things first, Miranda needed to get clear of the two *new* Rovers fast approaching, threatening a pincer move on the transport.

The rest came from instinct and adrenaline.

During mission prep on Earth, Miranda and her passengers received reams of background material downloaded direct to their holophones, covering the entire known history of humanity's interactions with the red planet. Miranda believed it a safe bet that she and the ex-cosmonaut Alexei, who waited back on the ship stationed several miles from their position, monitoring the planet and the ship's exterior via drone, were the only ones who had actually reviewed the material. Even then, she had doubts about the Russian. He struck her as the type to focus on his role in a mission and nothing past it. Despite their shared experiences in space travel, he possessed what she considered an *Earthman's* point-of-view. Head down, focused on what was in front of him. Even he hadn't seemed appreciative enough of the stars above and all around them.

Chased by defunct mobile robotic units, moving at greater speeds than she'd witnessed in grainy videos from the past, Miranda kept one eye on the orange blip telling her where to go, while at the same time focusing on what she steered the vehicle through. She reached back periodically to offer "reassuring" pats of the air.

The Rovers' tank treads ground Martian rocks into Martian dust. Mechanical arms designed to capture geologic samples or manipulate scientific equipment instead stretched out and groped across the ever-shrinking space between the robots and the transport.

On the nav-screen, the beacon shifted to the side, moving out of line with the transport's progress. Miranda cranked the steering wheel hard to the left, trying to compensate and remain on target. All she heard was her own breathing. Her head throbbed with pain. Something twitched behind her eyes.

Then, a Rover's mechanical claw slapped down onto the roof of the transport, rending plastic and metal apart like tissue paper. It extended its reach beyond what engineering should have allowed. Hell, what *physics* should have allowed. Its tin-man arm stretched and flopped—an obscene protuberance.

Like a snake.

The beacon grew larger and larger, matching the transport's increasing proximity to their destination. Miranda whipped the steering wheel back and forth, side-to-side, trying to shake loose the grasping, desperate mechanical claw. Then, she felt another hand—a human hand—on her shoulder, and it all became too much for the calm-under-pressure space veteran.

When Miranda looked behind her, her face shield collided with the helmet of one of the rich kids. They'd disobeyed her order to stay seated.

Jazon. Their name's Jazon.

"Get back d—"

But she didn't get to finish her warning and they wouldn't have heard it anyway. Reflected in her face shield, Jazon's eyes widened. Miranda turned forward in time to see the bunker entrance. Light panels made it shine, a refuge in the crimson sands.

She missed the jagged-edged obstruction sticking out from the ground though.

Everyone felt it when one of the transport's front wheels rolled across the scrap metal. The sharp exhalation of air from the punctured tire sounded like defeat. Then, Miranda experienced lift-off again. She held on tight to the wheel, feeling the layers of her spacesuit pressing against her, squeezing her. Up, up, then over, and…black.

But not for long. A small voice she'd ignored for a long time screamed inside her head.

Get up! Get up! They're not going to help you.

She pressed her thumb against the release button of her safety belt and dropped onto the roof of the flipped-over transport. Extra weight pressed down on the back of her neck. Miranda shrugged her shoulders, trying to get free from whatever held her down. The new spacesuits offered more flexibility than the bulky white monstrosities displayed in museums from the shuttle program days, but she still fought to get her arms behind her and push.

Red lights and various panicked read-outs flashed across her suit's monitors. One warned her blood pressure was too high.

No shit. At least I don't have it as bad as Jazon.

They were literal dead weight on her back. Their domed helmet sat shoved down to their stomach, their neck and back broken. Shuffling away from the corpse, Miranda heard rustling at the back of the transport. The other survivors followed her lead and unbuckled themselves.

Miranda watched them gather. Not a single one looked to the front of the transport. It turned out the voice in her head was correct, they weren't going to help her.

But it doesn't mean I'll let myself get away with not helping them…

Mars's lower gravity meant Miranda covered ground more quickly than on Earth. One step, one leap, and she found herself among her charges. Three domed heads turned in unison. The glare from the bunker's lights stopped Miranda from seeing their faces.

She gestured toward the bunker, then signaled for everyone to get low. The terrain from the crash site to the bunker appeared level. They could get there fast, but they'd be exposed, vulnerable to further attacks from the Rovers.

Pattie grabbed the front of Miranda's spacesuit, catching the astronaut by surprise. Miranda couldn't hear anything the girl said, and the red dust streaked across their helmets made lip-reading all but impossible. However, given the girl's emphatic pointing to the transport, Miranda suspected she was upset about Jazon.

But there wasn't time for mourning or panic. Miranda took hold of Pattie's hands, squeezing them hard enough to make her point stick. Then, shaking her head from side to side, she pointed to the bunker once again. The other two got the message. Ariyah and Brynden started a cautious crabwalk-shuffle across the open terrain.

Hearing the rumble of Rover treads, Miranda let go of Pattie and moved to follow the others. Before going too far, she scooped up a handful of loose Mars rocks. For lack of a better weapon, Miranda opted to settle for rock-flinging if needed.

The bunker entrance was dead ahead. It looked like an obscenity amid the otherwise untouched planet surface. Miranda took the security of obscenity any day.

"Mom…"

The word, uttered behind her, stopped Miranda in her tracks. It was impossibly familiar. She flashed on images of cold cheeks and bloated, swollen purple lips. A small mouth whispered, already dead before the syllable finished.

Pattie'd taken her helmet off. Stumbling forward, the girl mumbled for *her* mother. "Mommy, Mommy…" She made broken baby-doll sounds, like someone had held their hand down over a toy's voice-box, muffling its one recorded message.

Pattie's skin changed from its trendy dyed silver sheen to a cherry red. Fire engine red. Red like Mars, the way humans imagined it. Blood boiled under her skin.

But she kept walking.

Miranda knew she couldn't help. Given the exposure time, Pattie was dead already. Her eyes bulged from the sockets. Steam rose off the whites of those eyes. Then, a red beam, visible to the naked eye, hurtled toward her exposed head.

The Rover's laser obliterated Pattie's skull, producing an organic fireworks display with chunks of red, white, and goo tossed into the Martian sky. Miranda watched the three Rovers emerge from behind a dune. They resumed their slow, steady, but inevitable progress toward Miranda and the other survivors.

More laser blasts followed in a staccato pattern, blowing up the rocks near Miranda's feet. She didn't know how fast the altered, aggressive Rovers moved. No idea how much time she had before they'd catch up to her. She threw out any notion of crawling or taking cover. She ran.

And she didn't look back.

"We're going to die."

Ariyah hadn't asked a question, but Miranda chose to answer all the same. "Probably."

Her response stunned the girl into momentary silence. Miranda looked to the other survivor sitting up against one wall of the bunker's airlock hub.

Brynden's helmet was off, as were Miranda's and Ariyah's. He leaned too close in the direction of the outer door—the entrance to the bunker they'd barely made it through and managed to shut before the Rovers got them. A black singe mark from a laser blast across her suit's left shoulder provided all the evidence Miranda needed of how close they'd come.

"Get away from that door!"

All it took was one shouted command, and the boy (*No, not a boy. Not a man either. He's trapped in a boy-like existence his parents chose for him because they believed it preferable to him ever having to try...*) slunk away from the door. Miranda almost felt sorry for him. And for Ariyah, who remained still, following her encounter with frank, tired-of-the-bullshit Miranda, only to wrap her arms around her belly and rock in place.

Miranda took a deep breath, letting the recycled air fill her lungs. "Listen, those things out there, they—"

"What are they? Are those *ours*? Are those *our* space robots?" Ariyah fired off a litany of questions like they'd provide extra protection.

Miranda shook her head, waiting to speak.

"Yes. No. I'm not sure. I think they started as ours. But they've *changed*. Like something modified them. Or infected them. I'm—this isn't my area of..."

Brynden's eyes widened with sudden understanding

"Nanobots. Nanotechnology?" he offered, helping Miranda find the words that eluded her.

"Yeah. Like Devon said."

She left out: "before they killed him."

A sudden squawk from the bunker's communications hub on the other side of the room made Miranda and her charges nearly jump out of their skins and spacesuits.

"Colonel Miranda?"

The speaker's heavy Eastern European pronunciation of the "dah" at the end of her name brought a whoop from Miranda's lips. She crossed the room and jammed down the mic button on the control panel.

"Alexei?!"

"Da."

"Thank God, Alexei. We've...something's gone wrong here. I'm not 100%, but we suspect something's taken over the old NASA Rovers and...and—"

Above Miranda, a holoscreen flickered to life, displaying a pair of live-camera feeds. On one: their rocket's exterior, as filmed by Alexei's drone. On the other: a close-up from the capsule's interior, a tight focus on Alexei's face. He grinned. "It's okay, Miranda. It's okay. Devon came back and told me everything."

Miranda fought back the sudden urge to vomit. From behind her, Ariyah's low moan of dread provided the perfect soundtrack to their rapid descent into a mind-shattering hell.

Alexei's smile grew wider, wider, wider still. Wrinkled flesh split apart, revealing wires, cables—silver, black, yellow, and red—gushing out like blood vessels stripped from a cadaver. The droning hum of the wires reminded Miranda of wasps, undercut by the roar of static. The remains of Alexei's face (or what the nanobots fashioned themselves into *resembling* his face) hung loose like a discarded Halloween fright mask. One of the Rover's cameras blinked out white flashes. Another mechanical arm came onto the screen with Devon's bloody head attached.

A mockery of a human voice—sounding at once like the deceased Alexei, Devon, Pattie, and Jazon, but also nothing like them at all—spoke to Miranda and the others.

"More."

A single word. A demand, a threat, a promise. An intergalactic statement of purpose.

Miranda checked the exterior feed. Nothing better waited for her there. Thick-cabled metallic legs sprouted from the base of the rocket. The nano-infected ship flopped onto its side, sending rust-colored dust into the poisoned air. After flexing its new limbs, the behemoth scurried across the Martian landscape, like a giant cockroach. Miranda knew the power contained within the rocket. Enough to take them from Earth to Mars and back again. And now it was under the control of whatever nanobots had possessed the Rovers.

It headed for the survivors—headed for "more."

Ariyah tugged on her arm. A whispered question passed from the girl's trembling lips. "Where are the machines that built the bunker? Where'd *they* go?"

Before Miranda answered, the sound of stumbling feet behind them made them both turn. His eyes glazed, Brynden stomped forward with a drunk's flat-footed momentum. "They're inside—"

A buzzsaw-like blade attachment at the end of a construction bot whirred upward from the bunker floor, splitting Brynden's chest and cracking his ribs. The blade's rotating teeth split his chin apart and then his tongue, but not before he finished his sentence with a wheezing gasp.

"—me!"

Brynden's hollowed-out corpse hit the ground. Ariyah's screams echoed off the bunker walls like a hurricane siren. Tank treads made a rumbling approach from one of the "secure" tunnels underneath Mars. A million ideas about what step she should take next raced through Miranda's head.

She wanted to grab the screaming girl, tell her it'd be okay (even if it wasn't the truth), and remind her to put her helmet back on. After all, they couldn't be sure if the new nanobot-corrupted machine and its advancing companions had entered the bunker through a breach, or if they'd been waiting inside all that time.

But before she could do anything, Ariyah pressed the emergency button and opened the outer doors, exposing them to the red planet's atmosphere.

Miranda didn't wait around to see what happened next with Ariyah. She had her own problems.

Having split Brynden apart, the nano-controlled bot set its sights on her. It swung its blade attachment in menacing arcs, high and low. Twisting and turning to avoid the razor-sharp edges, Miranda secured her helmet and ran for the tunnels. Right before she crossed the first threshold, a saw blade almost bit through one of the tubes on her pack. The pack remained intact, but Miranda felt a cold sting as the blade's teeth bit into her spacesuit. The sharp metal drove the material of the suit against her skin.

Ariyah's hoarse screams were a tiny wave lapping at the shore compared to the tsunami of noise that followed. The sound of an explosion—the nano-"possessed" rocket ship arriving as Miranda expected—came next. Everything was out of order. Miranda leaped out of the way of the incoming wall of neon-green chemical flames.

She'd made a lucky one-in-a-million throw and connected by a million-to-one chance. Her body hit a door that slid open on contact. Miranda tumbled in, relatively untouched by the flames. She crawled over and hit a button, slamming the door shut behind her. Panting, catching up with her few remaining breaths, Miranda wondered what the alien nanobots would strip-mine from the gray dust remains of Brynden and Ariyah. She imagined ash and subatomic nanites swirling, swirling around the command center. Tangled up and mingled into something new. Something *more*.

Miranda waited for her turn.

Miranda took her helmet off. She didn't know if the automated processes intended to repair any breaches and re-purify the air in the bunker worked or not.

Her unease grew as she watched the Rover's drill core a hole through the door. She considered how they'd taken off their helmets in the bunker. *They—those machines—they could've already been inside with us. Probably already inside with us. So small, we'd never see them. So small, we'd breathe them in.*

The metallic ache in her mouth came from somewhere. A feeling like a million dentist's picks scratching at her fillings. Miranda wondered how many of the alien machines existed in her tears.

The red light of a laser sight covered her forehead. A perfect red jewel. Miranda stood up, steadying herself on the column she'd used as cover. "Please."

The Rover advanced.

"Please."

The Rover stopped. Its camera tilted so it looked more like an actual canine. Miranda set aside the fanciful notion and prepared to make her last request.

The words came in a flood.

"Please, at the hospital, they put us in this room in the middle of the ward. There wasn't even a window in the room. All my baby wanted…she wanted to see the stars."

"I wanna see where you're going, Mommy."

Miranda wiped at her cheeks, raw and red to match the face of Mars. "But they kept us in the room and wouldn't let us take her out to see the stars."

On her knees, she crawled through debris and blood, holding out a beseeching hand to the Rover.

"Please don't kill me here. Please don't let me die without seeing the stars."

"Red Rover, Red Rover, send everyone on over…"

The rockets from the next expedition settled onto the planet's surface.

The passengers stared through the ship's windows, aghast at what they saw. The long metal spike stuck straight up and defiant, seeming to crawl with something no one onboard could comprehend. When stared at too long, it appeared to ripple, to breathe.

On top of the spike, the woman's body, stripped bare and drained, fluttered and flapped, with Martian winds buffeting it like a flag. From atop this shimmering spire, her flesh towered above even the tallest mountains of Mars. So tall it looked like her wriggling fingers might touch the stars above, pulling them down from the vast black nothingness of space.

Around this macabre flagpole, the Rovers gathered. Waiting to be called.

SON OF DEMETER

Bryan Young

I was always told that hypersleep was a blank, black void, absent of everything. I wouldn't think anything, nor would I feel it. I'd wake up as if no time had passed but fifty years would have gone by. Being a colonist aboard an ark ship was sleepy work.

But I was awake.

I saw nothing, but I felt a lot. And perceived more.

The walls of the pod pressed against me. The tight underclothing we wore pressed tighter than the walls. The scent of chemicals piped into my nostrils with tubes made the whole thing feel clinical. And a still blackness consumed everything.

I tried opening my eyes, though they wouldn't—couldn't—open. But I knew what I would see. Or at least, I assumed I knew. Less than an inch from my face would be the glass window. Someone would be able to look in at me if they were awake and needed to check my vitals. Since I wasn't a member of the crew, I'd be asleep the entire fifty years and then I'd be back with my daughter again. Just the two of us against the world, ready to take on anything.

Was I really awake?

Was I dreaming instead?

I tried pinching myself, but my hand didn't respond. I was locked in my coffin-like space so tightly, I couldn't move my hand if I wanted to.

And I wanted to.

Was that something crawling on my arm?

It felt like a spider, each of its eight legs coming up and down along my bicep. It moved upward and forced a chill I didn't know I could experience.

I tried to shoo away the spider, but I was powerless. The phantom spider moved back down my arm with impunity and I was left to struggle with its tickle against the back of my left hand.

Something must have gone wrong.

Perhaps the chemicals they used to knock us out before the cryo-process had been mixed poorly?

There was no way I was supposed to be conscious..

I wondered what kind of spider it was. Was it something harmless? A daddy long legs? Or was it something much more deadly? A brown recluse? A black widow? Would it bite me? Would I wake in fifty years with a rotted hand from the venom of a long dead spider?

How would a spider even get through the clean area? Foreign objects were strictly forbidden in the hypersleep loading chambers. Biological creatures, doubly so. It should have been detected on the sensors and vaporized. But the twitch and tickle against my hand said otherwise. There was something in here with me.

Its gnarled teeth plunged into my hand, pumping its venom into my hand. Infecting it.

This was no dream.

I knew that.

The pounding dread ensured that I knew.

But how? Why?

If I was conscious, did that mean my body was aging? My poisoned hand wasn't the only thing that would decay through the journey. In fifty years, they'd pull from my pod a mummified corpse, frozen and dead. Would I starve to death first? How long could I last in a fevered dream like this?

A skitter at my bare feet changed my thoughts. The presence of the spider was gone, replaced by the speed and size of a tiny rodent somewhere down below me. It ran over my toes and my instinct was to recoil, to flinch and draw my body into itself. To scream.

My god, how I tried to scream.

But, like the worst of my nightmares, nothing came out.

And no one knew I was in trouble. No one would ever know.

What had I done to deserve such treatment?

There had to be someone responsible. This doesn't happen on an *Independence*-class colony starship by accident. Unless it always happens. And we're all lied to about the nature of hypersleep. Unless this was sabotage.

I wondered where the ship might have been on its journey.

Had we left moments ago?

Or would we be arriving imminently?

Were we somewhere in the middle and there were still a couple of decades left?

The rodent stopped its marathon across my feet and finally picked a toe and began to nibble. Its teeth pierced into my small toe first, perhaps that seemed like the easiest target. As much as I wanted to cry out when the spider bit, this was worse, a hundred-fold. Its teeth gnawed nimbly into my flesh, his bones tearing down to mine.

I screamed again.

Or tried.

I was still asleep.

Or half awake.

My mouth wouldn't open, air wouldn't pass through my vocal cords.

The rat cut deeper with its teeth. Into my phalanges, then deeper, sucking the life from my metatarsals.

I wanted to pity whatever poor soul would be forced to open my tube and remove my bones, picked clean by the rat, but all I could feel was the pain. It shot like a laser bolt from my foot to my brain, traveling faster than I could comprehend.

Why did someone put such a creature in my pod?

I kicked, or tried to, hoping I could stop the skittering teeth across my skin, sucking the flesh and blood from me. But my leg didn't work.

Defenseless, I tried a different tactic. Dozens of electrodes were attached to my head and my chest; if my mind screamed loud enough, then perhaps some passing technician might hear the beeps warning them of abnormal life signs. It was slim hope, but better than nothing.

The pain made it easy to conjure the mental energy to scream. The panic that I couldn't give voice to the scream added to my urgency.

I bellowed with my mind, shrieked and screamed with every ounce of energy I could muster.

I felt it in my lungs. Just a bit. As though they knew what they were being called to do. They inflated. But, like my voice, couldn't quite let anything out. My breath stayed there until it slowly trickled away like a pinhole in a boat. Tightness constricted inside me, as if hands were grasping at the lining of my throat.

The rat bit again, slicing into the next toe. Ravenously, as though they were long-sought delicacies.

How could I get it out?

How could I end the pain.

I wasn't meant to die like this.

Was I?

Suddenly, the feast of feet stopped and I knew the pain was so severe that I had numbed myself to it. As if my frontal lobe suffered an overload and shunted the pain away. I'd pay for it later, but for now, my feet were nothing but dead. Maybe the rodent carried on its morbid work, or maybe it didn't. It's not like I could have done anything about it anyway.

I closed my mind's eye, as though that might somehow calm me. A darker blackness shrouded me and I took in a deep breath, or tried. My lungs still wouldn't respond the way I wanted them to. My deep breath turned into a shallow one, then tighter, as if I was being held underwater.

Drowning.

Dry, in a hypersleep pod, I felt suffocated.

Drowning.

Panic slapped me.

Beat me.

Hit me.

More.

The water level rose.

But then subsided.

I took a breath.

I didn't want to die this way.

Don't.

The water didn't come back.

My breath returned.

I had to think fast.

How could I escape?

I tried mind-screaming once more. I thought I heard a beep. But I needed more than a beep to be more than a blip. I had to do something before the spider-mouse-rat transformed into something else. Something larger. Something deadlier.

This couldn't be normal. There's no way anyone would willingly travel this way if this was what they could expect. That left sabotage. What, or who, would do this to me?

Why would anyone forsake me?

My concentration flagged when I felt something skitter across my cheek and rest on my face just below my eye. Small, clawed feet, sandpaper rough, stopped right there on my crow's feet.

No.

I wished I could wince and tighten my eyes shut, to protect them.

Or to shoo away whatever monstrosity stood there, over my face.

Because I knew this next part wasn't going to be pleasant.

That's when the claws tightened, bracing themselves for what would happen next. And without a sound, a beak pierced my eyelid and dug into my soft, seeing orb. Still, no light nor reality penetrated my mind. The blackness grew darker, red bled into it. Sparks came with every peck of the beak.

Something wasn't right.

I wished the sharp beak would pierce further into my eye, through it, into my brain, pecking away at it. Tearing up shreds of it and eating them, just so it would end the pain. There was nothing that made me want to continue living in this dark limbo of pain and torture.

Perhaps it was poison, I wondered, as the beak sheared again into my face. I heard the slurping crack as it broke the bone around my eye socket. The pain didn't even faze me anymore. It was just a part of this existence.

Once, twice, thrice the beak came down. It didn't feel like anything but pressure against my face. Someone, or something, pressing the edge of a knife against my eye and feeling it press into my head and brain.

Plenty of biological agents could provide effects like these.

Because there was no way this could have been real. Had my hand really been gnarled with venom? My toes gnawed off by vermin? My eyes pecked out by a monster?

Why was I still alive? How could I be if it was real?

It was real enough.

Focus determines reality and all I could focus on was the horror.

The despair.

The pain.

Years passed. Or, at least, what felt like years. Pain came and went. It manifested itself in different ways. Spiders sometimes, crawling across my body. Stings of scorpions at my feet. A clawed monster scooping out the contents of my chest to eat like so much bloody ice cream. I don't even want to mention what the centipedes crawling into my ears felt like, or the maggots dissolving my groin.

And more years passed this way.

And finally light pierced my gaze. Bright, white light. It hurt almost as much as the torture, blinding. But sounds returned. Sounds of activity filled my ears like the centipedes had, but for the first time the sounds weren't coming from inside my own head.

"Wha…?" My mouth worked. My voice. I could scream again if I needed or wanted to. Or at least I felt like I could.

I shut my eyes tighter against the onslaught of light, convinced this was another trick. The blinding light was just another way to torture me, to force me to live my eternity in constant fear. They changed their tactics over many years, why wouldn't this be some new technique in the arsenal of my pain?

"Get him to the medcenter," a voice said.

I still couldn't make out shapes or color. Every time I tried to crack my eyes open, I had to seal them back up for fear of being blinded by the intensity of light. Like I was staring at a cold sun.

Was this all real? If I really was going to the medcenter… How bad was the damage? Was I a decimated corpse? An emaciated skeleton picked through with just enough vitality to keep alive after such an ordeal? I couldn't feel my flesh. My skin felt outside of me. I wore it as a jacket and my bones slid underneath it.

I couldn't even remember what the medcenter looked like. Or how far it was from the time I'd been put down.

Down.

Out.

Hands on me, at my shoulders and legs. They propped me around and laid me down on something.

I bobbed up and down as we went.

A stretcher?

I didn't want to get my hopes up. Life had become nothing but pain. Why would this be any different?

The bobbing stopped and I was tossed like refuse onto a bed.

"Whhha... whe... ho..." I could make sounds, but they didn't mean anything. I couldn't ask questions. I couldn't communicate.

Another nightmare.

I'd been given a voice, but was unable to use it properly.

"Don't speak," a voice said.

Hands gripped my arm. The one that had been bloated and killed by a spider's bite. They turned and twisted it, tapping it for something. Then a needle plunged into my arm. It bit me, and I wanted to twist and shout and scream, but I had no strength to resist. My arms flopped. Which was more than they'd been able to do in a hundred years. My dusty voice tried resisting, but coughed sand.

A moment passed.

Then another.

And I expected the needle digging into the center of my dead arm to explode or rot away from the final poison they were injecting into me.

Instead, a warmth grew from the epicenter. It radiated outward.

Medcenter.

Medicine.

How were they turning this against me?

How would this end in pain?

In my mind, I was black and white, a skeleton, dead. Death and life at once. But as the elixir of life pumped from their machine into my veins, it radiated color outward, bringing me back to my normal state. It fed up my arm and reached my heart with a warmth I hadn't known in a lifetime. My heart worked overtime, nothing more than a machine pumping medicine to tainted blood.

One by one, life returned to my limbs, first one leg, then another. My toes wiggled, uneaten.

When the warmth of a fireplace on a winter's day reached my head and my eyes, I dared to try opening them again. The light was bright but not blindingly so. I peeked, hoping to see what there was to see.

Three technicians stood over me.

The first people I'd seen in an eternity. Since I was knocked out. Chewed up. Spit out.

"Doctor…?" I asked.

But no one responded.

One of them brought out a pen. They clicked it and a light appeared at the end. With rubber-gloved hands, she pulled my eye open and pressed the light near me, blinding me again.

Examining.

Exploring.

Wondering.

Diagnosing.

"And the test?" One said.

"Negative," another responded.

"As I thought," the third stated.

But what test? Was that all this was? They'd put me through this as a test?

I growled, angry.

I didn't like being a guinea pig.

Hadn't they done enough to me?

They left the room. At least, I think they left the room. The bright lights turned to blackness again and I must have drifted back into sleep.

I didn't want to sleep anymore. I'd been asleep for what felt like a thousand years, I didn't want to go back to that place. Sleep was where hurt came. Where I was defenseless. But I couldn't help but surrender to the color radiating from my arm.

I woke up screaming.

I don't know how long I was out. But the second I was conscious enough to stop sleeping, I did.

The lights in the room were dim already, but brightened slightly when I woke. An alarm sounded. Not the sort of banshee shrieks and daemonic klaxons I expected after my ordeal, but a subdued pinging. Nurses entered the room. Three of them.

Two came to my side and did their best to lay me back down, the third went to the bag above my head and started to inject something… "No… Don't…"

"Sir, please," one nurse said.

But the other ignored them both. "Get him back down. He's in no state—"

"No!" I roared, shoving one away from me.

But I was nothing more than a paper tiger. I'd not really gotten a good look at myself and seeing my arms flail, I realized I was loose skin wrapped around bones. Had the nurses been children, I still wouldn't have been able to fend them off.

Their concoction hit the IV and I was sedated again. Drifting off toward pain. And sleep.

I heard them talking in my hazy stupor.

Words I didn't quite understand.

"Affected."

"Apologies."

"Aggravate."

Who was apologizing? What was happening. I was definitely affected. But by what? I was definitely aggravated.

Though I fought against it, trying to think through what was happening, sleep took me again. I couldn't fight very hard against anything.

I woke again.

Less screaming.

Less panic.

They must have put something in that cocktail dangling above me to keep me sedated, because I wanted to worry. I just couldn't muster the energy. Or maybe I was just tired.

Then sleep took me once more.

I didn't struggle against it so hard this time.

It felt more peaceful.

Restful.

Easy.

"Wake up, Mr. Garcia," a voice said through the void.

I hadn't had a voice do that before. In my decades of torture, the only discernible voice I heard was my own.

"Mr. Garcia," the voice said again. "Please, wake up."

My eyes fluttered easily, taking in the bright light around me. I flinched, but only barely.

"Where am I?" I asked, my voice dragged across broken glass to speak.

But I could see I was in a hospital room of some type, with silver bulkhead walls and no windows. There was a doctor, or who I presumed to be a doctor in front of me. She looked groggy, as though she'd been woken up early, too.

"You're in the infirmary, Mr. Garcia. And I'm Dr. Broadnax."

"You're who?" Speaking was difficult and it hurt, but it hurt more to be silenced.

"Dr. Broadnax. We need to discuss your options."

"Options?"

"Yes. Well, you see, you're in a very unusual situation."

"Someone… was trying to kill me," I said.

She smiled. "About that… That's what we need to talk to you about."

"Yes, I want to… press charges…"

"Well, it's…" The doctor took a breath. Unsure of how to speak, of what to say. She looked to the side and scrunched her nose in thought. Then the words came to her. "Why don't we start with where you are, shall we?"

"Okay."

"You're aboard the Space-Ark Demeter."

"Yes…"

"And we're currently about three hundred thousand miles from Earth."

"From… Earth?"

"Yes, we've just broken Lunar orbit for our first slingshot into the stars."

"But that means…"

"Yes. We're only a few days into our fifty year voyage."

I gasped. I'd been tortured for centuries. At the very least, I hoped I'd just wake up in my new home and the agony would be over and I'd never have to endure such a thing again.

"So, this is why we need to talk about choices. You see, we ran some tests and discovered that your psychometric and biological profiles had an error in them. We ran some tests and we've found that you're mildly allergic to the agents used to induce hypersleep comas."

"Mildly?"

"Yes. Despite your elevated vital signs and internal perception, you're no worse for wear. So we have two options."

Bile filled my stomach and threatened to erupt.

"What about my daughter? Is she like this, too?"

The doctor flipped through a few screens on her pad and continued confidently, "We've monitored her since your tests came back. She's had no signs of these effects and is hibernating normally. Though allergies can be genetic, she doesn't seem to share this one."

I covered my mouth with my hand. The only thing worse than enduring a lifetime of this agony was thinking my daughter would have to as well. My voice grew hoarse and my vision blurred with tears. "What are the options?"

The doctor took in a sharp breath, "We can put you back to sleep and you can endure the rest of the journey as you have been so far. When you wake, you'll be reunited with your daughter. We're wary of that option, though. The psychological stress might be irreversible after a week, let alone fifty years."

The blood ran from my face and I felt like I would pass out considering such a thing. "And the other?"

"The other option is that you can live out your remaining days here aboard the Demeter. We can look into resynthesizing the coma agent in a way you're not allergic to, but I'll be frank: the chances aren't good for that, given our limited medical capabilities and access to new materials here on the ship."

My future flashed before my eyes. Growing old aboard a starship. What would that look like? Would I become a burden? How would I deal with social interaction? The ship rotated its crew every year. I'd be saying goodbye to everyone I'd ever known with an alarming regularity. The next time they'd see me would be during their second rotation twenty-five years later.

And I'd have already said goodbye to my daughter for the last time.

Or I could endure torture? A hundred thousand years of mind-numbing, mind-destroying agony just to see her smile once more.

"Can't you just turn around? Send us back? We're still close to Earth…"

"Unfortunately, we've already begun our slingshot maneuver. The window for aborting the mission has closed. I'm sorry."

I had to make a choice.

It was really no choice at all.

I looked down to my hand, which seemed much more solid than it had the last time I had fallen asleep. Even wasting away had been an illusion of the drugs. "My name is Santiago Garcia, Doctor," I said, trying not to cry while extending my hand to shake hers. "And I'd like you to put me back to sleep…"

THE SCREAM

Timothy Lanz

With its powerful curves, the *Reach* was a stallion of space rather than a workhorse. The German transport charged toward the cold reaches of the outer solar system, away from the cloudy marble of Venus. Captain Rebekka Klein couldn't leave the screaming hell of that world fast enough. Her wish would have been granted sooner but for the massive bulk that trailed behind her ship, dangling at the end of a hundred-meter-long titanium cable.

She pressed the intercom. "Retrieval: status please."

She drummed her fingers and wondered nervously what was taking her crew so long to respond. But if she was honest with herself, nerves were the thing that she loved the most about being the ship's mistress, and also what she hated most. On any given day, she never knew if she'd be riding *The Reach* or if it would ride her.

"Retrieval, this is the cap—"

The *woosh* of the flight deck hatch cut her off. Helmut Rudnik, her first officer, stumbled into the co-pilot's seat. Perspiration dripped down his blotchy red face. His chest heaved.

"The payload is onboard and in decontamination."

His voice was ragged, almost hollow, and he stank of more than fatigue. She squinted at him. "Why didn't you answer the intercom?"

Rudnik rubbed his eyes. His mouth hung open to answer, but a life support alarm started flashing and interrupted the conversation.

"Shit," Rebekka said.

Rudnik leaned forward slowly, as if some heavy weight hung from his shoulders. Rebekka consulted the system overview. Status lights for the cargo bay flashed amber or red. "Shit," she repeated.

"One moment, Captain," Rudnik said and punched a few bunch buttons. All the system lights blanked out, then lit up green a moment later.

"You reset the alarm monitor."

"Yes, Captain."

"Instrumentation fault?"

"Yes."

Rebekka side-eyed her first officer. "How did you know?"

"It's radiation from the payload." He slumped over his console and buried his face in his hands. Dog tags slipped out of his flight suit and dangled gently.

"Radiation? I thought we were collecting an atmosphere processor?"

He gave her a meager shake of his head. The little muscle on his temple twitched.

Rebekka cocked her head. "I don't understand."

Rudnik looked up and stared out the cockpit. "It's interfering with internal systems."

She scrutinized the side of his mottled face. "Oh shit, you've got radiation burns." She reached out to touch one of the blotches, but he pushed her hand away with more strength than she expected.

"There's no time for that," Rudnik croaked, his voice thin and raspy.

Rebekka's eyes widened. "What the hell is going on?" she demanded. It was then that she noticed the engraving on his dog tags: *Tel P-7*.

"You're a telepath?"

Rudnik nodded again, still staring straight forward. "Seven rating," he said. "Not the most powerful, but strong enough."

"I didn't know. I mean, I knew you were a veteran of the psy—"

"Don't say it," Rudnik said through clenched teeth with a suddenly stern voice. He rubbed his eyes. "We all had our duties."

Indeed. There was hardly a spacer alive who wasn't connected to the last world war, either directly, like her first officer, or by lineage, like herself. But to find a rated telepath in the ranks was noteworthy, since most of them had gone into quiet seclusion after the war's end.

"Why didn't you tell me?" Rebekka asked.

"I'm not required to report it. Anonymity was the only useful gift Germany ever gave us, anyway. A kind of thank you for locking us in underground vaults for three years and using us as weapons."

Rebekka's voice shook. "I don't understand."

"I was a soldier, but my mission wasn't to kill. It was to probe the North American Alliance's plans or confuse them with mirages and false impressions. The generals drove us mad searching for some elusive advantage." Rudnik sighed and massaged his temples. "And the Alliance poured millions into hunting us down for extermination. So, our government locked us away, for our own protection. Of course, we Germans did the same thing to the Alliance telepaths. We were always on guard against each other and sometimes we met on invisible battlefields. We carry our scars on the inside."

A green glow on the cockpit window caught Rebekka's attention. It wasn't the sharp reflection of status lights but diffuse and of a sickly cast. She wrinkled her nose as the rotting-egg smell of sulfur filled the cabin. Her eyes darted back to her first officer. "Rudnik, look at me."

He turned away from her.

"What about the rest of the crew?"

"We have a mission to complete."

What was he talking about? "The mission's done. We need to get you all home."

"No, Captain. I'm setting a course for Jupiter. I'll take over from here."

"What the *fuck?* Are you insane? Look at me, Rudnik. What happened to the crew?"

Captain Klein's vision blurred. The cockpit flickered and the universe changed around her. A mirage faded from view and was replaced with a different reality.

The alert siren rang out, startling her. The red hue of emergency lighting replaced the normal glow in the cabin. The alarm panel lit up like a volcano, reporting high levels of radiation, unauthorized opening of the cargo bay door, and a warning message that the current payload mass exceeded the ship's fuel capacity. Rudnik now sat upright as if the weight of his fatigue had melted away. He reached over, shut off the audible alarm, and punched

The Scream

up the rear-facing camera onto the display. The half-disk of Venus was slowly shrinking, but it was still large enough for her to make out three—no four—tiny silhouettes of spacers floating in the void in front of it. None of them moved.

"Why?" Rebekka whispered.

"The war never ended for the telepaths. And on Venus, I finally found our advantage."

"You son of a bitch!" She lunged for her controls and the keyboard rattled under her shaking hands as she typed in her security lock-out code. She froze before she could press enter. But not from fear, nor from the vapor rising from Rudnik's eyes, now glowing with a spiteful green light. But from the psychic impulse that locked almost every muscle in her body.

Nothing came out when she tried to scream.

"Your lock out-code was the last thing I needed. Thank you." He stood, looming over her, no longer the image of a sick and dying man, but like whatever comes after that. His jaw opened, seeming to unhinge, wider, wider, and wider still, as if he would swallow her whole. But the same green light vomited forth from his gaping maw, covering her in a substance with a consistency between liquid and gas. Yet it clung to her as it melted her flesh away in a lingering agony like boiling acid until finally, nothing was left but a stain on the deck plate underneath the pilot's seat.

There is nothing like making love in zero-g.

The thought shot up in Martina Rigg's brain like a swimmer breaking the water's surface for one last gulp of air before drowning in a wave of ecstasy. Martina arched her back while her lover writhed on the bed as they slid against each other, faster and more insistent with each passing moment until pleasure overtook them.

Afterward, Stevie nuzzled into Martina's neck. "I love it when you turn my quarters into a bordello," she whispered.

Martina smiled and kissed the top of her head. She watched lurid Jupiter peeking through the cabin's single window, the only thing invited to intrude on their lovemaking. They were awash in its reflected light and Martina's lovely brown hands seemed to massage it like lotion into Stevie's beautiful dark skin.

Stevie was the first to break the magic. "Won't you reconsider?"

Martina pushed away from her lover. "Is that what this was? I can't believe you."

"Please don't go."

"Why? Why do you want me to take myself off the flight roster?"

"I just have a bad feeling," Stevie said. "You could get hurt."

"Come on, it's basically a milk run."

"It's more than that, Riggs." Stevie stood and crossed the room to fetch her uniform. "Didn't you think Captain Stern was being awful cagey during the mission brief?"

Martina propped herself up on one elbow. Her hair flowed messily over her shoulder. "Captain's an old man. Probably was a corporal in the last world war." She patted the now empty bed next to her. "Come back."

"He's moving the *Trust* 100,000 kilometers closer to Jupiter. You'll barely be within the edge of our sentry net."

Martina shrugged, then stood up and put her legs through the trousers of her flight suit. "Well, Lieutenant Commander," she said, adding a touch of sarcasm to her formality, "why didn't you say something?"

Stevie sighed. "I did, later. But the ExO shot me down, said he'd already brought it up to the captain, and his decision was final." She walked over to Martina and gently touched her breast. "He said, the maneuver only appears risky because it's not our standard operating procedure, but it's within doctrinal limits."

Martina shivered at her lover's touch, then lowered her head to gaze into Stevie's eyes. "I have fifteen combat missions under my belt and the best wingmen in the fleet. You're worried over nothing."

"I don't care. I don't like it when they take risks with your lives."

Martina caressed Stevie's face. "But we'll have you backing us up from the *Trust*. We couldn't be in better hands."

"I don't know. Marti—"

Martina silenced her with a kiss. "We're on burial detail, I couldn't ask for an easier mission. No one is going to assault an orbiting cemetery. I don't think towing a few freezers full of dead spacers is going to present any problems, Steve."

They kissed again.

Stevie still looked at her with doubtful eyes.

"Conn, Ops. The intruder is back." Lieutenant Commander Stevie Murtaugh looked up at the captain from behind the crewmen and the workstations she supervised.

Captain Stern pulled his coffee cup away from his lips, the one inscribed *NAA Trust* and with the ship's unofficial motto, 'But verify.'

"Radar contact, just emerging from Jupiter's far side," she said.

"Transponder?"

She stared over a crewman's shoulder. "German registry, sir."

"Why wasn't this reported before?" Captain Stern glared at her over the rim of his cup.

Murtaugh bit her tongue gently, then responded in a crisp, flat voice. "Jupiter is too close, sir. The ship came in on a highly eccentric orbit; the planet covered its approach and the magnetosphere masked its transponder." *And you were the one that ordered us closer to the planet,* she added in her mind.

The captain pinched the bridge of his nose and Murtaugh feared she might not have kept her voice as neutral as she intended, but the ExO jumped in. "We're getting video from our sentry. Putting it on the main view now."

Bloated Jupiter filled the view screen, but a small dot raced above its milky white and blood red clouds, not far from the Great Red Spot. The ExO enhanced the image to reveal a medium sized craft, probably a heavy equipment hauler. It appeared discolored, as if surrounded by nebulous gas. When it passed in front of a wisp of white cloud, a green hue was plainly visible.

"Conn, life support."

The ExO raised a quizzical eyebrow, but Captain Stern answered casually. "Yes?"

"Sir, we're detecting increased radiation levels onboard."

Captain Stern rubbed an eyelid absent-mindedly. "How's that again?"

"All the Geiger counters started going crazy. We've started checking readings in several compartments and they're all going up."

"Sir, should we ready our kinetics?" The ExO asked.

Captain Stern snorted, fingering the thin chain hanging around his neck. "Hardly. Until we know more, I don't need a trigger happy missileer with his hands on the button." The ExO's eyes widened. A missileer's badge glinted on his breast pocket. "Ops, raise them on the radio," the captain ordered.

"No response, Captain." Murtaugh glanced at her tactical overview for the Jovian system. There were four gold blips scooting across the display, away from Jupiter and the *Trust* and headed toward Ganymede. "Shall I recall the Reaper flight?"

Captain Stern regarded her dispassionately. "Is there anything they can do for us right now?"

She swallowed. "No, sir."

"Then let them bury the dead."

Murtaugh held her hand over the transmit button, wrestling with doubt. With a touch and a word, she could recall the honor guard en route to the cemetery at the Ganymede Lagrange point and bring Martina back to safety. But she didn't know which of them was safer, didn't know if she should disobey her captain or not. She just didn't know.

The ExO, however, had seemed to make up his mind already and jabbed his finger into Captain Stern's chest to underscore his point. "Intruder is a German craft without authorization to be here, or even a filed flight plan. Your actions are highly irregular."

Captain Stern dropped the dog tags he had been playing with to slap his subordinate's hand away. They tinkled gently together. "Are you questioning my judgment?"

"If these are your actual orders, sir, I'm saying you're a suitable case for treatment."

"Commander," the Captain snapped, "you're relieved. Lieutenant Commander Murtaugh, take his place."

Murtaugh's hand hovered over the tactical display controls. She watched the ExO take a step back and nod once, then turn to leave. The crack that came next startled everyone on the bridge, even though half of the crew expected it. The ExO massaged his hand and Captain Stern slumped in his chair, unconscious.

"Commander Murtaugh," he started.

"Sir," she said, interrupting. "I've already loaded a firing solution."

The ExO smiled. "Light 'em up with active radar. See if they get the hint."

An incoming transmission light illuminated, nearly ten seconds later. Murtaugh hadn't realized she had been holding her breath. "Conn, incoming video from the intruder."

A man in a civilian flight suit appeared in the now static-filled display. The color was off, but his skin looked splotchy and his eyes shimmered weirdly. "Where is Captain Stern?" the man asked, his German accent thick. He was hard to understand, in part from all the interference, but also because he clenched his teeth when he spoke, as if in great pain.

"My name is Commander Canyon," the ExO said. "I didn't know you were familiar with Captain Stern, but I am in command of this vessel."

The shimmer disappeared and reappeared as the other man wiped his hands over his mottled red face. "We are a civil service craft and not a valid target. Don't fire."

"You're here without leave and leaking radiation. Where did you come from?"

"Venus. This is a maintenance courier. It has been a long journey and—"

"You're lying. We're not about to welcome you with open arms."

Sweat beaded on the intruder's forehead. "I repeat, we've just completed the Venus-Jupiter transfer."

Commander Canyon shook his head. "Oh, I believe that. But you're not a courier. You tried to slip into orbit undetected. But we saw you. Lost you for a bit, but obviously not for long." He glanced at the unconscious form of Captain Stern. Commander Canyon smirked. "Maybe you had help. But whatever. I don't think you have enough fuel to leave. So, you can surrender, or I can fire a missile on you. That's got to be a better way to die than burning up in Jupiter's atmosphere."

The German pilot hunched over his controls, head down. His shoulders heaved with his breathing. Finally, he looked up and the weird light in his eyes intensified. "Fool," he said. "I'm dead already." He slammed his palm down on a button, then wrenched the flight stick.

"Sir," said Murtaugh, "he's changing course. He's deploying a ballute and dropping below the upper cloud bank."

Before Canyon could respond, the German pilot lifted his head back and opened his jaw impossibly wide. Weird light bubbled forth from his mouth, oozing languidly like an old man ejaculating, until it coated his entire face and body. The glow seemed to consume him, eating away at his flesh, like plastic stretched over a fire, and as awful as it was, it wasn't the worst thing. As the man's bones emerged from beneath his melting skin, a terrible sound erupted over the radio, with the force of a hurricane. A million hinges, moving for the first time after rusting away for decades in a scrap heat couldn't have grate more and an army of children dragging their nails along a chalkboard until they splintered off in bloody messes couldn't have hurt worse.

Terror held them, and no one saw Captain Stern raise his hand from the captain's chair. The skin sloughed off to expose the bony skeleton underneath, and it was limned in a glowing green miasma as he seized his former first officer.

Martina Riggs was beginning to think she shouldn't have dismissed her lover's concerns this morning. Sure, her mission started well enough. All four Reapers had glided in perfect formation toward Ganymede, looking something like a flight of sleek attack helicopters from the 21st century. They were poised like eagle's talons, ready to pluck an unsuspecting fish from a river, but everything went to hell thirty seconds ago. A malevolent green flash had washed over her cockpit and left her feeling like someone wanted to murder her. Her radio was inop—spitting a howling scream that made any transmission impossible. She switched it off, but swore her ears were still bleeding. For the first time in a long while, icy fear sat in her stomach. But her training had taught her to ignore that emotion, to even deny its existence most of the time, so she wasn't sure what to do with it now.

Another flash on her starboard wing caught her attention, the more familiar orange and red of an exploding spacecraft. She checked her rear facing radar, the *Felder* had veered into the flight path of the *Dio*. She screamed a question into her mic, then remembered her comms had been knocked out. She hesitated to turn the radio back on, just to check. She didn't want to hear that sound again. But it didn't matter. The debris pattern in her radar's scope didn't look promising for survivors.

The sudden pinging of an alarm arrested her attention. The upper third of her cockpit was filled with a view of the underside of the *Fagen* gliding past, dangerously close. Her fear gave way to an emotion more suited to her pilot's machismo: frustration. She hated not being in control. Why the hell wasn't her wingman staying in formation? She wrenched the stick to port, making way for the other Reaper which banked erratically, ten meters of titanium cable swishing behind it like a hyper dog wagging its tail. At the end was the freezer, the nickname for the coffins that spacers were buried in. It looked out of shape. Was the hatch open? She throttled up her own ship, the *Hagar*, and climbed for a better view.

Both spacecraft hurtled toward the cemetery. The green flash had faded, just barely visible beyond all the floating coffins. Something caught her eye among those long rectangular tubes, some instinct made her examine them closely. Like the freezer she was dodging, something looked out of place. What was it? Was their shape morphing? Or was something playing tricks on her eyes? Here and there, she saw tiny sparkles, like candles being lit against the backdrop of stars. As the graveyard in space zoomed into view, she perceived color in those lights, growing brighter until they resolved themselves in intense green.

Martina completed her climb, slightly above and behind her wingman, and what she saw made her stomach clench tight. A spacer, in an identical flight suit to hers, had crawled up the spine of the craft and now hunkered like a spider, hammering its fists on the canopy. It turned its head to stare back at her and its face contorted, forming hateful shapes made visible by its glowing eyes and mouth. Though Lieutenant Riggs knew there could be no sound, she was convinced that the creature had heard her approach and was screaming at her.

"Get back to the *Trust*!" she shouted, forgetting again that her radio was off. She increased speed, hoping the *Fagen* would follow her, but its pilot executed a sudden barrel-roll. She figured he was trying to shake the thing, but three turns later, it still clung on, smashing the canopy until its fists were pulp and spidery fractures appeared in the glass. It had to be indescribably strong to break that material. The next blow punctured it and a wisp of white appeared as the tiny amount of residual atmosphere inside rushed into space.

"Eject, eject!" Martina cried.

Her wingman must have thought the same thing, for in the next moment, his canopy flew off and the tiny booster rockets in his seat ignited. But his attacker leaped in anticipation and caught hold of him. Struggling, they spiraled off into the black and she craned her neck even after they became lost to her view.

When she looked forward again, she found herself surrounded by freezers on both sides. She was close enough to distinguish the pinpricks of light that made up the eyes, the noses, and the mouths of hundreds of dead spacers, all contorted like a mob howling for her blood. Some were still emerging from their tombs, others stood astride their coffins to watch her, like sentries of eternal hate. Some of them squatted and then jumped, propelling themselves toward her in what would have been a suicidal leap for anyone still alive. The act should have been futile at her speed, except that she had strayed so close. Ahead, space became crowded with the undead. She was flying toward a grim mockery of a flock of birds on Earth.

"Oh, fuck no," she said, "I'm not going out like that."

She meant to pull out, get the hell out of there, but an unexpected clunk reverberated through the hull of the craft. Too late, she cut the tow cable. The rapid sprinting footsteps along the spine of the *Hagar* counted down the time she had remaining. There was no way in hell it would last long enough to make it back to the *Trust*, but—maybe—she could stretch it out long enough to make it over there.

In this case, 'over there,' was a lonely freezer, vacant as the night. Its previous occupant had hurled himself toward her and missed. She was dead if she didn't go now. So, in a cold sweat, she seized control of her fate and banked her craft until the freezer was overhead. She pulled the ejection cord.

Her heart rate surged. Not just from the high-G thrill ride of shooting through space strapped to a tiny booster rocket, nor from the certain knowledge that spacer survival training was a joke, but because she had been caught off guard by one tiny detail. Her emergency radio. It automatically activated the moment her ejection seat ignited.

A raging storm that sounded like squalling metal assaulted her ears and she lifted her hands, but of course her helmet was in the way. She thrashed her head inside of it. Dead faces raced by, a blur of shadow and malevolent green. They clawed for her as they passed, some missing only by a hand's span. Her breath came in shallow gasps, like the last shudders of that poor dumb canary in that fucking coal mine. But each zombie was locked in its own predetermined trajectory, and nothing they could do would ever alter that. At least some laws of nature were still merciful. By a miracle, she cleared the gauntlet unscathed.

They streamed beneath her feet and twisted their necks to glare at her; the momentum caused their bodies to spin like injured fish rolled by strong currents. The screaming noise in her helmet never quieted, but it seemed to her that she heard the volume fluctuate if she stared at a face as it turned toward or away from her.

It wasn't much, but it was enough for Martina to take control of herself. She manipulated the thumb stick that maneuvered her ejection seat thrusters, eyed the direction she needed to go, nudged her chair in line with the freezer turned life raft, then nulled out her velocity. She knew the odds of her actually successfully navigating a line-of-sight trajectory like this had been astronomical—but hey—she had to be good to have survived fifteen combat missions.

Martina unstrapped from her chair when she was ten meters away, then kicked it away when she was less than four. It wasn't a textbook distance—miss by a meter, miss by a mile as the old saying went—but she didn't want to push the freezer out of orbit. It might take the *Trust* a while to start a search operation. She grabbed the outer railing, heaved herself on top, and breathed a little sigh.

But there was no time to rest.

Another fluctuation in the constant scream made her glance round in every direction. There, maybe a hundred meters away, two spacers stalked from one side of a freezer to the other. Keeping her profile low, she scurried toward the yawning hatch—a cockroach fleeing the exterminator's flashlight—and descended. She hoped nothing saw the puffy white hand of her spacesuit emerge, grasp around for the handle, and pull the lid shut behind it.

Martina wasn't prepared for just how dark the inside of the freezer was. A sudden claustrophobic moment sent her into a thrashing panic. She slapped again and again at her chest panel control until her helmet lights illuminated the cramped space. At the same time, the screaming in her helmet quieted. *Idiot,* she thought. She had forgotten her training, and the volume control for her internal speakers. She turned it down as far as it would go, which for safety reasons was well short of quiet.

Still, it was light years better than what she had already endured. She checked her emergency transmitter. Would anything be able to pick it up over all that screaming noise? She checked her battery levels. Eighty percent. She dimmed the lights to conserve the battery and thought about Stevie. *Where are you?*

Martina sobbed and her body trembled. The last twenty minutes had erased everything she considered sane and comforting. She had come to space to fight a war and found Hell instead and the only thing she wanted now was Stevie back. Would it even help? She didn't know.

"Stevie! Where the fuck are you?" The *Trust* had to have observed the recent shit storm she'd survived, even if it couldn't pick up her transponder. What the fuck could be keeping them?

She took a deep breath, spoke into her radio mic with as much control as she could muster. There was no side-tone in her ear, she knew she wasn't getting out. She tried again. And again. No change.

Once more.

Nothing.

She started shrieking, wailing, screaming, doing anything to hear that sound, like when she held a conch to her ear, letting her know she was transmitting. Finally, she slammed her fists against the side of the coffin.

Something outside knocked back.

She gasped. Was she being rescued? Then her heart sank. It had been a single knock and was followed by another and another. Something walked on top of her borrowed tomb.

No, no, no. She wasn't ready. Stevie!

Martina fumbled at the hatch, scratching and thrashing for a lock that didn't exist. It didn't matter because the thing that pulled it open, ripped it clean off its hinges and flung the slab into the void. Above her stood a once dead spacer, eyes, nose and mouth burning with a bale fire from inside. Only now, she saw that whatever the glowing light was, it had putrefied the body until only a few bits of flesh clung to a skeleton of frozen bone. And when it looked at her, she felt like the most despised thing in all the universe.

Before she could make a move it seized her in a powerful grasp, hauling her upward and smashing her helmet's face plate with its skull. Dozens of cracks appeared all at once. The pressure change disoriented her as the vacuum pulled on the shattered glass. She heard the hiss of leaking air. She smelled burning almonds.

The creature's next blow shattered the helmet. The air was ripped from Martina's lungs. The glowing green light from the undead spacer oozed into her helmet, covering her face like buttery slime. Martina braced for the abyssal cold, but instead felt heat, more intense than anything she had ever experienced. Was this what Hell felt like? The green ooze stuck to her skin like napalm, filling her with an agony that overrode all her other senses. Why was it taking so long to die?

But that was when she noticed the screaming had stopped and space reigned silent once more. Silent, but for a faint voice that she recognized.

"Stay here with me, darling."

Martina knew she had to choose between death and whatever this was, though she didn't know how she knew that. She also knew she had only a moment to decide, so she did.

The green light slid into her space suit and melted the flesh from her bones. Every agonized second lasted an eternity. Then the light crawled up her skeleton and up her spine to sit in the pit of her brain. Even without flesh, she felt the true cold of space. So cold it burned, but not as much as she burned from within.

She stood on top of her would-be coffin with the other spacer and waited for the *Trust* as it idly drifted toward them. Stevie was coming. Together, they would look out at mighty Jupiter and the stars beyond and hate everything they beheld.

THE WEIGHT OF FAITH

Carson Winter

The sky was hazy, the way a muddy creek looks when you stir up the bottom. Lightning flashed in amber explosions across the horizon. The ship hummed, then fell silent. I gazed upon the vista and drank it in, to make it a part of me. Aramie came out after, stretching her legs. She bounced and a smile crossed her lips. Dust hung in the air just as she did, before settling slowly.

"I'm so light," she said, testing her legs. She leapt into the air and slowly fell back to the Aleppian soil.

I pointed to a crest of rock on the horizon. "They should be over there. It's a small township. No more than fifty or so."

When she saw that I was not amused, her lips became a straight line. "How many generations deep?"

"Ten now, roughly."

"So they've had time to develop."

"Yes, they're a ripened civilization. They're a culture now."

"All their own."

I meant it sarcastically, but when she agreed, I was forced to explain. "Well, not all their own. They have influences. They're connected with the rest of the human diaspora. Just like we are."

"Yes, sure. They can experience off-world art and communication. But otherwise, fairly undocumented. Fairly self-sufficient."

I ground my teeth, but didn't say anything further.

We climbed the ridge. The ground gave way easily. Everything felt easy. My limbs felt light. I thought of making a joke. *I've lost weight.* But I didn't say anything. This was the fifteenth planet I'd visited in the last three weeks—the fifteenth chapter in my own personal legacy as an astro-anthropologist. The first I'd visited with Aramie. I watched her out of the corner of my eye, watching her own eyes drink in the landscape. She was green, easily awed in a way that I found repulsive. She did not fully understand the importance of our work—*my* work—and yet, she was here. A powerful father, impressive test scores—I didn't know. But as the pre-eminent researcher in my field, I felt she should learn *something* from me.

"What do you think?" I asked.

"It's different. Alien."

"We're not supposed to say 'alien,'" I corrected.

"Right, sorry. It's different."

"No harm done," I said. "But to them, we're alien. If we slip, it can set things off on a bad foot." I smiled at her to maintain appearances—to prove that I wasn't mad. "It *is* different though, very different."

The township sprawled across a plain where leafless trees grew like skyscrapers. The buildings were irregular—some of them looked like typical family homes, some were domed and pointedly retro-futuristic. These were likely cultural remnants left over from their initial landing, some two hundred and fifty years ago. Ship design back then took influence from visions of the future from more primitive times, a sort of tribute to humanity's early aspirations. Here, these NASA-white structures flourished amidst a hodgepodge of other architectural influences.

Aramie said what I was thinking. "Some of the newer buildings seem to be homemade versions of architecture from more densely populated planets."

"Keen eye," I said, keeping my voice even.

"Do they know we're coming?"

"Yes, the message I received was quite enthusiastic."

I breathed their air. Sweet and clean, unpolluted. "It really is beautiful," I said. "I feel so light."

"New Aleppo was named after a very old city on Earth," I said. "In the early days of space colonization, it was decided that new settlements should be named after the ancient human history of our progenitor."

"Boston à Veres, Neo London, and now New Aleppo."

"Yes, in that order, almost exactly—ignoring the several other thousand settlements. New Aleppo is relatively recent."

The town was empty. What amounted to streets were wide and dusty, which only increased the feeling of desolation. Aramie squinted her eyes. "Where did our Aleppians originate from?"

"The Susa-Fredericksburg metropolitan area on Gorrla. There is little information on why they left or how they founded New Aleppo. Primary documents suggest it was a religious revolt, that they left for spiritual reasons and ended up here."

"It's close. It was likely visible in the night sky on Gorrla."

"Yes, most likely. We don't always choose our homes. Sometimes, we take what is given. This story has played out a hundred thousand times, in galaxies far and wide. Humans look for something better, but settle for something closer."

We stopped after a while to listen. Aramie said, "Are you sure this isn't a ghost town?"

"They've sent communications within the last month. They're here. But we don't know what time they keep. They might be in bed."

"It's light out."

I nodded. "Yes, but there are other planets where it's normal to sleep when it's light out. This ecosystem might demand alertness at night."

Up ahead, the pathway widened even further. "Do you see that?"

"What do you call it, a cul-de-sac?"

"Could be. Or a town square. What's that in the middle of it?"

Some object, what looked like a great, irregular stone, stood in the middle of the clearing. I broke into a light jog, practically floating in the low gravity, toward my target. Child-like jubilation crossed my lips. Aramie felt it too. I turned back to see her, a wide smile as she stretched her legs and leapt ten feet at a time.

"Like walking on air," she said, when we both stopped in front of the stone.

The stone was taller than Aramie and I together. It was as wide as I was tall. Rust splotches colored it.

"Is that some sort of lichen?" I was quizzing her.

She shrugged. "Doesn't look like it. It does look organic though."

"Could be a religious relic."

"Or art."

"Yes, or art. Or both. Religious art is common."

"You said they were religiously persecuted. Do you know why? What did they worship?"

"Details are muddy. There were a thousand small cults on Gorrla. It was a melting pot for a lot of post-terrans. Many generations removed from Earth, raised on different planets with different cultures. There's a never-ending list of belief systems formed in the Susa region that likely had their roots in different home planets before they got there. It's hard to—"

Behind us, a third voice spoke. "You won't find many of us too keen to be referred to as a cult."

Aramie and I both turned on light feet. The man who stood behind us was small, wiry, remarkably thin. He looked terminally ill, starving. His cheekbones were sharp like the edges of obsidian cliffs. His lips pulled back to show yellow teeth and retreating gums. He was hunched over, holding a stick to keep up on steady legs.

"I'm sorry," I said to the man. "Cult has different connotations in my field. I only meant a small religion. My name is Travers, this is Aramie. We communicated with some of your interplanetary radios and mentioned we would be visiting, for research purposes." I held out a hand.

The man raised his feeble arm and waved my hand away. "We don't shake hands here," he said. "Hurts too much." He swirled his finger around in the air. "Both of you are strong, are you not?"

Aramie shrugged. "We are relatively fit. I wouldn't describe myself as strong. There are stronger."

"Both of you are stronger than anyone here," said the man. "We don't usually have visitors."

"Sir, what can I call you?"

"Canus," he said.

"Canus, are you a leader here?"

"I suppose I am."

"Political or religious?"

"Chosen by God. So both."

"Would you care to speak with us?"

Canus was ageless. His body was so ill that I could not tell if he were very old or very diseased. He spoke in a breathy, light tone that made me think of a breeze, albeit with an edge of sternness. "Yes, of course. But I am too tired to go back to my home. We can sit here and talk, if that's agreeable."

Aramie and I assured him it was as we gathered our recording equipment and explained to him the purpose of our mission. What struck me most about Canus was how shameless he was of his appearance. But the longer we spent around him, the harder it was to muster shock. Canus was a flimsy being of bone and skin, but he was still a man. He sat on the dusty earth, his back against the large stone behind him, each breath a battle.

"Are you ready, Canus?" asked Aramie.

I didn't expect her to take the lead, but I bit my tongue.

"Yes, yes."

"Alright. We're ready too. How old are you?"

"Twenty-seven," he wheezed.

"And you said you were a leader. What title do you hold?"

"Title?"

"Mayor, chancellor, king, president," assisted Aramie.

"The Ultimate," he said.

"Where are the others here? Inside?"

"Yes, that's where they are."

I looked at my *colleague*, rage boiling over into my voice. I jumped in. "On some planets, people become nocturnal. Is this the case here?"

"No. We sleep at night. But everyone is inside all the same."

"Why is that?"

"Before, it was because that is where we were most comfortable." Canus indicated his body. "We are not strong like you. We are weak. The gravity, or lack thereof, makes us grow weak. We only leave when we have to."

"And now?"

"What?"

"You said before. But why now?" I asked.

Canus sighed. "Now, they are inside because they are all dead. I killed them." Canus held up his hands. "I am no threat to you," he said. "Stay. Please, stay. I beg of you."

I could not read the look on Aramie's face, but I was pleased that my voice was captured in the recording, that I was woven into their history. To Canus, I said, "We have no authority to enforce laws."

In an effort to prove how little she knew, Aramie blurted: "I can go back to the ship now. I can call for help."

"If it would make you feel more comfortable, you may. I obviously can't stop you. But I'd rather you wait."

"Why?"

"I want to tell you my story. That's why you came, correct?"

"We came all this way," I said to Aramie. "We're here to record history, not punish crimes."

She bowed her head, unreadable. "Tell us," she said.

Canus' head lolled on his twig-like neck, a motion meant to be a nod. "Okay," he said. "It won't take long." He cleared his throat. "I was born here, you know. I've been here all my life.

"You don't think about that, I guess, until you're ready to die. That you are a clay mold shaped by your surroundings. But yes, that's what I am."

"And what are you?"

Canus let out a weak smile. "Envious."

"Envious of what?"

"You."

Aramie: "Why us?"

"You've been kissed by a God you don't even worship. While we languish in his ire. It's enough to make anyone envious."

"What is this God?"

Canus sighed. "You can only feel a weak echo of our God here. A weak echo indeed. We've grown to worship what we don't have, as if that would give us more of it. But that's not the case. We see you on the television, we see your narratives. We see the casual assumptions you place on others."

"What assumptions?"

"Vitality, health, strength."

Aramie studied him for a long while, during my line of questioning. "Your God is gravity," she said, coming to a conclusion that was by now obvious in mind.

"Yes," he said. "In so many words."

"Gravity is a fundamental force," I said. "It's a necessary component of nurturing life. It's all around us and binds. It makes sense that a sect within the human diaspora would worship it."

"We worship what we don't have. In the old days, it was tolerance. Or power. Or kindness. We humans are lacking many things. Therefore we have many things to worship. Gravity is ours."

"And you say that it has blessed others, but not you?"

"Look at me," he said. "I am the strongest in Aleppo. That's why I was chosen as the Ultimate."

I did look at him.

Aramie said, "The low gravity environment lowers muscle mass. I would think a sect of gravity worshippers would choose a high-G environment."

"We don't know why our elders colonized this planet. It was likely for no great reason. They left one place in hopes that there would be something better somewhere else. There was not. And we have now lived for generations, slowly dying out as a feeble race."

His candor unnerved me, but he was unwavering. "Is that why you killed the people in this settlement?"

Canus scoffed. "People? I'd hardly call them people. People are strong. They can run. They can lift. They have physicality and mirth—the sort we only see in those who live their lives beyond us."

"You didn't answer the question."

"Excuse me," he said. "I did it because we agreed to it."

"What sort of community agrees to collectively end itself?"

"A weak one."

"How was that decided?"

"Through sheer, pervasive fatigue."

"What does that mean?"

"It means we were tired of living our lives here. We were not strong enough to do much more than subsist and watch other worlds from afar, burning with envy. We are bedridden, most of us. Some of us, like me, are stronger, but our strength is a pale imitation of yours. We've been talking about it for decades, maybe longer. I heard my parents talk about it, suggest it. I grew up to do the same. We had the low population now to do it ourselves. I was able to go from house to house, without too much trouble, and end each of the Aleppians, until I was the last."

"The Ultimate."

"Yes."

In all of my studies, I had never heard of a civilization that *decided* to end itself. Electricity pulsed through my veins. A smile turned at the corners of my lips until I remembered Aramie was with me, nodding solemnly to Canus' story.

"It doesn't matter what we worship anymore. Gravity does not care for us, it has cursed us. I am here to die."

Aramie asked, "Was it you that answered the research proposal?"

"Yes."

"Were they already dead then?"

"Yes."

"Why did you call us?"

"Because I want to die."

I watched Aramie, crouched beside the spindly monster. I chose my words carefully. "You're seeking help."

"Yes," he agreed. "And that's why I called you. As I am the reaper, I deserve my own death too. Even though I am stronger than them, I am not strong enough to kill myself."

Aramie turned to me, the look in her eyes was unreadable. She said to Canus, "Tell us what you want."

He adjusted his weight with great effort, turning his head toward the large stone behind him. "It would be a great honor, if at the end, I could be killed by my God."

"The rock. Is it of religious importance?"

"Yes. Symbolic. I cannot lift it myself."

"And you want us to."

"Yes."

I stared at the thing. Tall, undoubtedly dashed with brains in stronger times. I played coy. "There's no way. We can't lift this."

But she said, "We couldn't lift it on either of our home planets. Together, we might be able to lift it here."

For the first time, she surprised me.

"You'd only need to rock it, lift an edge enough that I can place my head under it. God will do the rest."

"That's murder," I said, because we were still recording.

"It's assisted suicide," said Aramie. "We have his voice right here. Asking for help."

"You're not entertaining this, are you?" At the same time though, I pointed to the recorder.

She flipped the switch and the time stopped.

"I am."

"Why?"

"Research. To complete the story of the Aleppians."

I thought about that for a moment. "We would be remembered," I said.

"True."

Canus looked up at us with sunken eyes. "Please, try."

Aramie was already at the large rock; I was too. I imagined our trip to Aleppo going very differently. But seeing Canus lie down beside the great rust-colored stone, begging for death, repulsed me. I began to see him as less and less human. I stood beside Aramie, and placed my palms flat on the stone. Below us, Canus closed his eyes.

We pushed.

Our muscles flexed. Sweat dewed on our forehead.

We pushed.

I bounced forward, trying to use gravity to my advantage.

We pushed.

Aramie and I stood back, catching our breaths. We shared a look of defeat.

"It won't move," I said. "We aren't strong enough."

"No," said Aramie. "We aren't."

Canus shook his head slowly, as if in a bad dream. "No no no."

I cleared my throat. "I'm sorry," I said. "We wouldn't have killed you anyway. We're not murderers."

"No, we're not," said Aramie, turning the recorder back on. "We were just seeing if it was possible. We wouldn't have done it."

"No no no."

"We must go now," I said. I swallowed. "Thank you for speaking to us. Interplanetary law enforcement will be arriving soon."

Canus screamed, a plaintive cry that seemed improbable from his tiny frame. He writhed on the ground, in the shadow of the stone. We raced on light feet to the ship.

Aramie and I did not speak for a long time. Not about Aleppo. We sat in silence until we docked and boarded the space station. When we passed through the gravity lock, we felt our feet plant themselves firmly to the ground. That was the first time we acknowledged any of it.

We tested our weight, jumped into the air and came down immediately. "It's good to be back," she said.

I looked at my own body, the cords of muscle I never once considered, never once trained. "I think we're where we're supposed to be."

We stood there for a while, under the white lights of a long circular corridor. In silence, we measured the weight that pressed on our shoulders.

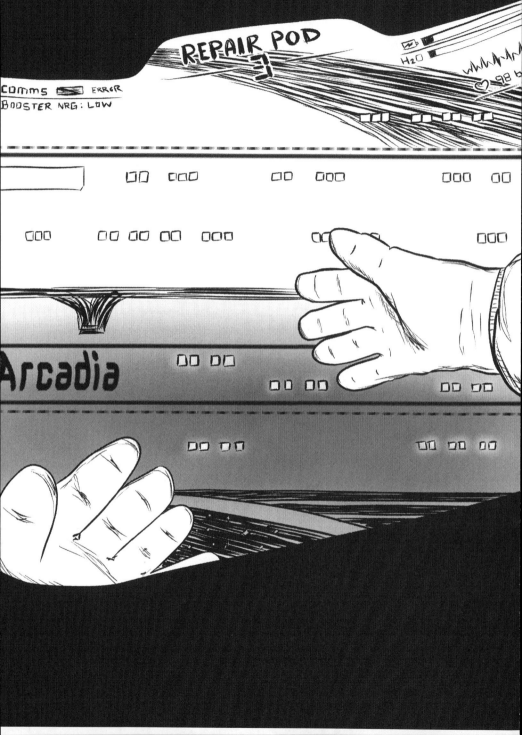

THE FACELESS

Ryan Marie Ketterer

Five. More. Hours.

That's it. Just five more hours, and then I'm off work. And not just until my next shift, but off work for a whole seven days.

I have to remind myself not to count down the minutes during this mission, otherwise my nerves will consume me.

Time off isn't common in my line of work, at least not while working for Starsight. Great pay, long hours, and a whole lot of shady behavior. But not tonight. I finally have vacation time approved, and nothing—even their "convenient" accidents— are going to prevent me from that.

Tonight's mission is simple: replace the power controllers on the starboard side of the *Arcadia*, a luxury spaceliner. I've run this one a million times and it's the perfect, mind-numbing task to help kill the remaining hours.

My repair pod glides quietly alongside the *Arcadia*, which is nearly the size of one of Benkora's moons. Tiny circular windows line the sides. I try to spot vacationers enjoying their stay—a kid waving or a party-goer enjoying a drink—but the windows are stark, empty.

I shove aside my creeping sense of desolation from staring at the barren rooms. I tell myself the mood will pass. I pretend that this solitude doesn't affect me, doesn't seep under my skin and cause my muscles to contract and tighten.

I zone out while my pod auto-drives several kilometers to the powerbay. I dream about the drink I'm going to order for myself from one of the tourist bars—probably a Cosmonaut, a blueberry-flavored drink with edible sparkles to mimic the stars. I envision the hammock I'm going to sink into, one of the many over in Benkora's dome where the *Arcadia* will be docking in two days' time. That time can't come soon enough. Luxury cruises run out of Benkora on a weekly basis, traveling between its seventeen moons, and I am typically on *every. single. one.*

So yeah, thanks for that living module, Starsight, the one I never even get to use.

"Repair Three, come in. Over."

The staticky words from my comms unit startle me from my daydream.

"Repair Three here. Over" I reply.

"We're picking up a minor disturbance at your four o'clock. Cap is saying to pull back, not worth the risk. We're going to delay until the debris clears. Over."

Debris fields were common, and normally Starsight wanted us to work them. Like the last one, that almost killed the maintenance worker from Repair Pod Seven.

"Tell Cap it's now or never. Tomorrow is my day off. I'll be extra careful. I promise."

My bones rattle with the static coming through the line and my heart rate starts to increase. A debris field isn't *that* bad. I've done it before.

All it takes is one tiny rock piercing my suit...

I let my pod continue towards the powerbay. From one of the lower-level windows on the ship, a man stares at me. *Economy.*

Even at my poorest, I would never stay in Economy. I'd rather not go on the ship at all. Why bother paying all that money to be at the bottom rung of the ladder?

I wonder if he can see me. I raise my hand to wave, but he continues to stare. An unnatural yellow light reflects from the window, a glint of some sort from the man? I'm too far away to tell.

Suddenly, my comms come back to life. I didn't realize I'd been holding my breath, and let out a long sigh.

"...*bzzt*...Cap doesn't...*bzzt*...back here..."

"*Arcadia*, come again." A pit forms in my stomach. Just my luck—nothing ever goes how I want.

The static from the radio increases in volume, before abruptly popping. I throw my headset away and grab my ear, now wet with blood. The pain is like a hot iron straight into my brain. My world begins to spin.

The communication status light is no longer green. It's yellow.

Am I seeing things? I didn't even know that light could be anything other than green or off. I steady myself on the wall of my repair pod, hoping my vision stabilizes.

I grab the headset, afraid of that ear-piercing screech, and slowly put it back to my non-bleeding ear. Silence.

"*Arcadia*, do you copy?"

Silence.

I am about to repeat my message when my pod begins an automated announcement.

"T-15 minutes until docking at *Arcadia* starboard powerbay. Please prepare for spacewalk."

The spacewalk was already going to be scary in an active debris field, but now? The edges of my vision continue to distort from the damage to my ear. How was I going to accomplish this?

I think about my vacation, reminding myself to pull it together. I deserve this vacation. Starsight or some minor debris field wasn't going to take it away.

I put on my helmet, and it activates as soon as it locks itself in place against the collar of my spacesuit, tightening ever so slightly against my throat.

The heads-up display turns on: oxygen level, comms status, my suit's booster energy levels, amongst other things. Comms status message is just jumbled letters, something I'd never seen before. Typical—good ol' Starsight. I shouldn't need comms to get this job done anyways.

"T-5 minutes until docking at starboard powerbay."

My pod's docking system unfurls into the black void and maneuvers its way into position.

"Docking at the starboard powerbay commencing."

My pod begins a countdown and fear crawls through my veins like tiny fire ants. There are hundreds—maybe thousands—of rocks traveling slowly around the pod.

I do my best not to acknowledge the disturbance. My brain buzzes with everything that can go wrong—*what if a rock gets lodged in a thruster? What if one jams the airlock door open?*—and I block it out the best I can.

The pod docks and I release the airlock. I attach my tether to the outside of the pod and step through the door. I float amongst the rocks, some smacking into my suit.

Calm down, I remind myself. *Deep breaths.*

I activate my suit's booster system to propel myself towards the powerbay. I do this every few months, replacing the power controllers so the *Arcadia*'s main propulsion and drive systems can continue to function without issue. As such, I'm very familiar with the procedure. The entire thing takes about a half hour—switching the *Arcadia* to reserve power, replacing the three controllers, and switching it back—and is entirely uneventful.

Even though I've finished the operation, I still need to get back to my pod. My stomach is in knots due to the constant movement back and forth coupled with the vertigo from my earlier ear injury.

I propel myself back to the pod door, collecting the tether as I do, when an abnormally large rock drifts towards me. I freeze, forgetting all my training. The rock will collide with me, no doubt, and I'll go careening off in a random direction into space. Without functioning comms, I'll surely die in the middle of this awful black void.

And then my reflexes kick in and I dodge it, releasing the collected tether from my hands and propelling myself back slightly. The sudden movement causes a flutter inside me, the type that is usually followed by vomit, but I take a deep breath in an attempt to regulate my breathing.

I've put more distance between myself and the airlock now, in order to evade the rock, which travels innocuously in front of me. As I'm drifting backwards, waiting for it to pass, I see the tether. It's snarled, somehow caught on itself. I won't have enough slack for—

My body jerks at the end of the now far shorter tether, nearly tearing itself from my suit. I wrap my hands around it and hold tight, though, now more concerned with becoming a floating popsicle than I am with the chunks of that morning's breakfast coming back.

Somehow, the tether doesn't rip from my suit. I am lucky.

Then I think to myself: where was that rock heading, anyway? I look to my right, towards the *Arcadia*, and there it is.

The asteroid collides with the powerbay docking system that connects Repair Pod Three to the massive cruise ship. Fragments of metal launch towards me.

My pod—my lifeline—has been forcefully undocked from the *Arcadia* and is now free-floating away—with me still attached to it. I use my boosters to escape the worst of the barrage, trying to get back to it at any cost.

The fear coursing through my body has turned to desperation. If I am going to live through this, I will need a lot of luck. I swallow, nearly choking on the dry air inside my spacesuit, when an alarm in my helmet starts sounding. The buzz is incessant. The booster energy level display in my HUD is flashing red.

I start hyperventilating.

If only I listened to Cap. If only I had turned back, I wouldn't be here.

I was so desperate for time off I was willing to continue this absolute non-emergency mission for what? A fucking daiquiri?

Of course Starsight would want me to think like that.

Despite the lowered energy levels, I propel myself forward, pulling on the length of knotted tether, as I get closer to the pod. If I can get back inside, then maybe, just maybe, I can call for help.

As I approach the handhold next to my pod's airlock, my vision blurs. Bile rises in my throat and the stars around me spin. I misjudged my initial speed and slam into the pod, somehow managing to grab onto the handholds next to the pod's airlock. I try and fail to unlatch the tether due to my impaired eyesight.

Just as I manage to pull the metal latch from the loop, an enormous asteroid collides with the back of the small ship, sending it end over end away from me. This one is even bigger than the first, crushing the propulsion system on my pod. I scream as I realize I lost my only means of transportation, my throat raw.

While the pod spins away, I look back to the *Arcadia*, my last chance of survival. The massive spaceliner is shrinking, growing further from me. I flail my arms, trying to move towards it, until I remember the motion is completely useless. My booster energy display is still flashing red. Will I have enough to make it all the ship?

I need to try. I use a small amount of energy to propel myself toward the *Arcadia*. What other choice did I have? I'm just going to need to hope I make it, and can find a spot to latch onto the spaceliner, and maybe get someone on comms.

My long float to the *Arcadia* takes forever, or at least, that's what it feels like. My sense of time and direction is greatly diminished. I wish I could propel myself faster, but I need to conserve my booster energy levels.

All of a sudden, what once felt like a slow float towards the *Arcadia* is now not. I'm about to hit the side of the spaceliner as fast as a goddamn pod racer. I brace my body, arms out and waiting to grasp anything.

My bones crunch as my body slams into the metal hull of the ship. There are no longer an abundance of handholds on the outside of the ship, what with a recent focus on sleek, modern designs. I curse Starsight as I slide along the side of the spaceliner, past window after window.

Lucky for me, there's an abnormality on the ship's underside.

The secretion processing unit.

Just a fancy way of saying a poop chute.

Crashing into the side of the massive, square component slows me down even more, and I manage to wrap my fingers around the corner of it.

Deep breaths.

Breathing heavily causes a sharp pain in my abdomen. My ribs are probably broken. A lump rises in my throat and I close my eyes, trying to regain whatever composure I might have left.

My grip on the edge of the poop chute is strong enough to bring me to a stop. Now I can take time to assess my situation. I open my eyes. Oxygen level is at an unusually low 41% and my booster energy levels are near nil. And, of course, my comms are still dead.

There's not much I can do about that now, so I need to find a way to survive on my own. Starsight trained us, the whole luxury spaceliner maintenance crew, for this very scenario. All I had to do was run through the process.

First step: power down the electronics in my suit. That doesn't include my oxygen, but it does include everything else, including my boosters. This full system restart should resolve nearly every issue I might encounter.

Gripping the edge of the SPU, I wait for my suit's systems to all come back online. A rumble reverberates up my arms. As the vibrations become more intense, I tighten my grip. The cruise ship is about to move. *Not possible, it's maintenance day.*

And that's when it happens. The semi-regular process of shooting poop, as it were. I'd never actually seen it in action. Thousands of gallons of waste from the massive *Arcadia* explode from the SPU.

I am off to the side, still gripping the edge of the unit, so I manage to avoid being carried away by the excrement, but I don't avoid the mess. Frozen poopsicles launch all around me, getting caught in the folds of my suit; some even manage to smack into my visor before I can turn away.

My systems are back online, but my booster energy is still nearly empty and my comms are dead. I'm stranded here, alone, covered in shit, without any way of calling for help.

I have one option left, my last resort. My magboots are activated via a voice command. I use my arms to shift my lower body around, and place my feet as solidly as possible on the underbelly of the *Arcadia*.

"Activate gravitational anchors."

The boots connect to the hull with a strong, magnetic force, and I can now walk across the expanse of the ship. Use of the magboots without a tether is strongly discouraged—it might scuff the precious paint job—but desperate times, and all that.

I keep my body as low as I can, my knees bent inside the cramped spacesuit, as I round the curved edge to the side of the *Arcadia*.

Just a little further, and I'll be able to alert someone, maybe a vacationing customer in their room, through one of those tiny windows, that I need assistance.

When I reach the lowest windows, the Economy class, I search for a light, any sign of life. In the distance, there is a pale yellow glow and I begin to carefully trek in that direction. Occasionally, my magnetized boot lands on the tempered glass of a window and I slip, each time a grim reminder of the possibility of dying alone. I make sure each step is careful, deliberate.

Somehow, I manage to avoid completely falling from the *Arcadia* and make it to the room with the yellow glow. I crouch lower, peering into it.

Several men stand in a circle, huddled together, arms draped over one another's shoulders.

Weird bachelor party.

I bang on the glass, and as I do, realize that unless someone is looking at the window, my commotion will exist only in the void of space. I bang anyways, knowing that this is my only chance of finding help, of signaling someone.

The huddled men rock back and forth, their heads downturned, completely oblivious to my pounding.

What the fuck are they doing?

I pound, each time my fist hitting the window a little harder.

The men continue to sway.

"Help me! I'm stranded out here!"

I don't know why I scream, there is no one to hear me. My voice is muffled with my hearing on one side nearly gone, and a taste of bile rises in my throat.

And then the men stop.

They release one another and turn, simultaneously. Their eyes are yellow, as if jaundiced, and they look directly at me, expressionless. It's as if they knew I have been here all along.

The one closest to me steps forward. As he walks towards the window, his face droops, melting, like liquid gold. Hunks of the man's flesh fall to the floor, the red fascia of his cheeks now exposed. His yellow eyes remain on me, unmoving.

My screams turn to sobs and I lean away, my arms and body flailing as my feet remain anchored to the *Arcadia*. I am still magnetized to the ship.

The faceless man raises his hand and brings together his finger and his thumb. He makes a simple flicking motion, and as he does, the magnets that keep my feet firmly attached to the ship release, and my body flies off of the spaceliner. I spin wildly.

Static begins crackling in my one functioning ear, but I am unable to check comms—I am spinning too fast. I close my eyes, trying to hold in the vomit bubbling inside my mouth, coating my tongue.

I use some of my booster energy to slow my spin, and finally stop my motion completely. I am hoping—*praying*—I didn't use it all.

I open my eyes. My booster energy level is down to 1%. Vomit drips down my chin and I cough, spraying the inside of my helmet.

I look frantically between the streaks of bile for somewhere on the ship to attach to.

Except...

Where is the Arcadia*?*

I can't see behind me, not without using more booster energy to rotate back, so I must just be turned around, right?

"Fuck!"

I spin myself, using the last of my energy, but there is nothing here, nothing at all.

The *Arcadia* is gone. Benkora's moons are gone. It's as if all the stars have been eaten, consumed.

The static returns in my ears and I nearly cry.

"*Arcadia*, please come in," I garble, frantic, through the helmet's microphone.

Static.

"*Arcadia*, do you copy?"

Static.

And then...

"...repair...*bzzt*...three...*bzzt*...*Arcadia*"

"Repair pod three, here. I copy!"

I know yelling just uses more oxygen, but I can't help it.

The static cuts off completely, and the comms readout in my helmet starts cycling through unfamiliar letters.

Something falls below my face, and there is a sizzling noise. The smell of roasted meat curls up my nose. I angle my eyes down as much as I can and see what appears to be blood. That's when the pain sets in, and I realize my skin has begun to slough off my face. I scream, grabbing at the outside of my helmet frantically as if I could stop it.

A laugh comes over the comms, now crystal clear.

"Strange is the night where the black stars rise."

There is another cackle as more of my skin continues to fall, the pain unbearable.

"Have you seen the Yellow Sign?"

The glee of the only voice I'd heard in hours continues, mumbling in a language that was unfamiliar. Chunks of my face continued to drip, cooking inside the ever increasing heat of my helmet. My throat is raw and I am numb. My vision goes black.

"You must die unheard in Dim Carcosa."

PLANTED IN THE SOIL OF ANOTHER WORLD

Dana Vickerson

The setting suns dip below the horizon as you stand on the hab's front porch and watch for movement. You need to be ready. You *are* ready.

A cramp makes you wince, and you place a hand on your huge stomach, willing the little one inside to stay calm.

It won't have to wait long.

Your husband is ten yards from the porch before you hear him. You don't have time to wonder how he moved so silently. You only have time to step back into the hab and lock down the sliding doors. He beats on the glass and screams your name from the other side.

The soil underneath my fingertips was the color of rust. I loved to sink my hands deep into the dirt and pretend I was reaching underneath the skin of a great beast. Our little moon was like a big animal, and we were just holding on, trying to survive.

I wiped the sweat from my brow and pulled the irrigation lines further into the patch of flowers. They had no name, because they'd yet to be classified, but I called them Red Stars because they had long stalks that burst at the end in crimson petals the shape of five pointed stars.

They seemed to like the drip lines. I'd laid them out for the carrots and cabbage, the crops I had yet to successfully grow, but everywhere I added our precious water the Red Stars popped up. They utterly fascinated me, and not just because they were different from any flora in our books from Earth-Long-Ago. Because they looked so *alive*.

Sweat ran down my back, and my body ached for rest. I stood and looked over the garden and a knot settled in my throat. Every one of my beds had failed to thrive. We knew this was a possibility, of course, but that didn't make it any easier. Some botanist I was.

Mountain *would* pick that moment to come looking for me. He had a way of showing up when I was deep in thought or self-recrimination. Me, standing around dumbfounded by my lack of horticultural skills. Him, sweet and lumbering and serious.

"What's got you making that face, Pebble?"

I gave him a weak smile. "Carrots and cabbages failed to sprout. I need to try again." I didn't add at least the potatoes seemed to be growing. No need to jinx it.

"You said that last time." His voice wasn't reprimanding, but it still stung.

"Well, I need to try again if you ever want to stop eating vac-pac for supper." I looked into the paddock at our lone cow. The pigs and chickens had failed to reproduce then grown sickly, so they became furnace fodder. I eyed the cow, wondering how many more times I'd have to inseminate her before we had to burn her, too.

Not the glamorous life of interstellar settlers you read about in books. I would say it's not what I signed up for, but I didn't sign up for shit. This occupation, this life, was predestined for everyone on Station. Shoot the ships out in all directions as Earth-Long-Ago burned in our rear-view. Find habitable planets. Start over.

Three generations later and we finally found a little moon with enough atmosphere and mineral content in the soil that it seemed like the place to make a go of it. Too bad Mountain and I were proving the flaws in the calculations.

Mountain wrapped his big arm around me. I'm not a small woman, but he made me feel tiny by comparison. I let the weight of him ground me as I tried to forget about our withering crops.

"No need to be prickly. I'll send up for more seeds. But that wasn't why I was coming over here." He raised a clear three gallon bucket. A few inches of water sloshed around the bottom. "Did you use all the tanks for the garden?"

I watched his eyes survey my dead plants, the soaked soil, and the Red Stars.

"No, that would be stupid. How would we shower or cook?"

He looked at me with an expression I'd never seen before, and it gave me an unpleasant twinge in my gut.

"Well, stupid or not, this is all that's left."

That look made me question if I *had* used it all on the drip lines. But no, I'd need ten times the amount of irrigation snaking through the garden to use it all.

"A leak?"

"Checked the lines and the main valve. Everything's clear. It's just gone."

"Well shit. How long until the aqueduct replenishes?"

"Forty hours."

The idea of no showers or water to boil for that long did not sound appealing. At least we had drinking-pacs. Enough, at least, for this minor disruption.

I wrapped my arms around his waist and pulled him toward the hab. "Well, you better get used to the way I smell, because I've been sweating in the garden for hours."

He pulled me close and inhaled, undeterred.

We left our muddy boots on the hab porch and went in to find food that didn't require water.

The contractions feel like they're timed with the pounding of his fist on the hab door. You want to let him in, but you're afraid. The pain in your groin feels like it will rip you in two, but you press your face to the glass.

Your breath fogs the window, but beyond you see your husband. In a broken voice, he asks that you let him in.

He says he is better now.

I was just getting used to the smell of myself as I slid into bed, but when Mountain pulled me into his chest I resisted.

"Not tonight. I feel gross."

He nuzzled my neck, and I could feel the day old stubble sprouting from his cheeks. No water, no shave. "Come on. I don't care how you smell. I kinda like it."

I pushed him off and rolled over. It wasn't just the smell, and he knew it. The comp had access to my cycles, so he did too.

I was ovulating.

"But we have to keep trying," he said, his voice low.

"You can wait a few days." When my window had passed.

"You know, sometimes I think you don't want to get pregnant."

My body went rigid. I *didn't* want to be pregnant, but it was something I was having trouble vocalizing. I knew he'd get upset. Tell me it was our purpose.

"River died. Did you know that? Over in Post 7. Eight kids and they just kept going."

He slid a hand over my hip and pulled me back to him. "That won't happen to you."

My fingers itched to get back to the Red Stars, but I didn't tell Mountain. I just nestled into him and hoped he understood I didn't want to talk anymore.

As he fell asleep, he murmured in my ear, in a voice that didn't even sound like his own, "What else are you gonna do out here? Sit around and grow fucking flowers?"

My fingers twisted the sheets, and I spent the rest of the night listening to his breathing, thinking that the man I married would never talk to me that way.

You open the door, and his hands are on you in seconds. He falls to his knees and presses his face into your stomach, whispering to the life inside. He says he's sorry. He says he will be good. He says he's finally ready.

The suns came up a few days later with a force I hadn't yet seen on our little moon. I stepped out of the hab and the cool air was immediately sucked away, leaving a balmy film on my skin. My flowers would be thirsty. I hopped down off the porch and headed to the sprawling patch, excited to look for new growth. The tips of my fingers tingled, eager to slip underneath the soil.

Except my flowers were ripped to shreds.

The irrigation lines were a tangled heap. The stalks had been pulled out and tossed aside, exposing long, twisted black roots with irregular bulbs on the ends. My nostrils flared.

How could he?

I stalked past the potato beds, their leaves just starting to poke above the soil. I thought about ripping them up and pouring lye over everything. To hell with Mountain and his little homestead.

It was hard to see past my rage, but I managed to find him in the paddock. His broad back faced me, and his thin shirt was soaked through with sweat.

"How could you?" I spat.

He rounded on me. I watched him register the anger on my face, but his hard features remained a wall between us. "Don't blame this on me, Pebble. You're the one stalking around like a fucking zombie." He ran a hand through his hair and I could see how angry he was. I faltered, but he kept going. "First you use up all the water, now you leave the paddock open."

He stared down at me like I was some stranger, when *he* was the one acting weird. Why was *he* so mad? It was infuriating. And what was he even talking about? Paddock?

The air between us was charged. "I don't know what I did to piss you off, Mountain, but stay out of my garden."

"Garden?" He looked genuinely confused. I watched a bead of sweat roll down from his dislodged, ginger curls onto his shoulder. "What are you talking about?"

"Don't play dumb. You tore up the flowers in my garden."

"I didn't go near your garden."

Behind him, I registered the open paddock and the dead cow.

I shook my head but didn't want to let go of the argument. "There's only two of us for miles, and I sure as shit didn't do it."

Mountain nodded slowly. "I think I know what happened here." He took my hand. I wanted to pull it back, but I let him lead me through the gate. A rusty stain crept up my forearms, but Mountain didn't seem to notice.

We stopped in front of the cow. Our last animal. It was on its side, swollen tongue hanging limply out of its mouth, huge belly distended off its bony corpse. Its dead, staring eyes were glazed over with a milky film.

"I think it got into your flowers."

I stared at the tongue, so flat and lifeless. Another failure threatening to doom our Post and send us back to Station. The possibility that our life here might not work out, that we'd have to tuck tail and head back to the inky blackness of space—where there is no soil or lovely, red pointed flowers—sunk deep under my skin.

I didn't want to go back. The outpost might be desolate, but it was *ours*. Station was just a heaving, crowded mass of people, all trying to flee the tin can.

"Shit," I said, still not sure if the cow or Mountain was responsible for the destruction of my lovelies.

Mountain ran a big hand over my shoulder and sighed. "Better take it to the incinerator."

"No." We'd burned all the rest. Spread the ashes over the fields, hoping it would enrich the soil. Maybe we could do better. Maybe the soil needed more. A gentle crawling sensation worked up my fingers. I wanted to dig.

"Bring it to the garden."

You take your husband by the hand and lead him through the hab to your bed. In his absence, you have made the space ready. You lie back on the clean sheets and spread your legs.

His movements are jerky and unsure.

A trail of dirt follows him from the front door to your bedroom, but you don't mind.

You're just happy to have him back.

Two days after we buried the cow, my flowers were back. They were so beautiful. Tall, bright green stalks ending in an explosion of sharp, blood red points. Some were tiny, just little babies, but some were as big as my hand.

Knees in the dirt, hands sunk deep into the soil, I closed my eyes and could almost hear how happy they were. Humming is the only way I could describe it. Satiated.

The Earth-Long-Ago seeds just weren't strong enough to thrive in this new world. Maybe that was our problem, too. We hadn't fully adjusted yet. Hadn't *adapted*.

There was still time.

I caressed a particularly lovely flower and was rewarded with the most enticing smell. Musky. Animal, almost. It hung in the air, weaving in and out of my nostrils like a promise. I inhaled and felt a twinge deep inside.

As I walked the rest of the garden, I ran my nails up and down the itchy skin of my arms. Surveyed the failures lying limply in their beds. I was no longer thinking of them as *my* failures. *I* wasn't the problem. Just look at the flowers. They were beautiful. They were thriving.

No, these tomatoes and carrots and cabbages were weak. Not meant for life on this moon. Honestly, the thought of eating a carrot felt revolting. The flowers outstretched themselves to me, just begging to be plucked. I took a petal into my mouth and was rewarded with an intense wave of pleasure. Yes, we could eat the flowers. They were all we needed.

After several more petals, my mouth was numb with ecstasy, and my stomach felt comfortably full. Distended, almost. I rubbed the swell of my belly and floated through the garden, lifting a limp stalk here, pulling an errant weed there. The sopping wet ground squashed beneath my bare feet, weaving in between my toes. When I got to the lone potato patch, I stopped.

My fingers wove through the dry leaves and I pulled, taking the nubby potatoes and their puny stolon with them. They were so thin and pathetic. The muted purple flowers sprouting from the top were nothing compared to my Red Stars. I would fill this garden with *my* flowers. The whole Post. We'd have everything we needed.

When Mountain found me, I was sinking the misshapen tubers deep within the soil beneath my lovelies.

"What are you doing?"

"The flowers are hungry." I gave him my best smile. *Everything was fine now.*

"Jesus Christ, Pebble. What's wrong with your teeth?"

I tilted my head, not understanding.

"They're black."

The contractions come faster, and you grit your teeth and scream as the wave crests and crashes over you. There are only a few moments of reprieve before another one comes.

The room hums in anticipation.

Your husband sits at the end of the bed, hands outstretched.

Mountain pulled the sheets up to my chin, even though I felt unbearably hot. I wanted to push him off. To go back to the garden, but he insisted I rest. He laid a clammy hand over my forehead and furrowed his brow.

"I still think you have a fever. You haven't been acting like yourself."

"I'm fine," I said, pushing his hand away. I wasn't a baby.

He glanced at his watch, then back at me, like he was trying to decide something. "Listen, Pebble. I need you to rest while I'm gone."

"Where are you going?"

His face dropped. "Post 7. We just talked about it."

We had? Surely I'd gotten into bed at some point, but I was having trouble remembering. I scratched my arms.

"Of course," I lied. I kept my face open, hoping he'd elaborate.

He looked relieved. "Okay, so you'll take it easy? There should be enough vac-pacs to feed you for a couple days, minus the ones I grabbed for the trip."

A couple days? Were we that low on supplies? Was that why he was going? I gave my head a slight shake, trying to clear the fog. I hoped he didn't notice.

His posture was strange. Foreign.

Alien.

I searched his eyes for some clue, but he kept them averted. He talked through the supply run, the hab security system, the aqueduct levels, which were low again. Things I needed to know, but I wasn't listening. I just kept watching his mouth. Something felt wrong. I couldn't stop thinking about the dead cow. The bloated pink of its tongue.

"Think you can manage?"

His words popped my thoughts, and I tried to remember what we were talking about.

When did I get into bed?

"Definitely," I said with a smile.

You scream through the searing pain and feel everything inside you drop. It's coming, and you don't know if you're ready, but you know you have

no choice. This gift is yours, one you will share with your husband, and it's too late to go back.

He crawls up your heaving stomach and kisses you hard, leaving the taste of dirt on your lips.

It drove me insane to be away from the flowers, but Mountain made me promise not to go outside. I said I'd rest, that I wouldn't leave the hab, then I watched him leave.

Agony is the only way I can describe how it felt to pace and stare out the windows at the landscape that unfolded in all directions. At my flower patch overflowing with life.

Calling me.

My nails dug lines down my arms, searching for the itch, until I winced at the pain.

Blood pooled on my fingertips, and I saw the rust had spread up past my elbows. I went to the bathroom to get something to clean the mess.

When I flipped on the light, I noticed how my t-shirt stretched tight over my stomach. I pulled it up and saw the swollen mound. I smiled. There was no fear. This was what I was here for.

I put my palms on either side and felt my insides respond to the touch.

In and out you breathe as the life inside you struggles. You push a hand down between your legs and feel the limbs break free. You want to tug, to pull it out, but you know that's not the way.

It has to come on its own.

And when it does, your husband will be there to catch it.

I didn't let Mountain back in the hab right away. He stood on the porch, ashen faced and dirty. The buggy sat empty on the primitive road. No supplies.

He pounded on the glass. "Pebble, are you ok? Let me in."

I just stood there. Was that blood on his hands? He seemed bigger than usual. His skin sagged, as though it didn't fit him properly. I didn't think it was just dehydration or lack of nutrition.

Something was wearing his skin.

I shook my head, which made him pound harder. "For fuck's sake, Pebble. Let me in!"

His eyes were wide, crazed. I retreated to the bedroom and tucked myself deep under the covers.

I don't know how he got in, but he did. He stood before me. Clothes torn. Filthy.

"They're all dead," he whispered as he fell to his knees. "Everyone."

I didn't ask him what happened. I slid out of bed and watched his eyes register my stomach. His grief was replaced by confusion. Then he saw my arms, and his face fell.

"Oh, Pebble. We have to leave. Something isn't right here. We need to go back to Station."

He pulled me to him, not as a lover does, but as a shepherd herds his flock. Rough. Clinical. His fingertips searched my skin, tracing the spiderweb of black veins just beneath the surface. I let him. I needed to know if this was really *my* Mountain. My rusty fingertips hovered over the skin of his cheek, but he wasn't looking at me. He was looking at my belly.

"Jesus, Pebble."

His skin was definitely wrong. I knew if I pulled hard enough, I'd find what lurked beneath. I pinched below his jaw, but he pulled away before I could tug at the mask.

"You didn't leave the hab?" His voice was gruff. His eyes wide, like a spooked calf.

I had the strangest vision of myself in the dim evening light, lying naked in the flowers. Their petals caressed my toes, my thighs, my growing bump. The thought was thrilling, but I knew it was just a fantasy.

My legs and back itched, and I wanted to scratch them, but Mountain took my hands. "Pebble, are you…How could you be this—" He placed a hand on my bump. There came a forceful push and a rolling deep within my core. I smiled as Mountain jumped.

He did not smile.

I rubbed the tight skin over my belly button, which had taken on a slight red tinge. "It feels weird, but I like it."

Why wasn't he excited? He'd wanted this so bad. The real Mountain did, anyway.

"I'm going to go call down the shuttle. Do you want to start packing?"

Why would I pack? We weren't going anywhere.

"Sure."

I hummed quietly to myself and stepped onto the porch to greet my flowers. A single vine twisted up the first two steps, and I followed it down and to the thick patch of Red Stars. Their petals thrummed with greeting. Oh how they missed me.

Mountain's heavy footsteps on the porch a few minutes later weren't enough to pull me from my reunion—hands sunk deep into the soil—but his booming voice, thick with anger, was enough to get my attention.

"Pebble, what happened to the comms? It looks like someone took a hammer to it."

Your Red Stars. Your lovelies. You stare at them as you make your final push. The searing pain threatens to tear you in two, but the flowers sing their sweet notes, soothing you.

Your husband doesn't speak, just hums along with them. The whole room vibrates with song.

Not even Mountain's anger could puncture the serenity I felt standing waist deep in the ever expanding growth of flowers.

"Pebble, I don't know what's going on, but we need to leave. Christ, it smells like death out here. These fucking flowers, they were everywhere at Post 7. In the dirt, growing through the hab. Through the bodies…" His eyes grew distant.

He was lying. Trying to trick me. Trying to get me away from my lovelies. That was never going to happen.

A faint noise sounded from a little ways off, and Mountain and I both looked over. My smile spread wide as I took in the beautiful gift.

The cow came toward us in halting steps. I could hear Mountain take a sharp inhale, but it was the most beautiful thing I'd ever seen.

Its skin was no longer smooth white. Mottled rust webbed over its body and black veins pulsed just below the surface. The most incredible thing about it, though, were the Red Stars. They erupted from the cow's eye sockets and trailed down the side of its face, swaying as if to music or a breeze that was not there. There were smaller pockets of the flower pushing through the cow's sagging body, but I couldn't look away from the eyes.

They were trained on me like a flower watches the sun. I stretched out my arms, and the cow stalked closer, lifting its head in acknowledgment.

In revelry.

The shot was so loud that I stumbled to the side, almost falling over one of the discarded vegetable beds. Where the cow had stood was now a black, open wound. The ringing in my ears was so intense that I thought I might puke. I stumbled through the waist-high flowers and found the cow's corpse split open. There was no blood, just iridescent black roots woven throughout its flesh.

Standing on the porch, shotgun in hand, was Mountain.

"How could you?" I screamed. I cradled the cow's head in my lap. Caressed its eye petals as they fluttered closed. My beautiful gift, ruined. The man I married would never do this to something so wonderful.

I knew then. That was no man standing on the porch. It was a monster.

I looked up at the thing that was not my husband and bared my teeth. He seemed to want to aim the gun at me. I willed him to do it. The flowers would protect me. They pushed all around me like an ocean of blood. They would swallow me up and take me away.

Me and the life I carried.

Mountain dropped the gun and stumbled down the steps, picking me up in one smooth motion.

"We have to go, Pebble. We have to get you out of here."

I let him believe we could still be ok, but I knew everything had changed.

Your husband holds the tiny creature in his arms, and you lay back on the pillows. Your sweat has soaked them through, but you could stay there forever watching him look down at this little being.

The red petals bursting from your husband's eye sockets flutter and sway as the creature reaches its tentacles up to greet its father.

The thing wearing Mountain paced the hab muttering to himself. He didn't seem to notice me watching him. I wasn't a threat. A puny pebble could not take down a mighty mountain.

I curled up on the couch and closed my eyes, listening. The thing stalked back and forth, and his words drifted to me in broken whispers.

"…back to Post 7, maybe their comms is still working…"

"…she can't travel like that…"

"…have to fix it…"

From the control room, I heard swears and clunking sounds as the thing busied himself with fixing the comms. I let my bare feet drift to the floor to land on the lush carpet of vines that flowed in through the open hab door. They poured out in front of me like a river, twisting their vines up to brush my fingertips with their red petals. My lovelies. My protectors. They were with me, and it was time.

The thing didn't hear me enter the room. It was on its back under the console, feet the only things visible. As vines wove up its legs, I found the hammer I'd discarded in the toolbox. It still had pieces of the comm wiring woven around the handle.

The braided vines pulled the thing out from under the controls, and although it thrashed, my plants were stronger. They laced up its wrists, pinning the alien thing down onto the floor, its Mountain mask distorted in a scream.

"Pebble! What are you doing?"

It looked at me as though I were the monster, but I was just protecting myself. Protecting my baby.

I sank onto my knees, bearing all my weight down on the thing's chest. Its Mountain eyes were so wide, watching as I lifted the hammer, never looking away. Never flinching, as though it didn't believe what I could do. The cloudy sheen of death ghosted across its irises. Mountain was already gone, so what I had to do next didn't matter. He'd never returned from his trip, and this new thing was a threat.

"Pebble, please—"

The hammer should have felt heavy, but it was light as a feather. I brought it down in one hard *thunk* squarely on the thing's forehead. The petals seemed to vibrate with every blow, and before long they were coated in the thing's blood. Draining it.

The flowers helped me carry its huge body out to the garden. They filled the air with that heady, delicious scent. Outside, the ground beneath them practically opened on its own.

When the soil had taken in all of the thing that had been my husband, I sat on the porch and waited.

I did not despair. The cow had died, but it had been brought back. Glorious and renewed and *mine*. The Red Stars would return Mountain to me, the real Mountain, and everything would be as it should be.

Just in time to welcome the child.

Your husband slides into the bed beside you and lays your new baby on your chest. It attaches to you through a hundred tiny, piercing suckers. You feel the tendrils of the root system take hold in your flesh. The flowers climb on every surface of the hab, up the walls, across the ceiling, enveloping your new family in their beauty.

You feel nothing as you bleed out on the bed. Just gratitude. Just love. Your flesh is their flesh. Your joy is their joy. The Red Stars drink up your blood and grow larger, hum louder.

Your husband slips an arm around you and leans in. You turn to his beautiful face and gaze at him through the unfurling red petals of your eyes.

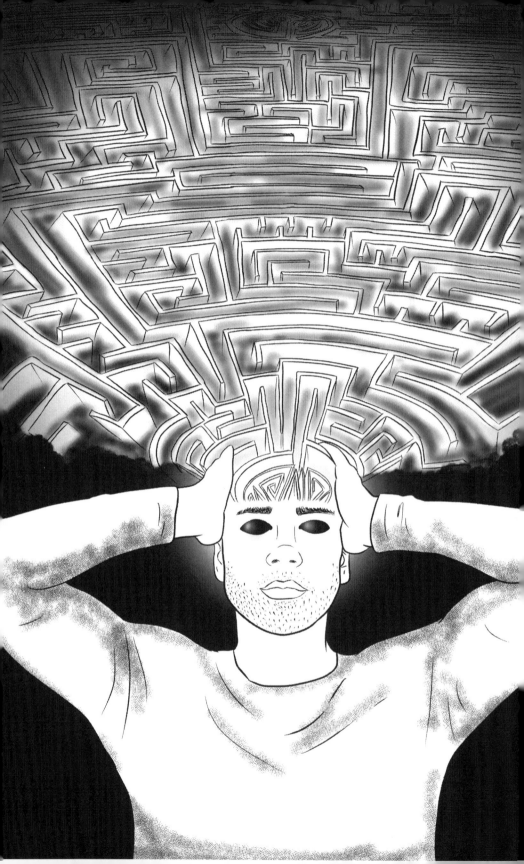

THE VELA REMNANT
David Worn

Space is filled with the radio screams of dying stars.

Hidden within the cacophony are periodic spikes emanating from rapidly spinning neutron stars known as pulsars. Long ago, radio astronomers detected pulsars by listening for their tell-tale ticking sound. These ghostly metronomes cut through the cosmic static like a lighthouse in the night.

As if to say, "we are here, come find us."

—Dr. Jedidah Williams, *Introduction to The Whole Sky Pulsar Survey.*

Neptune Transit Station
959 light-years from PSR J0835-4510

Lana had always hungered for the stars. Had felt them calling to her, urging her to see what mysteries lay beyond the horizon of Sol. The risks be damned.

Therefore, no one was more surprised than Lana herself to find that after four years working aboard the commercial scouting ship *Rama*, she'd grown cautious. Space was dangerous. Rescue, if it ever came, was slow. Reliant on radio distress signals that, compared to the faster-than-light drive technology that powered their ships, crawled through space at regular old light speed.

So, when Captain Pereira first announced that they were being diverted back to Neptune station for a special mission, she'd been concerned. When they'd arrived and found out that this special mission consisted of ferrying UNSA personnel on some vague expedition, she was more than concerned—she was pissed. Like everyone else, she'd heard the rumors. The UNSA using its power and influence to requisition corporate ships for special assignments. Some never to be heard from again.

As Lana walked into the mess hall for a briefing with their new UNSA bosses, she couldn't help but scowl at the newcomers.

Next to her, her best friend and the ship's physician, Bertrand, swore under his breath. "So, these are the assholes."

The one standing next to the captain was clearly an admiral of some sort. The silver hair, the pips on his uniform, the way he waited for the briefing to begin—cool as a fucking cucumber. The second one looked like an academic, though Lana couldn't quite place the discipline. The last of the newcomers was engrossed in his tablet and—*holy shit!*

"Bert, I recognize that guy," Lana whispered.

"Which one?" replied Bertrand.

"Tablet."

"A former *lover?*" Bertrand said, exaggerating his French accent for effect.

Lana stifled a laugh. "Not likely. He's a man of God."

At the front of the room, Captain Pereira cleared her throat. The briefing was about to begin.

"Now, I know everyone has questions about why Corporate rerouted us to Neptune. The admiral here will explain the details of our new assignment. Admiral?"

He stepped forward. "I am Admiral Park of the United Nations Space Agency. With me are Professor Parrish and his associate Mr. Jessup. On behalf of the UNSA, we thank you for welcoming us on board."

The admiral motioned to Jessup who tapped a button on his tablet. The display on the nearby wall screen changed to a top-down map of the local stellar neighborhood. An icon indicated *Rama*'s position next to Sol.

"Our destination is here," said the admiral.

Jessup tapped another button and the map panned away from Sol. Ten light-years. Past Sirius and Epsilon Indi. Twenty light-years. Past Gliese 832. On the opposite edge of the map, the Aquilla Rift disappeared from view. Tau Centauri flew by. One hundred light-years. Lana's heart skipped a beat as the map picked up speed. Omicron Velorum. Five hundred light-years.

This has got to be a fucking joke.

The map slowed to a stop. In the center of the display was the Vela SNR.

"Pulsar J0835-4510. The beating heart of the Vela Supernova Remnant."

An icon appeared, highlighting the pulsar and listing its current distance to Sol.

Nine-hundred and fifty-nine light-years.

Nobody spoke.

Lana played the map back in her mind. Most ships, *Rama* included, had seldom ventured out past twenty light-years from Earth. Commercial crews like theirs were superstitious of straying too far from Sol. A thousand light-years into deep space was unheard of outside of a handful of UNSA long-range vessels. It was dangerous. One false move or a malfunction with the ship's drive and they'd be long dead before anyone ever heard their distress signal.

What the fuck had Corporate gotten us into?

Lana broke the silence. "Norton, can *Rama* handle the radiation?"

At the sound of his name, Norton, the ship's pudgy engineer, sat up straight. "It depends on how close we're talking. As long as we stay outside the remnant, we should be fine."

"We will close to a distance of ten Astronomical Units." the admiral stated.

"From the remnant's edge?" asked Norton.

"From Vela."

A murmur passed around the room.

"But that's the distance of Saturn to the Sun!" Norton pointed at the image on the wallscreen. "At that proximity, if we so much as graze Vela's gamma rays, we're dead."

Lana was next, she focused on Captain Pereira, "Captain, you can't seriously be considering this. If anything goes wrong out there, it'll be a millennia before Earth finds out about it. May I remind the admiral that we may travel faster than light, but our radio transmissions don't."

Captain Pereira raised her palm to quiet the room. "I'm sure the admiral has some idea in mind for keeping us safe. Isn't that correct, admiral?"

The Vela Remnant

"It is. The station's technicians have uploaded nav data into your ship's computer. It contains a flight path that will see us safely through the remnant. No one is going to get irradiated by a pulsar, I assure you."

"Now," said the admiral, "I know this is a lot to take in. I would be happy to answer any questions you have."

Lana raised her hand. "There are any number of pulsars closer to Sol. What is so special about Vela?"

"The UNSA is interested in gathering close-range telemetry. Next question."

Lana nudged Bertrand. "That wasn't really an answer," she whispered.

"The plot *thickens*," Bertrand replied, "now watch as I step in the shit."

He stood up.

"Admiral, why not use one of your own ships?" Bertrand asked. "Or does the UNSA prefer this mission be kept off the books?"

The captain took a step towards him. "Bertrand, *sit down!*"

"It's OK, Captain," the admiral smiled, "Doctor, it's nothing so sinister. All our deep-space vessels are otherwise engaged. If I may speak frankly, we're in the position of having too much money and not enough ships. Now, if there are no further questions—"

Lana's chair screeched as she stood up.

"Admiral, I have a question!"

Captain Pereira shook her head and put her palm over her eyes.

"Yes?"

Lana pointed at Jessup.

"Why did you bring a priest?"

Interstellar space
641 light-years from PSR J0835-4510

"What exactly am I looking for?"

Lana was hunched over Bertrand's computer in the ship's medbay. On the display was the first page of a scientific article.

Entheogenic alterations of consciousness from consumption of dimethyltryptamine (DMT) provoke a common hallucinatory experience across members of distant religious traditions.

"Do you see it yet?" asked Bertrand.

"Why are you reading this weird—*Oh shit!*"

"At last she has found it!"

Lana traced a finger over the names of two of the paper's authors.

"Edward Parrish and Mason Jessup of the Max Planck Institute for Entheobiology and Psychedelic Research. *My oh my,* Father Jessup, do you have some explaining to do."

"An admiral, a psychiatrist, and a priest. The plot—"

"Bert, don't you dare!"

"—*thickens!*"

"Asshole!"

Bertrand winked at her. "There's something else I want you to see."

He brought up the system's search tool. Although *Rama* no longer had access to the Sol internetwork, the ship's computer held a vast storehouse of scientific information inside its storage arrays.

Bertrand entered 'Edward Parrish' into the search field.

0 search results.

He then entered 'Mason Jessup' and got the same answer.

"I don't understand. You found the paper, they're clearly in the database."

"Yes, but someone blocked their names from showing up in searches."

"The admiral?"

"He clearly doesn't want us to know who we're traveling with."

Lana stepped back from the computer.

"What the fuck is an *entheogen?*"

"It means something like *generating the divine inside the self.* It's used to describe substances that make you see God and the little green men. LSD, psilocybin, DMT. It seems, the professor and the priest were studying the effects of DMT on true believers. Here, let me read you a section from their review paper: *There has long been debate among scholars of religion as to whether the psychedelic experience brought about by DMT consumption is equivalent to a genuine religious experience. In our view, experiencing the pure light of God is, at its core, a biochemical process. One that, with the use of DMT, we can bring into the lab with the hopes of unlocking a psychopharmicological route that will enable us to amplify the experience. To bring us in direct contact to the pure light of God.*"

"I don't like this, Bert. Not one bit." Lana paced around the medibeds. "Are there more articles?"

"Dozens from Parrish. Perhaps four of them with the priest."

"And they're all about drugs?"

"All of them."

"OK. Let's bring this to the captain. It's time our guests tell us what we're really doing out here."

Omicron Velorum Cluster
494 light-years from PSR J0835-4510

The crew of the *Rama* once again assembled in the mess hall.

Captain Pereira stood beside the admiral, her jaw clenched—she was pissed.

"I've gathered you here because Admiral Park and his associates have agreed to brief us on details of our mission that were—" She glanced towards the admiral. "—previously omitted."

The admiral grunted, straightened his uniform, and stepped forward.

"What you're about to hear is classified intelligence. Your corporation has already agreed to a non-disclosure agreement on your behalf. There is *no* opt-out." He looked at each member of the crew, holding Lana's gaze the longest. "Professor, the floor is yours."

The professor stood up, cleared his throat, and looked around the room before beginning.

"I am Edward Parrish of the Max Plank Institute for Entheobiology and Psychedelic Research. I study the phenomenology of religious experiences resulting from use of the compound dimethyltryptamine, otherwise known as DMT."

Jessup pressed a key on his tablet and the wallscreen displayed a three-dimensional rendering of the DMT molecule.

"DMT consumption induces a brief but intense hallucinatory voyage. Its key characteristics are depersonalization, altered time perception, death of the ego, and...encounters with supernatural entities."

The display filled with a grid of videos. Individuals of varying ages and ethnicities sat on hospital recliners as technicians administered injections. Something about their clothing caught Lana's eye.

They were all clergy members.

"For years my team, in collaboration with Father Jessup, has studied how DMT consumption evokes a common experience among adherents to many of the world's religions. What we discovered—"

"Excuse me," came a thick Ukrainian accent from the back of the room. It was the ship's technician, Boris. "Will this take much longer?"

"*Boris,*" snapped Captain Pereira, "take a nap if you're bored."

"Aye, ma'am."

The Professor coughed. "As I was saying, we discovered evidence of *external neural stimulation* during DMT usage."

Lana turned to Bertrand, who shrugged in response.

"Come again, professor?" she asked.

"Let me explain. This graph represents the overall entropy across the subject's neuronal connectome. In the awake brain, neural entropy increases in response to a novel stimulus then falls again as neurons minimize their prediction errors."

Jessup swiped on his tablet and another video filled the wallscreen. A priest in clerical clothing sat in a chair, his head covered by a metallic dome. Wires ran from electrode patches on his chest and hands to amplifiers outside the frame.

"The subject has just received 30 mg of DMT. In a few moments, they will begin to experience powerful hallucinations."

Lana turned to make a snide remark to Bert, only to find him completely engrossed.

"Now, look what happens to neuronal entropy." The professor pointed at the screen. As before, the graph shot up, wavered, then plummeted back down before repeating the pattern. "It's the same as in the waking brain! No other entheogen produces this effect."

Bertrand raised his hand. "Are you saying the subject's experiences are real?"

"I'm saying that on the basis of the neural data, we cannot distinguish DMT hallucinations from reality."

Bertrand whispered under his breath, "*I want to try it.*"

At the next table over, Norton shook his head. "What the *hell* does any of this have to do with Vela?"

"Look closely at his hand," said the Professor.

The video zoomed in on the subject's arm.

"It's twitching," said Norton.

"Correct. That patch on his hand is recording electromyography."

Another graph appeared on the screen and a series of staccato spikes scrolled in synchrony with the subject's twitches. Jessup swiped on his tablet and dozens more traces filled the wallscreen.

"Every one of our subjects exhibits this phenomenon. All of them tap at precisely the same frequency of once every eighty-nine milliseconds."

Lana's stomach dropped and she gripped Bertrand's arm.

"What's wrong?" he whispered.

"Vela," she hissed back.

Jessup tapped his tablet.

"Now look at this next trace."

On the wallscreen, the same spike train flowed by. However, in place of *millivolts*, the units were measured in *relative radio intensity*.

Jessup pressed a button, and a repetitive clanging noise filled the room, sounding like the amplified heartbeat of a small animal.

"This is a recording of Vela. What you're hearing is the radio pulse as our solar system is bombarded by Vela's emissions precisely once every eighty-nine milliseconds."

The rapid-fire rhythm continued to play over the loudspeaker.

Norton raised his hand. "They're not the same."

"That's correct. There's a small phase shift every seven repetitions."

The audio stopped.

"That was the official recording from the Whole Sky Pulsar Survey. Vela's entry was last updated fifty-four years ago. Thanks to Admiral Park, we were able to buy some time on the Square Kilometer Array in South Africa."

Jessup brought up a new trace.

"Our subjects' EMG traces and this new recording of Vela are a perfect match. It would appear that, sometime in the last fifty-four years, Vela developed a glitch!"

Lana pushed her palms into her eyes. *This was insane.* These idiots had them chasing after the hallucinations of a bunch of drugged-up priests to what? Investigate a pulsar glitch a thousand fucking light-years away?

Something about that number bothered Lana. She thought back to what she said at that first briefing.

We may travel faster than light, but our radio transmissions don't.

"Professor," exclaimed Lana, "Vela is almost a thousand light-years from Earth. That new signal you recorded is practically from the dark ages."

"Exactly!" The professor beamed at her. "Something happened at Vela a thousand years ago that created the glitch. That something happens to coincide with the first recorded use of DMT in sacred rituals across the world."

The professor looked at the darkness outside the viewport. When he turned back, he spoke softly, as though only to himself.

"What if our ancestors woke something during their astral travels? What if we're not alone among the stars? I believe Vela is an invitation. And soon, we're going to answer it."

Outer shell of the Vela SNR
49 light-years from PSR J0835-4510

In the medbay, Jessup attached EMG patches and EKG leads to Bertrand's hands and chest. Ever since the professor's presentation, Bertrand had gotten it into his head that he would try DMT. Lana had argued with him repeatedly over it. However, the professor proved receptive to the idea, hoping their proximity to Vela might reveal something new about the glitch.

"Bert, this is a really bad idea," said Lana.

"I'll be fine, *mon chou*. Trust me."

"It's OK," Jessup smiled reassuringly, "we're monitoring his vitals. If he starts having a bad trip, we can bring him down instantly with this." Jessup held up a blue jet injector.

The door slid open, and Norton and Boris walked in. Lana gave them a questioning look.

"What? We're not allowed to be curious?" replied the large Ukrainian.

Jessup lowered a metallic dome over Bertrand's head.

"Say something so I can calibrate the scanner."

"*Allons-y!* I want to go see the little green men!"

Lana paced around nervously.

"Does anyone else think it's a bad idea to drug our only physician while we're hundreds of light-years from Earth?"

"DMT is perfectly safe," said Jessup, "the only danger your friend is in is of discovering his authentic self."

Lana rolled her eyes at Burt, who winked back at her.

"Ready?" asked Jessup.

Bertrand gave a thumbs-up and Jessup pressed a jet injector against his bare arm. There was a faint hiss as the drug was delivered into his bloodstream.

"See you on the other side," said Bertrand.

He took a deep shuddering breath and closed his eyes. On the wallscreen, his heart rate increased, but otherwise, everything appeared normal.

"*Oh, c'est merveilleux!*"

"Bertrand, can you hear me?" asked Jessup.

"*Oui, monsieur!*"

"Can you describe what you see?"

"Oh yes. You are all made of such fantastic geometries!"

"Good." Jessup turned to the rest of them. "He's experiencing the early stages of DMT. These first hallucinations can be disorienting as they tend to have non-euclidean components."

Jessup studied Bertrand's vitals on the wallscreen.

"The next stage will begin shortly. We call it the *breakthrough*. Bertrand will experience his consciousness leaving the body to travel through what subjects often describe as *hyperspace*. From that point on, he will not speak again until the comedown."

Lana put her hand on Bertrand's arm and felt something tremble beneath her touch. When she looked down to see the cause, her mouth dropped. Bertrand's index finger twitched against the side of the medibed.

"Jessup, his finger."

"I see it." Jessup wasn't looking at Bertrand but at the EMG trace on the wallscreen. "Eighty-nine milliseconds exactly with a phase shift every seventh repeat."

"Just like Vela," said Lana.

Bertrand whimpered.

"Is that normal?" she asked.

Bertrand's lips were moving. Lana leaned in. It took her a few seconds to translate what Bertrand was saying into English. When she did, it made the hairs on the back of her neck stand up.

"He says he has to get away from the machines."

"That's not uncommon," said Jessup, "subjects often describe traveling through vast machinescapes on their way to the entities."

Bertrand's heart rate shot up and an alarm rang out. His hands jerked and he pounded out Vela's pulse train with such force that the medibed shook.

"Bert!" Lana cried, "Jessup, bring him down!"

Jessup looked back and forth between the wallscreen and his subject, a confused look on his face. "We should let him finish the voyage."

"*Fuck the voyage!* Give him the injection!"

Bertrand's body began to convulse.

Lana pleaded. "Do it now!"

Jessup plunged the injector into Bertrand's neck. His eyes jerked open and he gasped like he'd been shot with adrenaline.

"Bert, it's OK. You had a bad trip."

His face flushed with rage, and he yelled at her in French "*Tu comprends pas! Les machines!*"

He slid out of the brain scanner and shoved Lana aside.

Jessup stepped in front of him. "Bertrand, you're disoriented, please sit back down."

Bertrand snarled and slammed Jessup against a medibed.

Boris came over and put one large hand on Bertrand's shoulder. "I think you should listen to your friends and have a seat," he said, his voice low and threatening.

"*Non!* We have to go to them! We must join in the configuration!"

"Sit down, or I make you sit."

Bertrand headbutted the larger man. Boris fell back dazed as blood gushed from his broken nose.

"Stop him!" yelled Lana as Bertrand made for the exit.

Jessup grabbed the bundle of EMG and EKG wires dragging across the floor. Bertrand struggled against the makeshift leash, causing the patches to rip off his skin one by one like Velcro.

At the back of the room, Lana riffled through a cabinet and found the container marked *halodiazepam*. She ran past Jessup and stabbed a pair of jet injectors into the back of Bertrand's neck.

Bertrand whirled around, a hurt expression on his face. The madness that had fallen over him was gone.

It was just Bert.

Bracing himself against a medibed, he took a step towards her. Boris was back on his feet and moving to intercept. Lana waved him back.

"Bert?"

Bertrand's breathing grew shallow as the tranquilizer took hold. Before he slumped to the floor, he managed to speak a single sentence.

"*Lana, don't go into the labyrinth.*"

PSR J0835-4510
959 light-years from Sol

Silence hung over *Rama*'s bridge as the crew gazed in awe at the image on the main wallscreen.

Vela.

An immaculate sphere in a galaxy of imperfect forms. Its rapidly rotating neutron core, the only object in the cosmos dense enough to overcome the centrifugal forces that would have otherwise caused it to bulge out. And somewhere out there, its twin beams of gamma radiation painted an invisible arc of death across the night sky exactly once every 89 milliseconds.

"Distance?" asked Captain Pereira.

"Holding at ninety-seven AUs," replied Norton. "Background radiation is higher than I'd like, but we're okay."

The admiral turned away from the wallscreen, his expression sour.

"Where is the glitch?"

Captain Pereira shifted in her seat. "I'm sorry?"

"The glitch in Vela's period. Where is it?"

"Admiral, just what *exactly* do you think the glitch is?"

Lana turned from her station to face them. "Admiral, pulsar glitches occur when the outer core becomes coupled to the—"

"Dammit, I know what glitches are! This one is different. Something is causing it, check your systems and find it!"

Lana gave the captain a look and she shrugged in response.

"Lana, initiate a narrowband sweep around Vela. Four degrees of arc."

"Aye, ma'am. Commencing radio sweep."

"And get that damn thing off my viewscreen!"

Lana switched off the magnification and Vela disappeared from view. At *Rama*'s current distance, the pulsar, no more than twelve miles in diameter, appeared as a bright star in the night, no different from the millions of others that dotted the darkness of space.

After several fruitless minutes, the admiral began to pace the bridge. Every so often, he'd stand behind Lana's station and pester her for an update.

Lana's console beeped.

"Sweep complete. There's nothing–wait, hold on."

"What is it?" inquired the captain.

"Captain, there's a shadow in the x-ray band. Putting it onscreen."

The wallscreen filled with a false-color image showing Vela's electromagnetic emissions in a narrow band of x-ray. There was a dark streak that began a few degrees of arc from Vela and fanned out like a shadow.

"Switch back to optical," ordered the captain.

The screen returned to an optical view of Vela.

"Lana, are you sure that's the same area? There's nothing there."

"Holy shit! Yes, there is," exclaimed Lana.

She walked up to the main wallscreen and traced a square with her finger over an area of space. As soon as she finished, they all saw it. A perfectly square patch of darkness occluded the background stars. As though a hole had been punched in the fabric of space.

"How big is that?" asked the captain.

"Big, ma'am. Twenty kilometers per side," Lana said.

"What the hell is it?"

The Admiral straightened his uniform and smiled.

"That, Captain Pereira, is the source of Vela's glitch."

Rama came to a stop in the shadow of the black cube. Vela was on the other side, irradiating the night with violent gamma-ray emissions. Were it not for the dark object before them, *Rama*, its crew, and all its systems would not survive being this close to the pulsar.

On the bridge, Norton laser-scanned the anomaly, searching for any breaks in its surface. The crew was tired, none of them had left the bridge since they discovered the dark cube and traveled down the funnel of its electromagnetic shadow.

"Anything?" the captain asked for the third time.

"No, ma'am, the surface is perfectly smooth."

"Stop…Norton, go back!" said Lana.

Norton stopped panning the ship's laser scanner. On the wallscreen, a wireframe model of the cube, spanning several kilometers in height, filled the display. Lana pointed to a small break in the grid.

"What is that?" asked the admiral.

"It looks like a platform," replied Norton, "about two hundred meters wide and fifty deep."

"The mouth of the beast," said Lana.

The admiral gave her a condescending look.

"Bring us in closer," he ordered.

On the screen, the wireframe model updated as their forward momentum brought them closer to the anomaly. The dark surface of the structure was all but invisible, were it not for their sensors, it would be impossible to know it was there at all.

The object's awesome scale and unknown origin rustled something deep inside Lana. A fear she'd not felt since she was a child and still scared of what might be hiding in the dark. If only Bert were here instead of sedated in the medbay. He'd make some snide remark. *The plot thickens.* And it would quell the growing dread that festered within her.

"Captain," said Norton, "there's a break at the far end of the platform. It looks like…" he hesitated. "Ma'am, it looks like a doorway."

"Lana, is there *any possibility* that this thing could be a natural formation?" asked the Captain.

"No," replied Lana, "It's a perfect cube, identical on every side. There are crystals that form cubic lattices, but not at this scale."

"I see." The captain tapped the side of her chair with her index finger, a nervous tick she'd picked up since entering the remnant. "Admiral Park, it looks like we found your glitch. What now?"

"Land the ship."

The seven figures floated along the platform toward the doorway at the far end. The darkness was punctuated only by the occasional flare of light as one of the crew activated their suit's propulsion.

Lana turned back towards the ship. Even with all of its exterior lights, *Rama* appeared small and fragile against the immense blackness of space. Like a tin egg waiting to be crushed.

Bert was in there. Restrained and sedated. It pained Lana to leave him. What if he wakes up? What if he started raving again? They'd instructed the remaining officer on how to use the tranquilizers, but if Bert lost it again, would they be up to the task?

Ahead, the admiral and professor crossed the threshold and entered the cube.

"It's like a cathedral," said the professor over the radio.

The passage led into a cavernous corridor that stretched for as far as their lights could reach. Sheer featureless walls rose high above them, ending in a vaulted ceiling. Everything was made of the same dark material, as though the corridor had been etched into the anomaly

Norton held a utility torch and kept it aimed down the passageway. As the figures in front crossed its path, they cast monstrous shadows over the corridor. It was in one of those shadows that Lana first noticed the faint glow.

"Norton, turn off your torch. Everyone, power down your suit lights."

"What is it, Lana?" asked the captain.

"There's something up ahead."

As their eyes adjusted to the dark, they all saw the faint reddish glow at the end of the corridor.

"That's daylight," Boris stated plainly.

Lana looked skeptically at him through her suit's visor.

"What?" The Ukrainian shrugged inside his EVA suit. "It looks like sunlight."

The Admiral and the professor went first, their EVA suits back-lit by the crimson-red glow that emanated from beyond the opening.

"Isn't it beautiful?" the professor said over the radio.

Captain Pereira floated out onto the ledge next to them and gasped.

Lana and Norton went next.

"Oh my God!" exclaimed Lana.

The inside of the cube anomaly was hollow.

The dark walls spread out on either side into a vast featureless landscape. In the sky above and the ground below—for Lana's terrestrial mind knew of no other way to interpret what she was seeing—stood vast cyclopean structures that fanned out in a grid, not unlike the blocks of a city or the traces on a circuit board.

Or the corridors of a labyrinth.

At various points along the vast distances before them, circular spires rose from the ground like spokes on a wheel. They converged towards a point in the center where a large featureless Citadel stood. Above it, suspended in the center by some unseen force, was a cubic structure from which the crimson illumination emanated.

All along the colossal landscape, geometric planes of shadow spread out in an arc as the light source in the center slowly rotated. The overall effect was of a day/night cycle whose borders were visible only to someone from their current vantage point.

This majestic geography was mirrored on the ceiling above them, and as Lana looked from ground to sky, her head swam with vertigo as her mind desperately struggled to reconcile these two opposing vistas.

"The light," said the captain, her voice muted to almost a whisper, "it's scattering."

Lana saw it too. A faint haze that obscured the most distant structures.

She checked her wrist computer. "There's an atmosphere. It's thin, but… it's *breathable*. Wait—"

"Lana, what is it?"

She studied the readout. "The air is full of an organic compound."

Jessup floated over to her. "May I see?" He looked at the readout on Lana's wrist computer.

"That's dimethyltryptamine. DMT."

"Fuck," exclaimed Lana.

"Alright, everyone. Nothing's changed." said the captain, "Atmosphere or no atmosphere, this is still officially a spacewalk. Keep your helmets on and your suit pressurized."

The admiral peered over the edge. "We keep going."

"Are you crazy? Captain, fuck the chain of command. We have to go back! This is—" Lana let her eyes gaze again at the structures above and below "—incredible. But we're taking an enormous risk just by being off the ship."

"Lana's right," said Captain Pereira, "I'm pulling the plug. We go back to *Rama*."

"The hell we are!" exclaimed the admiral, "I am the ranking officer here."

The captain glared at the admiral through her visor and was about to speak when Boris's thick Ukrainian accent came over the radio.

"I'm sorry to interrupt, but has anyone seen the professor?"

"Anyone who wishes to go back is welcome to do so. We have about sixty minutes of O2 left. If we are unable to retrieve the professor in the next thirty minutes, we leave him. Is that understood?"

Everyone but the admiral nodded.

"We move out in pairs."

The captain and the admiral went first. They stepped off the platform and descended downwards. Next came Lana and Jessup, who floated off the edge and followed after them.

The region beneath the platform was in the night section of the central cube's rotation and they had no trouble spotting the professor's EVA suit lights descending into the gloom below.

To cover the ten-kilometer trip to the ground in time, the Captain ordered them to increase their velocity to sixty kilometers per hour. Despite their speed, the vastness of the anomaly's interior volume gave the illusion of a slow descent.

As the ground drew closer, the grid-like configuration they had seen from above resolved into a maze of enormous passages.

"Begin deceleration. Stay close. He's headed for that spire," said Captain Pereira.

The pairs of astronauts gradually slowed their descent to a gentle fall before landing on the ground at the base of one of the enormous spires. All around the structure, the grid of cathedral-like corridors fanned out in multiple directions.

The spire itself was taller than it had appeared from above. The red stone material of its walls was rougher than the smooth dark surface of the outer cube. It looked primitive by comparison. Lana thought it may as well have been constructed by a completely different civilization.

As if reading her mind, Norton spoke. "These buildings don't fit in." He shone his utility torch up the spire. "They look like...ancient temples."

As Lana's gaze followed the tower into the sky, she caught sight of rectangular slabs that jutted out at irregular intervals. *Those look like balconies.*

A flicker of movement. Lana strained to make out the far-off shape, it looked almost like—*is that a face?*

"Does anyone else see that? Norton, hold your torch still. There! A third of the way up."

The figure jerked away and disappeared inside the structure.

"I don't think we're alone," said Lana.

The admiral scoffed. "You're imagining things, this place is long dead."

The Captain sighed. "Alright everyone, I don't want us to be here any longer than we have to. Ten minutes to find the Professor and then we get the hell out of here, with or without him!" The captain pointed at the spire. "The admiral and I will search for an entrance, the rest of you, take a look down those passageways in case he landed over there. Stay together and don't take any risks."

Lana and Jessup trailed behind as Norton and Boris floated to the nearest entrance to the grid. As they moved inside, the dark interior swallowed them up. Only the beam of Norton's utility torch moving along the walls allowed Lana to pinpoint their location.

Boris's voice rang out over the radio.

"We found something. *Is not good.*"

Lana and Jessup entered the grid and floated next to the pair.

"You're going to want to see this," Norton said.

Norton shone his torch on what appeared to be a giant mound of dark flesh hanging from the wall. He lifted the beam of his torch higher and Lana's skin ran cold. Ten feet above the ground a human head stuck out of the cocoon of flesh. Norton panned the light back down and Lana made out the faint shadowy form of the person's body embedded inside the flesh sac.

"Show her the eyes," said Boris.

Norton raised his torch back to the figure's head. The woman suspended there was bald, her ash-colored skin was dry and desiccated. Deep cracks had formed around the creases of her mouth and nose. She appeared dead, except for the eyes. They were open. The pupils, dulled to a milky gray, moved back and forth. The speed was strobe-light fast. It reminded Lana of a flickering display.

It reminded her of Vela.

"There's more," said Norton and he shone his torch down the corridor. Mounds of flesh hung from the wall for as far as the eye could see. Each with a human occupant.

"Where did they all come from?" asked Lana.

"I have a theory," replied Norton, "we're not the first ship to come here. How else would the Admiral know what to look for? The UNSA must have sent ships before us. *Expendable* ships like ours!"

"It doesn't make sense," said Lana.

"Why not?"

"The size of this place. Not just here, but look above us. If the rest of it is anything like this, then not even a thousand ships could fill this place!"

They stood in silence, gazing up at the mirror image of their location nearly twenty kilometers above.

"The labyrinth," murmured Lana.

"What's that?" asked Norton.

"It's something Bert said…" Lana thought back to that frantic moment in the medbay. Back to the last *sane* thing Bert had said before succumbing to madness.

"He warned me not to go into the *labyrinth*."

Over the radio, Jessup could be heard sobbing. His EVA suit helmet was turned up towards the woman in the cocoon. Lana floated over to him.

"It wasn't supposed to be like this," he said, "we were supposed to find evidence of the divine." He swept his arm towards the rest of the corridor. "Not this! *There's no God here.*"

"Father Jessup," said Boris, "no offense, but I say fuck your God and fuck the professor. It's time we leave."

"Amen to that," said Norton.

A burst of static rang out over the intercom, followed by shouting.

"Shh, it's the captain. Everyone listen," said Lana.

"Professor, I want you to come with us, that's an order."

"They're coming."

"What the fuck is that?"

"Professor, get away from it!"

"I have traveled the stars—"

"Admiral, leave him, we need to go NOW."

"—to find you. I deliver myself into—"

"I don't understand. Its face looks human."

"Now, admiral!"

"—your hands. To join you in glorious union."

"Professor, no! Keep your helmet on!"

"Admiral! Behind you."

A howl of wind followed by an alarm indicating someone's EVA suit had been compromised.

"Captain? It's Lana. Where are you?"

"We should leave," repeated Boris.

"Not without the captain!"

Lana activated her propulsion and shot out of the corridor, back towards the spire. She engaged the lateral thrusters and her forward momentum caused her to arc around the circumference of the building towards the direction the captain and admiral had traveled.

Behind her, Boris copied her maneuver. Halfway around the spire, Lana found an opening in the smooth walls.

She slowed her approach and oriented herself to the opening. Boris pulled up alongside her.

"Are you sure about this?" he asked.

"No."

"Good, neither am I."

They floated into the opening. The inside of the spire was completely dark, their EVA suit lamps cut tiny pools of light in the blackness. As best Lana could tell, they were inside a large atrium.

"There!"

On the ground, several meters ahead, was an EVA suit helmet, its visor cracked. Lana swept the area with her suit lights but saw no trace of the admiral or the captain.

"Norton, we could sure use your torch in here."

Norton's voice crackled over comms.

"I'm on my way."

Lana turned to find Boris staring up at the wall. It was another one of those cocoons. She came closer and her suit lights illuminated the face of Captain Pereira. Her neck and skin were stained with blood and a dark purple fluid that seeped from the flesh around her. The cocoon glistened and pulsed with life, it slithered around the exposed parts of the captain's body. Entombing her.

The captain stared at Lana, her face grimacing as if under an enormous strain. Her mouth twitched as she tried to form words.

Lana. Go.

Then, her pupils dilated and her head jerked up towards the ceiling. Her eyes began to move back and forth like a pendulum. Picking up speed with every passing second.

"We have to get her down!"

Lana rushed to the wall and pulled on the mound of flesh, trying to dislodge it. At her feet, thick flesh vines spread away from the cocoon and followed the edge of the floor, reminding Lana of the thick network cables in *Rama*'s computer room.

A tendril crept out of the captain's cocoon and wrapped itself around Lana's wrist. She panicked, and pushed away from the wall, trying to rip herself free. Her body floated away before the tension in the vine caused her to glide back. Her feet searched the ground but were unable to find purchase in this low-gravity environment.

Boris was at her side, pulling on the tendril. Pushing against Lana to create leverage between them. Slowly, the flesh vine uncoiled from her wrist, and she was free.

Engaging her suit thrusters, she backed away rapidly and bumped into something on the opposing wall. Turning around, Lana found herself face to face with the admiral.

They were too late. The admiral's skin had turned gray and his eyes already moved with Vela's rhythm.

"We have to leave them," Boris said.

Lana nodded her helmet.

She turned, away from the wall, but in the darkness, she'd lost sight of the entrance.

"Which way did we come from?" Lana panicked as she looked for the exit. Her heart pounded in her chest. They had to get out. Something had done this to the captain and the admiral. *The face on the balcony.* The admiral had said it had looked human. Lana could feel it in the darkness with them. Watching.

"Boris, which way?"

"I don't fucking know! This way…maybe."

Boris took off into the darkness and Lana followed after him when, suddenly, his EVA suit jerked upward. A cry of pain rang out over the radio.

Lana was blinded by a beam of light.

It was Norton, his utility light lit up the darkness of the atrium and she saw everything.

Flesh cocoons hung from the walls. Beneath them, dark cables unspooled onto the floor, joining up to larger trunks in glistening junctions of flesh. She saw Boris, hanging several feet off the ground.

And she saw the creature that held him.

Lana's stomach plummeted and her hands shook as she peered into its cold dark eyes. Its large, thin body was covered in tattered red robes. Its limbs were long and slender. Its expressionless face was enormous, and the skin shone like plastic, giving it the appearance of a giant theatrical mask made of flesh and bone. Although the creature was a giant compared to them, the configuration of features on its face was unmistakably human.

It moved like a marionette,its enormous limbs unfurling as though attached to invisible strings.

"Lana, get out of there!" Norton yelled over the comms.

Lana looked back toward the captain, her skin had already turned gray. She couldn't save her. But Boris…

Lana slammed the thrusters on her EVA suit and accelerated towards the creature. Sensing her gambit, Boris reached out. Lana collided with his arm and frantically searched for a grip on his suit.

There was a moment she felt her momentum slow. Where she was sure the creature had held onto them both. Then, they tumbled out of the entrance, nearly colliding with Norton and Jessup.

"Captain's dead. We're leaving NOW," said Lana.

Behind them, the entity emerged from the Spire. Then another. This one younger, its robes less worn. It moved quickly in their direction, its legs pushing off the surface in a series of low-gravity leaps. Its long arms reaching out for them.

"Up! Up!" Lana screamed into her radio.

Jessup fumbled with his suit's controls as the creature grew near. Norton grabbed his arm and pulled him up with him.

The four remaining astronauts gained altitude, moving away from the spire in the direction of the far wall.

Lana glanced down behind them. More of the plastic-faced entities had emerged from the entrance. They stood perfectly still, their dark expressionless eyes tracking their ascent.

Boris's voice crackled over the radio.

"That was some move."

"You're welcome."

"We're not out of this yet. You can have my thanks when you fly us back home."

As they increased their velocity, Lana scanned the faraway wall where the ledge to the corridor ought to be.

"Norton, I can't see the opening. Where the fuck is it?"

"Aim for the center," he replied, "This place is huge, we won't see it until we're close."

Lana's wrist computer flashed a warning. Her O2 was running low.

"We're going to run out on O2 before we get to *Rama*. Go to 100kph."

"At that speed, can we decelerate in time?"

"We don't have a choice. Go to 100kph!"

Ahead, a thin sliver of darkness. Different from the dark walls of the cube. *The corridor.*

"Something's coming," said Norton.

They all saw it. A light growing steadily brighter.

"Is that an EVA suit?" Lana asked.

"Lana, we have to slow down!" Norton cried.

"OK, reverse thrust now!"

Lana felt her suit kick against her as she activated her forward thrusters. The shape in the tunnel was coming up fast now.

"Who is that?" Norton asked.

The figure showed no signs of responding. It flew past and for a brief moment, Lana saw into the visor of its suit's helmet.

She had known it would be Bert. Had known it the instant they saw the suit lights in the corridor. Had known it before she saw the face in the visor.

However, the Bert she knew was gone.

The face that had flashed by had borne a look of pure madness—a wild and twisted grin that stretched his features into a grotesque mockery of the friend she had known.

Lana looked behind her. In the distance, Bertrand's EVA suit raced down toward one of the spires.

The radio crackled.

The voice that came over comms chilled Lana to the core.

"Lana, come with me."

She didn't reply.

"They're everywhere, you know. Here. Back on earth. They've always been there. In between and all around. And there are so many more of them. Lost between worlds."

Lana looked at her wrist computer. They were running out of time.

"They need us, Lana. We must join in the configuration. We are the key that opens the way."

They drifted over the ledge and into the corridor. Bertrand's radio signal grew fainter.

"You'll see. You have no—" Static cut him off momentarily, they were losing the signal. *"—when you get outside, you'll see."*

The radio went dead.

The exit back to the platform loomed ahead. Soon, they would be back on *Rama*. Soon, they would be going home.

We should be able to see the ship's lights.
Oh fuck!
Oh no!
Bert, what did you do?

Rama was gone.

The four remaining astronauts stood on the dark platform looking out into the void of space. They had tried to raise the ship on the radio but to no avail.

What could they do? Go back? The air was breathable, but it was filled with DMT. How long would they last before they ended up like Bert?

An alarm drew Lana out of her thoughts. Her wrist computer flashed red—her O2 was dangerously low. Looking over, she saw the same warning on her companions' wrists.

She felt like she should say something. *Really, Lana. A speech? Pereira's gone for less than an hour and you're already trying to fill her shoes?*

She laughed. Maybe she was already showing the effects of hypoxia.

One of the stars in the distance winked at her.

She winked back.

It winked again.

That's no star.

"That's *Rama*!" Lana pointed. "Anyone know how far that is?"

"Hold on," said Norton, "Let me think."

He raised his arm and lined up his thumb with the ship. Lana recognized what he was doing.

"Really?"

"It's all I fucking got OK? The suit doesn't have a range finder."

"How far?"

"Uhh, five klicks. Give or take a few hundred meters."

Lana checked her propellant. *Fuck.* She was almost empty.

If I miss, I'll just keep going and going...

Her O2 alarm beeped again. It wouldn't matter, she'd be dead from asphyxiation in a few minutes anyway.

"Stay here, I'm going to get our ship back."

Lana jammed her forward thrusters. Her suit lifted off the platform and into the vast sea of darkness. She planned to leave just enough propellant to correct her heading once she was close. The star that was *Rama* slowly grew larger.

Something was wrong. She couldn't keep *Rama* centered in her view. Her suit beeped as her propellant ran out. Lana tried to engage her lateral thrusters, but nothing happened. She punched the button again. *Dammit, come on!* But it was no use. She fucked up. Failed to leave enough propellant to adjust her trajectory, and now they would all die.

A pressure on her arm.

Turning her helmet she saw Boris looking back at her.

Lana beamed at the crazy Ukrainian through her visor.

"Are you sure about this?" she asked.

He shook his head.

"Good, neither am I!"

Boris put his arms around her and engaged his lateral thrusters. In the distance, *Rama* moved steadily toward the center of their trajectory.

Then it happened. Boris's thrusters cut out, and his wrist computer flashed a warning as he ran out of propellant. Lana looked over and saw that he was sweating inside his visor. He did not look well.

"Ran out of O2 long ago," he explained through gasping breaths.

"Boris, I'm sorry."

Rama was coming up fast. She could make out the airlock hatch, the cockpit, the mess hall viewport. They were so close. *Rama* drifted towards the center of their trajectory, but it wasn't going to be enough. They were going to pass her by. Just another second or two of thrust and they would have made it.

Boris's grip on her shifted and he pulled himself around so that their visors were face-to-face.

"Save them," then he added, "Ma'am."

Before she understood what he was doing, she felt him push against her and then let go. They floated apart. The force changed her trajectory. Sending her hurtling towards *Rama* as Boris drifted away into the emptiness of space.

"Boris!" she cried.

But there was no time, *Rama* was approaching fast. She was going to hit hard. Lana tried her forward thrusters again, anything to slow her speed, but there was nothing left. She would have to grab onto something or risk careening off the hull.

This is going to hurt.

Lana slammed into the ship, her torso colliding with the grab hold she had been aiming for. She felt a crack in her chest, and pain shot through her ribs. Her suit slid across the hull, tumbling over a curved section. Her hands frantically grabbed for a hold. Then she jerked to a stop as her boot became stuck on something, leaving her dangling over the ship.

The radio-telescope.

Her left foot broke through the thin plating of the dish, holding her in place as she flailed in a wild panic.

She tried to calm herself. Tried to ignore the primal fear she felt at hanging upside down over the chasm of space. Lana focused on her breathing. The air in her suit was stale, too much of her own CO2 mixed in. Feeling for the edge of the dish, careful not to puncture her suit, she pried away the metal plating that held her boot in place.

Lana crawled over the hull of the ship. The lack of O2 left her feeling woozy and confused. At the airlock hatch, she stopped and puzzled at the controls. *How the fuck do I open this?* She could no longer remember.

Boris would know.

She looked out into space. In the distance, his EVA suit had receded to a pinpoint of light, to take its place among the stars. Lana blinked and when she opened her eyes the star was gone. She was out of time.

She closed her eyes and concentrated on the controls. The word "disengage" came into focus and she jammed the button.

A hiss of air and the airlock door unsealed.

They found the comms officer on the floor of *Rama*'s bridge. Norton helped her back to her seat as Jessup examined the wound on her head.

"Bit of a concussion, but I think she'll be OK."

An alarm went off.

"The airlock!" Lana exclaimed.

She sat in the captain's chair, pulled over the systems display, and swiped the camera feed onto the main wallscreen.

It was one of *them*.

The enormous creature was hunched over, its thin limbs furled up as it tapped at the airlock controls with the long digits of its finger. Somehow it knew they were watching and it turned its enormous head towards the camera.

"There's more!" cried Norton.

Behind the creature, at the end of the platform, they could see the dark entrance to the anomaly. Inside, bathed in shadows, more of them were coming. Their enormous plastic faces stood out like ghosts in the darkness.

"Norton, get us out of here now!"

"Aye, ma'am."

Rama's maneuvering jets fired, lifting the ship away from the platform and out into the shadow of the cube. The creature held on, its thin fingers finding purchase on the handholds at either side of the airlock. Its giant human face betrayed no emotion as the ship accelerated outwards.

Lana watched over the camera feed. She was certain it would hold on forever. Would find a way into the ship. And then what? Would she too entombed inside a cocoon of flesh? Her body taken over and her mind jacked into the machines? Like they'd done to Captain Pereira.

Lana swiped at the captain's systems display. *There has to be something in here. Something I can use.*

There it was, buried in the airlock emergency control panel. Explosive Hatch Release.

"Hold on everyone, this might rock the boat."

Lana punched the button and a deep thundering pulse came from the bowels of the ship. It rattled the hull and their course shifted slightly.

On the camera feed, the creature was gone. Far behind them, they could see its giant body spiraling out into space. Its limbs unfurled to their full length and it thrashed like a worm dying in the sun. Then, a bright flash lit up the bridge as the creature fell out of the electromagnetic shadow of the cube and was consumed by the fire of Vela's gamma rays.

Lana sat in the captain's chair, moving around equations and data structures on the screen as she computed a course away from Vela and out of the remnant. Her left hand rested at her side. A slight, almost imperceptible twitching animated her fingers as they tapped out a staccato pulse against the fabric of the armrest.

THE WRECKAGE OF HESTIA
Jessica Peter

We made love under the mercury-vapour lamps of the dining hall. They cast a greenish pall over Henry's skin that made him appear sickly, but we laughed and came together in a few sweat-soaked moments that made us forget the rest. Only when we lie together on the table afterwards did the oppressive solitude creep back.

Henry drifted off for a nap as I listened to the soft hum of the survival systems. Oxygen, depressurization, electricity. Yet beyond the hum, each room echoed with emptiness, every motion I made came back to me tenfold. This encampment on Hestia was supposed to fit thousands of refugees from the water wars, but after that first accident up here, all the colonists had fled back home.

They hadn't built this place with *living* in mind, just surviving. It turned out surviving wasn't enough. They'd rather take their chances with the dying Earth.

I could almost hear their voices embedded in the walls.

Henry murmured in his sleep and pulled me towards him, so I cuddled in. We weren't partners, just two lost souls who could come together in romance or whatever else and come apart just as easily. Two people who enjoyed the convenience of another warm body. We'd both had the same amount of nothing waiting for us back on Earth—me with a dead partner, dead family, dead-end job—so we'd volunteered to stay on to maintain the encampment. A skeleton crew for the skeletal encampment, on the chance that others would return and fill it with something resembling life again.

I knew better. They wouldn't be back.

A muffled thud came from outside the room. I bolted upright, but Henry only shifted.

"You okay, Sophia?" He opened his groggy, sated eyes.

"Did you hear that?"

His gaze sharpened and he fumbled for his station-issued boxer briefs. "No?"

"Maybe something fell?" In most other places, that might not matter. Here, where damage to the structure might take our oxygen with it, it could be a disaster.

We pulled on our clothes, me worrying my bottom lip as Henry quieted into his usual cool focus. We each grabbed our oxygen helmets by the door, but avoided the bulky spacesuits. If decompression had started, we'd have felt the effects.

"Split up?" His fingers tap-tapped on the helmet.

Dread coursed through me. To think, back on Earth, I used to love the chance to be alone. "I'll go counter-clockwise," I said.

I started with town square, the massive and ironically circular central area of empty storefronts and dead trees covered with a thick glass dome. It had been a wonder and a marvel when they built it, and even now it seemed the integrity of the glass would never fail. I checked it anyway; it held fast. As always, looking out at the darkness of Hestia's night that lasted sixteen Earth days gave me a tickling feeling up my spine.

Like I was being watched.

I turned from the dome, ignoring the creeping sensation, and set out toward D Wing. Ten identical wings radiated from town square like spokes on a wheel. I started down the first corridor, fluorescent lights turning on as I did. Toward the berths, there was a soft rustle like fabric against a wall, as if someone was walking just ahead.

My gaze snapped down that hall. It was dark, and I couldn't bring myself to step into it to activate the lighting. There was nothing down there. There couldn't be.

The fine hairs on my arms lifted. I squinted into the darkness, but nothing moved, nothing shifted.

The radio inside my helmet crackled.

I jumped, and then felt sheepish. "Henry?"

"You were right about the thud," he said, ignoring all radio protocol. Not that it mattered with just the two of us. "We lost a piece of the roof in G Wing."

"Are we destabilized?" There was a long silence. I could hear my own heart beating.

"No," he said. "But I think we'll have to shut down the wing."

I closed my eyes for a moment, embarrassed to find that my eyes were damp. As maintainers, this was failure. The encampment had the systems to keep thousands of people alive for decades. We should be able to keep it whole.

"I'll come help."

The next crackle of the radio signalled Henry's agreement.

I began to go, to join him, but the allure of finding the source of that soft rustle pulled at me. I'd been too long in near isolation. Was this it, the point where I finally cracked? Started hearing things? Lost it for good? The psychiatrist who'd cleared me for this role couldn't have known how it would be. The pressure of an entire empty planet, with only one other living soul on it.

I took a deep breath and strode across town square toward Henry.

He stood outside G Wing, his hands on his hips, his back to me.

As I neared, he turned towards me and pointed one thumb behind his back. Through the door, I could see that there was a tiny shadow in the ceiling, visible only as a darker void on the slate grey metal. A hole.

I inhaled sharply, picturing the whole encampment crumpling like a tin can. I shifted this way and that, viewing the little gap through the thick glass of the G Wing door.

"We could try repairing it…but, yeah, maybe we have to shut the airlock," I said.

"Yeah." He rubbed his wrist with two fingers, a gesture I'd seen him doing more and more lately. "That's what I thought, but I wanted your opinion."

He didn't take his eyes off the hole as he spoke. The tiny blot that could wipe us out entirely.

And yet. Cutting off a wing was like cutting off a limb. It wasn't something to do lightly.

We stood in silence for a moment in a sort of mourning. For the wing, certainly. But also for the people that had once been here and had given up. For the Earth that they'd fled to that might not make it. For us too, trapped alone.

Then Henry spoke with his voice thick. "Let's do it."

We both held the wheel of the airlock together, as if this way neither of us could be to blame. The door shut with a pressurized hiss and light clank.

G Wing was closed. And then there were nine.

"I guess we head to bed for the night." The hole might be closed off, but he still didn't face me, didn't look in my eyes.

A sharp pang ripped through me. I didn't want to go to bed alone, not tonight. Our berths may be beside each other, but we didn't share. Most of the time that was fine. Tonight I wished that wasn't the case.

But I said nothing. I didn't want to interrupt our easy balance. Even more, I didn't want to infect him with my baseless fear.

I went back to my room where I thrashed through the night. Did I want to go back to Earth? I could, if I requested it. They didn't want people who were losing their minds being the ones left up here. But what had Earth held for me? Nothing but death.

My sister Olivia died before everything went bad, back when we were still kids. Mangled beneath the wheels of a car while I stood there and watched, useless, my feet rooted in place. My mother was dead for twenty long years now, slaughtered in her walk-up apartment in the brutal inner-city battles as people fought for water. My partner, who ironically died drowning on dry land as the white plague filled their lungs. They just missed being able to join me on Hestia. It was supposed to be our new life.

The encampment might be haunted and isolated, but it wasn't any worse than home.

I awoke hours later covered in dried sweat to what sounded like distant voices. It wasn't morning as I once knew it; not for the equivalent of another ten Earth days. But I sprang out of bed and pulled on yesterday's clothes. I rushed to Henry's and prayed he was still up, watching something on his video screen. But his room was silent.

I knocked.

"Come in." His voice was muffled through the door.

I entered to find him standing in his underwear, scratching his bare skin.

"Did you hear that?" I said.

"Another issue?" His gaze sharpened and his chin snapped up, instantly alert. I hated him a little for how confident and together he always seemed. "Are we losing something else? Maybe we need to do some repairs."

"No, no." Now I felt silly. I had to be imagining the sound. "Did you leave a screen playing?"

He shook his head. "I haven't been near a screen since the night before last. We were a bit occupied last night. What with the wing and…" he gave a wry grin, "…what came before."

I chuckled without any humour.

"We should split up and search again," he said.

Coldness filled me. Alone, again. "It's probably nothing." I tried to force casualness into my voice, but he gave me a narrowed-eye glance.

"No, I trust your instincts. Let's check."

His logic had me heading back to my room to grab my things. Of all the little sounds that this encampment could make, I couldn't have heard *voices*. Unless…an idea popped into my head and I ducked back into Henry's room.

"Maybe something's up with the radios to Mission Control. I'll start with the control room."

"Sounds good. Then you'll head counter-clockwise as usual?" He started walking down the hall the opposite way already.

"Yep," I said.

The radios would be an easy fix. They could easily explain what I'd heard. But discomfort still hovered in my gut.

I walked down the corridor to the control room, my footsteps click-clacking on the linoleum, the sound bouncing off the walls.

It was a moment before I noticed the darkness behind me. The fluorescent lights were supposed to stay on for fifteen minutes after motion, but the ones at the end of the hall were out.

My heart pounded and fear threatened to explode out of me, send me spiralling into incoherency. I forced it down.

This was a maintenance thing, it had to be. I'd deal with this later. So I turned toward the control room once more and walked.

The next furthest light went out.

My heart thumped harder, but I kept going. The darkness followed. I sped up and the wave of darkness did too. I sprinted down the corridor, the darkness getting ever closer, closer, closer like a predator nipping at my heels.

I hit the door of the control room and burst inside, slamming the door behind me and leaning against it, panting. My hot breath fogged the glass of the helmet, leaving me with the scent of my own rancid breath. A blurry rainbow of buttons in red, green, blue, and yellow blinked cheerfully from the full-wall control panels. I fought to regain composure.

A sharp crackle nearly made me hit the roof, until I realized it was my headset radio.

"Everything good over there?" Henry's voice was calm and normal.

I forced normalcy into my own voice. "Yes, fine," I lied. "Though we should check the lighting in the corridor to the control room."

Check the lighting. A harsh laugh wedged its way out of my mouth as Henry spoke, but it's not like I could tell him I was hearing things and afraid of the dark.

"Affirmative," he said. "Nothing in F Wing either. I'm continuing the circle."

My breathing near steady, I walked to the controls. "Houston, this is Planet Base Hestia, requesting connection."

The line was empty. No hiss. No crackle. No response.

I took another deep, shaky breath, hung up the receiver, and then tried again.

Dead.

My hand on the receiver was slick, and I realized I'd been standing frozen for several minutes, holding the useless thing in my hands. Our communications were gone. The immensity of the solitude struck me all at once.

Forget considering leaving. We were entirely alone up here now. So I did the only thing I could and turned the helmet radio back on.

"Henry, our comms are down. I can't make the check-in to Earth." It was a wonder how level my voice sounded with the panic thrumming in my chest like a trapped bird trying to pound its way out.

"That was probably what you heard then. The last crackle of the radios, whatever took the radios down. Solar flare or the like. We'll get it back up."

I gripped both hands into fists as if I could absorb his pragmatism. And his optimism. But the bird in my chest kept fluttering.

"Right," I said instead. "Let's regroup." I needed to see a live person.

"Affirm – " his voice ended in a hissing crackle, the radio still on but no sound from him.

"Henry?" Something felt very wrong, but radios weren't perfect. My hallucinations couldn't hurt Henry. It was all in my head.

But everyone *I'd* ever cared for was dead. What was the common denominator?

After a couple minutes, his voice crackled to life again and relief coursed through me. "Sophia, I need. . ." He trailed off into static.

"Henry? What's going on?" My voice was getting more and more frantic, not the perfect cool I wanted to convey.

He screamed once and fear for him battled with relief that he was still around to make the scream at all.

The scream cut off abruptly and ended in a gargle that made me think of my dead partner choking on their own lungs.

"Henry!"

There was nothing on the line but static.

"I'm coming, just wait. I'm coming!" I said.

Where had he been? He said he'd just checked F Wing, which meant he was working his way around and would hit G next. But that was the locked off wing.

I pushed open the control room door to the hallway, only half lit. The darkness gave me pause as my heart thudded in my mouth. But I had to get through it, for Henry. I charged down the darkened hall. The blackness stayed in its place this time, and I made it out into town square.

As I ran between the wings, I stopped short at F. How long ago was it that Henry had called saying he was here? It couldn't have been more than fifteen minutes. Yet the lights were out.

Even with my fear for Henry, the horror of it struck me.

What if I was alone in the dark?

A sharp hiss of static from Henry's radio reminded me I had to keep going.

He had to be just a bit further ahead. He had to be okay. I couldn't be on my own up here, cut off from anyone or anything. I wouldn't make it with my mind intact; I was already halfway there.

A childlike giggle echoed from the berths.

I let out a sob. I knew that laugh. It was Olivia. My long-dead sister Olivia. It couldn't be, but it was.

Another giggle from that familiar voice was soothed by a feminine murmur with words I couldn't catch. But the voice I knew as well as my own. It was the one that soothed my restless childhood nights with lullabies, that corrected my recipes on long-distance video calls, that admitted she struggled to understand my life choices but did her best. My mother.

I sobbed against my helmet, the atmosphere inside becoming thick and wet. I couldn't stay here with my ghosts. Henry needed me. I ran from the voices and the memories.

I slowed as I neared G Wing. I couldn't stop myself from looking through the small, thick window of the airlock door.

A figure walked past, blocking my view with darker shadow for an instant and I pulled away, heart pounding.

"Henry?" I cried through it.

But the airlock door was still sealed from this side. He couldn't be in there. No one could be. This was my mind cracking once again.

But where was Henry?

I turned and ran to the next wing, the final place where Henry could have been when he called.

But it was empty, dark.

Yet a soft whisper slithered out.

I pulled my helmet off so I could hear it better, but it wasn't Henry's voice.

It was my mother and Olivia. And if I strained, I could pick up the voice of my partner murmuring in the background. I used to hear them on video calls when we'd worked from home on the days we couldn't safely leave the house. I smiled against the tears. It had been too long.

Then, could it be? That group of friends, more like found family, that whole household who'd never been found after the tsunami that hit California.

All dead, all lost to me.

The whispers emanated from the darkness, building over each other, and bouncing off the walls, an ever increasing and mind-numbing crescendo. I couldn't bear what I might see if the lights turned on—and suddenly I couldn't decide what would be worse: if they were all there, or if they weren't.

I ran.

Through the broken and silent encampment, through the darkness that didn't end, and right back to the control room where I'd had the smallest measure of comfort.

The coloured lights gave me no comfort now.

I couldn't bear it anymore. I started flipping switches wildly, even the ones I was absolutely not meant to turn.

Everything went dark. The background hum that accompanied everything we did finally shifted to blessed silence. Then I slid down the wall of dead switches and curled myself in a ball, sitting and rocking with my arms gripping my knees like when I'd had nightmares as a child.

I could almost hear my mom's voice singing lullabies. Or perhaps I did hear it. Right outside the control room door.

Alone in the dark, I strained to hear their voices and waited for the end.

THE TROCOPHORE

Rachel Searcey

"Pay first, then we'll handle the thing in the warehouse," Garrett said to the leader of the colonists on Outpost 27. We stood in the shadow of the rusted exterior of the *Bellerophon*, sheltering us from the brutal light from both suns. The heat was smothering and the air was thin.

When the leader hesitated, Garrett continued, "You want us to leave? I got better jobs on other outposts."

"No, please. I'll talk to them," the leader said. He turned to the group of men and boys clustered at the edge of the clearing. They whispered amongst themselves. Voices were raised, but the man returned with a bag full of crumpled bills—old Earth money nobody used anymore.

"This all you got?" Garrett asked. "No credits?"

The leader shook his head, eyes wide and anxious, "I'm sorry. It's all we have left. Two weeks we've waited for someone to respond to our SOS. We have nothing to defend ourselves against the monster. It's locked in the largest warehouse. We can hear it moving at night. Our women and many of our children—" The man's voice broke and he began to cry. Sympathy twitched in my gut but I dismissed the feeling. Wasted energy when we had a job to do.

Garrett scoffed and tied the sack to his utility belt. "Show us the warehouse."

The leader wiped his eyes on the hem of his simple tunic and led the way.

Garrett gestured to Liesel, Griffin, and me and we followed, leaving behind the precious shade. I watched the money bag swinging from Garrett's hip. We wouldn't see our cut until we'd done our part, and only if we were successful and followed orders.

The "monster" was likely a native predator looking for food. We'd dealt with worse—mass murderers, rogue androids, space crazy colonists—but animals were tricky and unpredictable. We'd capture whatever it was and bring it to Sullen, the nearest planet, and Garrett would hand it off to the scientists there for a second payout.

A dry wind rustled through the broad, hyper-blue leaves of the alien trees surrounding us on all sides and sent a shiver up my spine, despite the heat. I prayed for an easy in-and-out.

A heavy wood plank had been lodged against the warehouse doors, locking the creature inside.

Garrett worked the wood free and the door swung outwards. The rotted stench of bodies in an enclosed space swept over us and I gagged, tightening my grip on the shock rifle slung across my chest. Nervous energy coursed through me.

"Kirek," Garret said to me, "you take point. Liesel, watch his back."

Liesel, long blond ponytail whipping in the wind, stepped to my side. His crooked nose, broken one too many times by Garrett, ruined his traditional good looks but he made up for it with staunch reliability. We were friends before we joined Garrett's merc unit. Griffin, on the other hand…

"Take the thing *alive.* You got that? The xenobiologists will pay big bucks for a live specimen. Hurry it up, Griffin."

The hover thrusters on the prison crate were broken and Griffin struggled to drag it over the rocky ground. It dug a gouge into the earth all the way from the ship. Sweat dripped from his brow and he swatted away bloated flies.

Garret snapped at Griffin, "You're in charge of the crate. If you fuck this up, we'll have words."

Griffin's bulldog jowls twisted into a frown. He crossed his meaty arms in front of his barrel-like chest and muttered, "Yessir."

What he lacked in discipline, he made up for in size. Griffin towered over the rest of us and he was useful for hauling gear. But he wasn't allowed a weapon, not after he shot up a family of colonists, including their small children, when he mistook them for a bounty. He claimed PTSD from military service. Dishonorably discharged from what I heard. He was always trouble, but Garrett refused to cut him loose—not with all the money Griffin owed him. Liesel and I worked well together, balancing out Griffin's incompetence.

I promised myself, *I won't end up like Griffin, a broken man with nothing to live for.*

I took the lead with Liesel watching my six. The crate bumped across the warehouse threshold and I winced at the racket, but bit my tongue. Griffin couldn't help the broken thrusters, I told myself. But fending off a starving alien animal, startled by our presence, would be disastrous. Better to catch it by surprise.

Garrett locked us inside the warehouse. He rarely accompanied us into the fray, preferring to collect the pay and keep his hands clean. He'd "done his time" as he liked to say. As if we hadn't.

The underlying reek of decaying flesh was stifling. Murky sunlight filtered through slit windows set high in the metal walls. Black clouds of flies emitted an unnerving hum and raised the hairs on the back of my neck. Rows of shelving filled the warehouse as far as I could see, stacked with preserves and canned food. No sign of the so-called monster.

My eyes began to itch and I remembered to blink. We had no idea how big it was or anything about its appearance. The colonists had been so frightened, they hadn't had a good look at it. Uncertainty was part of the job but the unknown never failed to unnerve me.

My foot slipped in something soft and I almost fell. A quick glance was enough to tell me it was a woman. Her midsection had been eaten away. Arms and legs lay at skewed angles, her head thrown back in a perpetual scream. Maggots writhed over the rotted flesh and now clung to my boot. A full body shudder made me lose my grip on the shock rifle.

Liesel, always watching out for me, put a reassuring hand on my shoulder while I steadied myself. "You okay, man?"

I nodded but was still on edge more than usual. *Get it together.*

"What the fuck…" Griffin knelt by the corpse. Anger flashed across his face. A familiar look we'd come to dread. "There's more over there," he said, pointing. "My God, it's a child. A little boy." He took off for the back of the warehouse.

"Griffin, wait," I said, but he'd already disappeared behind a shelf. "Goddammit."

Liesel followed me as we caught up to him. At Griffin's feet were the bodies of a dozen disemboweled women and children. Flies swarmed from body to body, pulsing in the still air. I stood in shock, unable to comprehend the tangled limbs, desiccated organs, and blood spatters as ever having been human.

Griffin bent over, hands on knees, hyperventilating.

"Hey! Don't look at them. Get a hold of yourself. Don't fucking do this to me." I took Griffin by the collar and pushed him towards the crate where he'd left it. I wouldn't let him fuck up my payday.

In the darkened corner, something twitched near the ceiling. I took a step back, realizing it was almost directly on top of us. I motioned to Liesel and we both trained our shock rifles on it.

Hooked tentacles clung to the rafters. It hung like a desiccated spider. Its skin was dry and flaky, as if it were molting. It looked half dead already. We had to get it down.

"Griffin," I whispered. "Ready the crate."

His fists clenched and unclenched as he watched the monster. Sweat poured from his brow, into his eyes, across his flushed cheeks.

"Griffin!" Before I realized what he was doing, he had yanked the rifle out of my hands and shot at the alien. He missed, the ceiling sparking where the charge hit the roof. Griffin screamed, swinging the butt of the rifle as if he was going to fight it one-on-one. He scaled a shelf, scattering canned food. I yanked on his ankle and he came tumbling down, along with the shelf which landed on top of him. I rolled out of the way.

Liesel fired as the monster twitched and flailed, revealing a screaming, jagged mouth tucked beneath its domed head. Over a dozen slit-eye pupils emerged from the wrinkled skin and swiveled in their sockets to focus on us.

I took my shock rifle back from Griffin, who was unconscious and trapped under the shelf. Liesel fired again when the thing dropped to the floor with a gelatinous plop, tentacle-like limbs twisting over each other as it righted itself, then scrambled towards us while shrieks erupted between rows of jagged teeth. I fired and hit true—its skin rippled with each pulse—the smell of burnt metal and hair filled the hot warehouse.

It collapsed into a shapeless, quivering mass.

"Don't kill it," I reminded Liesel. Griffin had already done enough damage.

Liesel nudged it with his foot and it shifted, let out a high-pitched whine. "It's still alive," he said.

Griffin woke up moaning and attempting to push the shelf off himself. "I think my arm is broken."

We left him until the thing was secured in the crate.

Liesel and I walked together back to the ship, both of us watching Griffin limp ahead of us, dragging the crate with his good arm.

"I could've taken the crate," I said to Liesel.

He laughed at me. "You're a regular Boy Scout."

I elbowed him in the gut and he play-acted like I'd sucker-punched him. When we stopped laughing, I asked him, "You ever encounter anything like this before?"

He shook his head. "It's the most fucked up thing I've seen in a while. And you know I've seen shit."

"Too bad the pay isn't better," I said.

Liesel shrugged. "That's just how this goes, man. How about we finish our card game and plan for shore leave on Sullen?"

As the only crew member besides Garrett with access, I transferred the creature to the *Bellerophon*'s brig—a six-by-six metal cube with a toilet and sink meant for humans. It lay on the floor in a lifeless puddle, closer to a jellyfish or octopus like I'd seen in the Earth history records.

Lukewarm water trickled from the shower-head, dripping on the mildew laden tiles. It was a relief after the stifling heat on the outpost. I dressed in a clean uniform and retrieved my wrist console from the charger.

After we had boarded, Garrett split up the pay between Liesel and I, since Griffin had forfeited his portion when he disobeyed orders. Topping off this shit show, his arm was in a sling and he was restricted to his bunk until we reached Sullen. Liesel and I took over his shifts. So much for our card game.

We alternated shifts, patrolling outside the brig. The eerie silence in the long passageway, marred only by our steel-toed boots pacing back and forth, was maddening. No music. No sitting. No distractions. *Period.*

The lights blinked out as soon as I put my hand on the door latch. If it was a power failure, the emergency backup generator should have triggered. Yet air poured from the vents and life support was still online. Someone had turned off the ship lights, but why? The darkness was broken by my wrist console flashing text across the small screen: BRIG BREECH.

Sweat prickled on my brow as I took in the message. It wasn't possible. The ship was a refurbished military cruiser on its last legs, but the brig was state of the art with a titanium door. It was self-contained and impenetrable. Did the monster escape through the toilet and worm its way through the pipes? Its fleshy body was boneless and amorphous. Was it intelligent?

"Kirek to Garrett, come in. Over." I perched on the metal bench, my boot beating an anxious pattern on the floor. "Kirek to Liesel. Do you read me? Over."

Was the monster slithering around in the corridors? The mangled bodies it left in the warehouse haunted me. The shock rifles were locked up on the bridge armory and only Garrett had the code. I tapped out a quick message on my console and sent it, watching the screen for a response. Seconds dragged into minutes and I couldn't wait any longer.

If the monster was loose and had hurt the others, I had to alert Sullen. Maybe they'd send reinforcements.

I can do this, I thought, wrestling down the panic threatening to climb from my bowels into my throat to strangle me.

The *Bellerophon* was longer than it was wide. The bridge at the bow, the engine room in the stern. Between them ran a lengthy passageway lined with self-contained rooms, including the brig to my left and the dorms to my right. All the doors were sealed, with no sign of my crew-mates.

Beneath the scent of machine oil and metallic ozone pushing through the vents, there was a coppery undertone I could taste in the back of my throat.

I hugged the wall and approached the monitoring system for the brig. The screen was broken but still functional. I ran my hand over the door.

Sealed, but damaged. There were deep gouges where the door met the frame. The video feed lit up, but the screen was black. Through the speaker, I heard a shuffling sound, as if sand were running over a smooth surface.

"Garrett, Liesel...come in. Griffin. Over." A loud clatter in the passageway from behind sent me sprinting. I wasn't about to face the creature on my own. I was no coward but I wasn't an idiot either. I slammed my palm into the panel next to the berth door and it hissed open to flickering darkness.

"Liesel? Griffin?" I whispered. I closed the door behind me, squinting in the dark at the mounded sheets on the bunks. The one on the bottom shifted and there was a gurgling noise, like the last dregs of milk being sucked through a straw. Liesel rolled over, but all I could see were his eyes framed by the sheet.

I knelt by the bed and put a hand on his shoulder. "Liesel, what's the situation? Garrett isn't answering comms."

My fingers sank into slick flesh. His body spasmed and the sheet slid to the floor. A ragged gasp of breath ended with choking and a spray of blood from what was left of his face.

His tongue flapped against the remains of his lower jaw, which hung by threads of sinew against his chest. His exposed esophagus struggled to suck in air.

The monster.

I crouched by the bedside, my hands shaking with fear and uncertainty.

"Liesel, hey, can you hear me?" His eyes roved in their sockets, aimless and pained. His tongue flapped as if he was trying to speak.

From a small drawer under the bunk, I found bandages in a bare-bones first aid kit. He'd lost a lot of blood already, enough to soak the mattress underneath.

My hands were sticky with fluids. I tried to keep them steady as I wound the bandages around the back of his head and under his jaw to keep everything in place. His teeth clacked against one another with a loud snap. He moaned with pain. I had no medical training but held onto the desperate hope my clumsiness wouldn't be what killed him. There were surgeons on Sullen who could help.

Liesel was the closest person I had to a friend. Both of us stuck in dead-end jobs, crisscrossing the ass-end of space to pick up low-lifes and maniacs and dump them on Sullen for a pittance. I didn't want him to die, not like this.

I scrubbed my fingers with a clean sheet, averting my eyes from the bloodied fabric. I leaned against the top bunk, feeling the cool metal pressing into my forehead. What the hell was happening? Every few minutes I'd glance at my wrist console, expecting answers, but none came.

"Liesel, I'm going to the bridge."

Muffled noises gurgled from beneath the bandages but I shushed him, placing a hand on his shoulder. Tears squeezed from his eyes as he attempted to rock his head back and forth as if saying *no*. Blood drenched the white bandages in a growing red patch until they were soaked through. My own jaw ached, watching him struggle.

"You need help. Sullen can send a medical transport to meet us halfway."

Once I was on the bridge, I could send a message.

Footsteps clattered in the passageway outside: Garrett's lighter tread, followed by Griffin's heavier gait, I thought. The bridge door clanged shut and sealed. But when I went to look, the passageway was empty.

Liesel's eyes fluttered and his head lolled to the side. I gave him one last look and then eased the door close behind me.

Shadows distorted into reaching tentacles with hooked claws. An illusion triggered by shock, nothing more. Keeping my back to the wall so I could see in both directions, I stalked towards the bridge, hoping Garrett had readied the shock rifles. I feared one of the doors opening behind me, and the alien's hooks dragging me into the dark, to eviscerate me like it did the colonists. Patches of sweat grew on my shirt and slid down my back and sides. I resisted the urge to scratch and kept my eyes moving between the locked bridge door and the passageway behind me.

I pressed my ear to the door but it was impossible to hear anything. I tried the latch and to my surprise, it wasn't locked. Inside, the weapons cabinet was open, but all four shock rifles were missing.

The monitors were cracked, sparking in the dark. We were still on autopilot for Sullen—ETA: ten hours. Whatever the monster had tried to do—wreck the ship, maybe—hadn't worked. The navigation system required a series of codes from Garrett in order to change course.

When I logged into the communications terminal, that's when I found Garrett doubled over himself under the console. I stifled a scream when I saw his face. His eyes and nose had been reduced to a pulpy mass, smashed in beyond all recognition. Fresh blood pooled on the metal floor, still dripping. With a shaking hand, I checked for a pulse, but he was gone. His body was warm as if he'd been murdered moments before I entered the bridge. The bastard meant nothing to me, but I respected the hell out of him. The monster had left him under the console and then fled. But where? How? My eyes darted to the vents, the trash chute. It could be anywhere.

My head was pounding. I didn't know what to do. Where was Griffin?

The lights came on and I blinked against the sudden brightness. I left the bridge and there he was, coming out of the brig. Griffin's uniform was dripping red, soaked through to the skin. He was no longer wearing the sling and his left arm hung uselessly at his side. He squeezed his eyes shut and stood there for a moment.

"Griffin! What the hell is happening?"

He swayed on his feet as if he were about to fall, but caught himself on the passageway wall. "Kirek, there you are." His voice was distorted and when I jogged over, I saw he was missing some teeth. Blood streamed from his mouth when he spoke. "I took care of it."

When he turned to look at me, I could see his right eye was swollen shut. He gripped one of the shock rifles in his right hand.

"I was in the head when I got the message," I said.

On the brig monitor, the alien was splayed in a corner. Blood splashed the walls and floor. Over the tinny speaker, it keened at an ear-drilling pitch.

Despite all the abuse it had endured, it somehow slid across the floor in jerky, sick motions and pressed itself against the door. My skin crawled to think of it on the other side, only a few layers of metal separating it from us.

Somehow, Griffin had subdued the creature. *Of all people.* Relief washed over me. We'd lost Garrett but Liesel would survive.

"How did it escape? Talk to me, Griffin."

The monster began throwing itself against the door. Griffin turned his bulldog eyes on me, jowls shaking. The pupil in his open eye was ringed with red and tears streamed down his cheeks. "This fucking job will kill me, Kirek." He smiled, his remaining teeth unearthly white against the gore smeared across his face.

"We can talk about it later." Griffin was headed for the deep end again and we didn't have time for his shit. "Liesel needs medical attention. He's still alive."

I realized I'd never sent the message and started to return to the bridge when Griffin pushed past me. He opened the door to the crew quarters and I followed. The shock rifle fell from hand with a clatter. He stood over Liesel, whose chest rose and fell in shallow breaths. In the glaring lights, it was impossible to deny he was near death. My stomach dropped at his pale skin and the blood-soaked mattress.

"I patched him up as best I could, but he needs a doc," I said.

Griffin reached out with his good hand towards Liesel, as if to remove the bandages. I placed a hand on his shoulder to stop him. "Don't. He needs rest."

I pulled on Griffin's upper arm to stop him but he lunged forward as if I weren't there. His hand circled Liesel's throat and I watched in horror as his fingers dug into the ruined flesh. He shrugged me off as I beat him around the head and neck with my fists, desperate to separate him from my friend.

I found the shock rifle and swung the butt at Griffin's head. He staggered under the blow, blood seeping from a cut in his scalp, but he remained standing. There was a wet crunch and Griffin released his hand.

He murdered Liesel.

I had no time to defend myself when Griffin's fist met the bridge of my nose, shattering it and triggering black spots across my vision.

On shaky legs, I backed towards the door, feeling for the frame. My heels hit the raised lip of the doorway. I stumbled ass-first into the passageway. Pain jarred my lower back with such force that my teeth chattered. Salty blood flooded from my nostrils. I tasted copper. Griffin's red-ringed eye zeroed in on me as he loomed in the door frame.

"It's for the best, Kirek. He was suffering. We all are." He leaned over and took me by the collar. "I will end your suffering, Kirek. And mine."

Blood oozed from cuts in his hand. Knuckles shredded from assaulting our crew mates. I imagined Griffin's knuckles smashing into Garrett's cheekbones, smashing the cartilage in his nose to a pulp. Griffin cornering Liesel in the bunk, digging his thick fingers into Liesel's mouth until he gagged. The sharp downward pull of hands as Griffin wrenched Liesel's jaw from his skull.

Garrett's punishments, doled out almost daily, the stress of this shit job—all fell on Griffin's already stooped shoulders. We knew he was fucked in the head but never expected him to snap.

My forehead crashed into his nose. He lurched backwards and clutched at his face. A plan began to form but there was no guarantee it would work. Ignoring the pain ricocheting up my legs, I ran for the brig, slapping my hand on the broken door panel. My fingers were coated with blood and my prints didn't register, flashing an error code. The floor shook with Griffin's pounding footsteps and I said a silent prayer while scrubbing my fingers on the one clean spot on my uniform.

He was breathing down my back when the brig door hissed open.

The monster was waiting.

The broken creature shifted—barbed tentacles rose into the air like scorpion tails. Griffin charged and I threw myself to the side, crashing to the floor. The monster's talons dug into Griffin's chest and face, gouging into his flesh. He screamed and pummeled the tentacles wrapping around him. They tumbled together into the brig and I locked the door behind them.

Griffin's screams rang through the thick metal. My body shook as adrenaline pumped through my nervous system and I felt nauseous. A ripple ran through my innards. I vomited, my body curled around itself.

I tried to stand but my legs gave way. I tumbled to the ground and blacked out.

When the *Bellerophon* auto-docked on Sullen, I woke up face down in my own vomit and my head ringing. Sullen traffic control's signal echoed through the empty ship. I cleaned myself up, trying not to think of the carnage Griffin had left behind. What he'd done to Liesel. Tears pricked at my eyes but I blinked them away and continued to the bridge.

I pulled Garrett's body from under the console and left him in the passageway. Steeling myself, I answered the hail.

"Message received. Kirek here, acting captain. We have a situation on board. Three crew members down, including my superior. Over."

My head throbbed as I waited for a response. I had a concussion, maybe brain damage.

"Roger that, Kirek. Permission to board and transfer custody of the bounty? Over."

"Permission granted, over."

I opened the bay doors to a private security troop in crisp new uniforms, followed by a medical crew. They brought their own state-of-the-art capsule, specially designed to contain alien life.

A xenobiologist in a black suit took me aside. "The creature did this?" She tapped out notes on her tablet and gestured to the body bags holding Liesel and Garrett. Her face twitched into a smile.

"No. Griffin, a crew member," I said, confused by her cheerful demeanor.

"Oh, well. And where is Griffin?"

I gestured towards the brig where the guards were clustered around the door. She raised her eyebrows at the implication. "We'll need you to open the door, but please stay out of the way while we handle the rest. With your superior out of commission, I assume payment transfers to you?"

I felt numb and her question barely registered at first. I nodded and held up my wrist console to her tablet. The funds transferred within seconds. More credits than I'd ever seen in my life. She laughed at my shocked expression.

"You could buy a new ship with the payout. This rusted hulk is on its last legs. We could work out a deal, if you're interested." Her smile broadened. "We always need new specimens and Garrett will be missed."

"I'll think about it," I said.

"Don't take too long. My contact info is on the invoice. Our lab is in Quadrant 7." She walked away from me and I caught up with her at the brig door. "Please unlock the door."

I placed my palm on the panel and the guards shoved me out of the way as it opened. From across the passageway, I watched them enter, expecting to see Griffin's disemboweled corpse on the brig floor and the creature on the attack.

Instead, the guards carried out a long, hard cocoon, the size of a man. It was mottled brown and crimson, slightly transparent. The creature was pressed against the surface and appeared to be suspended in some kind of gel. It twitched and rolled over inside the cocoon, revealing a half-digested human corpse caught in its tentacles.

Griffin.

I abandoned the *Bellerophon* and merc life, never looking back. I'd rather die planet-side than set foot on another ship carrying a bounty—human or not.

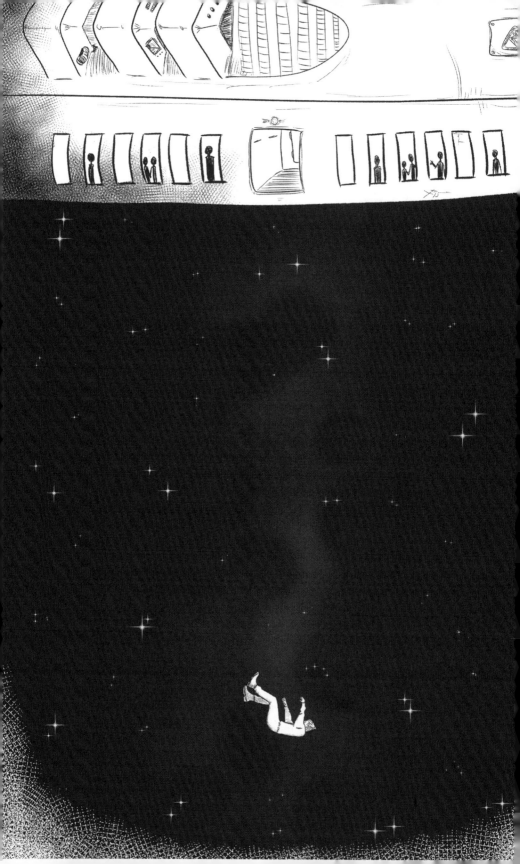

LOCKED OUT
Joseph Andre Thomas

Execution

Jaroenchai Degrom was led down the hallway to the airlocks, followed by Captain Behr and his command retinue. Jaro was dressed in his gray Colloquy Corporation jumper; his hands were bound and he was gagged, per Company Protocols. His deep, onyx-black eyes betrayed no emotion.

I watched from the back of the room with the technicians. I didn't need to be there, but Jaro was my friend. I struggled to place the emotion the sight of him brought up in me. Benigns, like me, were genetically edited for pragmatism and artisanal work, not emotional intelligence. Sadness? Frustration? Distress? Not that any particular emotion would help. Jaro did what he did in direct violation of Protocols. Everyone knew how that ended.

A guard opened airlock one, and the captain—flanked by two guards and Hila Rask, his counsel (like me, a Benign)—marched Jaro inside. Everyone stepped back, except Jaro and the captain. Hila raised a holographic slate and swiped it to the captain's wristscreen.

"Turn," said Captain Behr.

Jaro did, slowly. The captain's hulking shoulders and long, brown hair dwarfed the small scientist. Jaro appeared indifferent.

"Jaroenchai Navin Degrom," said the captain, reading from his wrist-screen. "You have been found guilty of illegal ship entry and are thereby charged with Corporate Treason, punishable by Article 3.11.A2. Therefore, by the power granted me by God and Colloquy Corporate Protocols, I, Goodman Behr, captain of the *Aphelia*, sentence you to die by airlock dispersion.

"Do you have any final words?"

One of the guards removed the metal gag around Jaro's mouth. He looked at the captain for a long moment, then shrugged.

He spared me a glance…and winked.

The captain waved a hand in the air. Guards removed Jaro's cuffs and shut the airlock door on him. Watching Jaro through the viewing glass, the air around him loudly siphoning out, I thought I might actually cry—an extreme rarity; it was nearly impossible for Benigns to show emotions physically. There was some talk around the ship that an exception might be made for Jaroenchai's transgression. He was essential to the *Aphelia*'s mission, after all—a Paradigm scientist heading the exploratory team.

Evidently not that essential.

I felt a tightness in my throat, as the airlock warning blared, and my friend was launched into the black vacuum of space.

98 Hours Before Execution

"Hah!" said Jaro, slamming a plastic stein down, sloshing beer on the mess hall table. "They've got the *gall* to work you for twelve hour shifts?"

I shrugged. "My gene editing is largely muscular and cardiovascular. It takes awhile to get tired. I used to work on a ship in the asteroid belt that would keep shifts going for sixteen, eighteen hours."

"Exploitation," said Jaro. He scanned the busy room, focusing on the command table. It was weekly social time, so we were allowed alcohol and double rations. We were seated at tables of professional cliques—science, communications, cartography, medical, and technical—each one drunk and loud, as usual.

"Benigns shouldn't be treated any differently than unedited," spat Jaro. "Even Paradigms."

Even though we were far from the command table, I glanced at Captain Behr's stern figure, worried he might overhear. Jaro'd had a lot of beer. I didn't stop him, though. Jaro was a Paradigm—a lavishly edited human like the captain and some other *Aphelia* team leads. Jaro was one of the few Paradigms who was friendly to Benigns, let alone willing to drink with one. When others on the ship saw us socializing, I was told I should feel "honored."

"I'm used to being worked like a dog," I said.

Jaro stopped his stein an inch from his face and narrowed his eyes. "Malik," he said slowly. "Did you just use...a *metaphor?*"

"No." I said, with a rehearsed smile. "It was a simile."

Jaro laughed loudly. He slapped a hand on my shoulder, and I smiled again. "They don't really respect you, do they?"

"I am paid well."

"That's not what I mean." He leaned in, drunkenly severe. "They don't... tell you anything?"

"I get my work orders."

"They don't tell you what we're mining."

My impulse was to respond that they were not *mining* anything. The *Aphelia* was an exploratory science vessel. A proper mining vessel would be thrice the size with quintuple the crew, at least. He was referring to the specimens we were collecting from Qallupilluk, the Trans-Neptunian Object (TNO) the *Aphelia* orbited. Qallupilluk was once a part of Nanook, a much larger, hypothesized TNO, likely a dwarf planet, that had been destroyed at some point in the distant past.

The scientists, like Jaro, had been using drones to harvest small samples of a unique mineral from the TNO's surface, which they called *savirajak*. The savirajak had a beautiful blue glow when brought up to the *Aphelia* by the drones. For precautionary reasons, it was quarantined in the lab until it could be examined in a controlled environment back at Base Tycho.

I don't correct him, though. Mining was the common, if inaccurate, term—metaphor?—used by the crew.

"What have they told you about *savirajak?*" he continued.

"It might be dangerous. Perhaps even toxic."

He burped. "Christ. No one tells Benigns anything."

I shrugged. "Benigns have been known to unintentionally betray confidence."

"You don't resent being left out?"

"No. I respect that you and the scientists will act in our best interests."

"You're one-in-a-million, Malik." He smiled; we clinked steins. "One-in-a-damn-million."

Execution

I left the airlocks and walked with the others into the ship's atrium, a cavernous room connecting both levels of the ship, with a fully-grown arbutus tree at its center. Though it was not customary for crew to attend the actual execution, it's common for them to witness the condemned's body float out to space. Thus, the majority of the nearly 300 person crew gathered around the viewing glass. I walked to the back of the room and heard muttering: that Jaro had it coming; that he was a good man; that he deserved it; that he didn't.

Out the window, Jaroenchai Degrom floated silently, pathetically into the blackness. He was still alive; his hands moved. Jaro signed *Help* repeatedly, likely the only word he remembered from training. Others in the room noted it, too. Many looked away, some cried.

"How long does it take to die out there?" asked an operator, glancing at the time on his wristscreen.

"For a Paradigm?" said a nearby scientist. "Perhaps three minutes."

Her estimate seemed accurate. Paradigms were edited in every conceivable way—physically, cognitively, psychologically. To edit an effective Benign was expensive; to meet the threshold for a Paradigm was obscene. The fact that the *Aphelia* had four onboard—three now, I suppose—spoke to the importance of its mission.

"Interesting," said the operator. "He's been out there five minutes."

As Jaro floated outside the viewing screen, about a quarter-kilometer from the *Aphelia*, he continued to sign.

...*Help*...

40 Hours Before Execution

I laid on my back in Ion Propulsor Two, cleaning hardened plasma buildup from the inner ring. There's a misconception that ion thrusters were "clean" energy, which may be true in the ecological sense, but shredding plasmics with a handtorch covered my mask in stinking, noxious film.

My wristscreen beeped and blinked red. Urgent. From Jaro Degrom.

Need a favor, was all it read.

I exited the propulsor. The job was only half-finished, but we'd be in stasis around Qallupilluk for at least another month. Plenty of time to complete the job. Wiping down my mask, I was surprised to see Jaro standing at the console in the center of the engine room—face uncovered.

"You need a mask," I said, indicating the thick air.

He waved me off. "The dangers of gaseous plasmics have been vastly overstated. Old wives tale! Listen, Malik. I need help."

As a Benign engineer, I had no business contradicting a Paradigm scientist. Jaro looked fine. Still, I guided him toward a nearby engineering bay, shut the door, and vented the Engine Room.

I removed my mask and washed my face at the sink. "How may I help you?"

"Well, er…" Jaro cleared his throat. He seemed uncharacteristically reserved. Nervous? "I'd like to get back into labs."

"On-shift is over," I said, flatly. The day/night cycle was irrelevant on an interstellar craft, but, for organizational and mental health reasons, it was Company Protocol to maintain that superficies. As Chief Engineer, I was one of the few who had access to every area of the ship at all times.

"I know, I know," said Jaro. "The thing is…there's something. Something big. *Exciting.* My research into the *savirajak*…I need to investigate. Won't be able to sleep anyway."

"I thought that the *savirajak* was being quarantined. That analysis would begin back at Tycho."

He cocked his head at me, smirking. "Malik…" His face was—questioning? He waited for me to come to my own conclusion.

"You have begun analysis already."

"And they say Benigns are slow!" Jaro smiled. "I think we've established that Behr and his cronies aren't exactly open books. Please, Malik. It would mean the world. And, hey, if anyone catches me, I'll blame it on that prick Smithe in maintenance, how about that?"

I hesitated for a moment, but nodded and followed my friend back to the science wing, letting him through the two security doors. He thanked me profusely along the way. Smithe in maintenance was indeed unpleasant, but blaming him would be impossible; my wristscreen would be logged upon entry. If anyone asked, I could say that I was doing routine equipment checks.

I opened lab four—Jaro's personal lab—and let him in. He thanked me again and pointed.

"Look—"

Floating in a glass observation container in the middle of the lab was a hunk of glowing blue mineral.

Savirajak.

"Isn't it beautiful?" said Jaro.

I stared for a long moment at its cerulean glow, almost hypnotized. I'd seen it being brought up from Qallupilluk by automated drones many times, but this was different.

"Yes," I said.

"You're a good friend, Malik," Jaro said, smiling as he stepped into the lab. "A very good friend."

4 Hours After Execution

The Atrium was like a warzone. Faces everywhere—confused, pained, and angry. But mostly, fearful—existential fear.

Four hours had passed, and Jaro Degrom had not died.

He had managed to grab hold of a drone charging cord and pull himself against a steel wing of the ship. He clung to the wing with his legs and continued to sign: *Help.*

Hypotheses were shared, accusations levied. A practical joke of some kind? Some elaborate ruse? A social experiment, some kind of test, orchestrated by command? One person loudly suggested that perhaps Jaro was wearing some kind of transparent space suit. If such a thing existed, I had never heard of it.

Those not panicked were ecstatic. Crying. Praying. Some called out to God, convinced that we were witnessing something genuinely metaphysical.

Captain Behr stood off to the side with his commanders, his face illustrating no emotion. There had been calls for him to do something—"Bank the ship sharply, commit to the execution!"—"Bring him back inside!"—but he had remained silent, uncharacteristically indecisive.

"This is concerning," said Hila Rask behind me. "Is there precedent for such an event?"

"If you do not know, I certainly do not."

She nodded. Her vocation, as Benign counsel, was to memorize Colloquy Corporation's 600-page Operation Protocols, as well as the Protocols of all major rival companies. Not just a database, but a lawyer capable of interpreting data at a moment's notice.

"If there's anything you want to tell me," she said, "do it now."

I turned to her. "What do you mean?"

She remained silent for a moment, then said: "There will be a team lead meeting in Command soon. Be there." And she was gone.

An odd comment. Of course I would be there. As Chief Engineer, I was a team lead. A suggestion of threat?

I stayed in the atrium for several more hours, watching my friend cling for dear life—if that expression still applies—onto the wing of the *Aphelia*. After some time, he stopped signing and began crawling along the exterior of the ship to the relative safety of the hull. When he was no longer visible, I moved back to work, answering tickets in tech and cartography. I worked like a somnambulist. The rest of the crew, too, returned to work in silence, their eyes wide—concerned, fearful.

At the end of my shift, I returned to the atrium, where many crew members remained gathered. The atrium had taken on a pious atmosphere. People knelt, prayed, stood in silent homage. Votive candles had been lit, Mezuzahs hung. Meditative and protective Buddhas. People held prayer beads, evil eyes, kara bangles. Others, more secular, brought some equipment out into one corner, attempting to scientifically decipher what was happening.

While it wasn't possible to still see Jaro naturally out of the viewing glass, a drone had moved near him, so crew could easily bring up the holographic feed on their 'screens. There had been some rudimentary attempts to shoo people away, but Captain Behr had neglected to order the congregation away.

The holoscreen above a workstation they'd wheeled in was by far the clearest I'd seen my friend since he'd been thrown out the airlock. I did a double take at the sight on screen.

Jaro's face was bright red, and bumpy.

I asked a nearby scientist what was wrong. She shook her head. "We don't know. Some kind of reaction to being in the vacuum for an extended period of time."

A nearby medical tech snorted laughter. "I've observed dozens of bodies after time *in vacuo*," she said. "That is *not* what they look like."

"Sure," said a man—another medical officer. "Tell us all about the very many people who've survived prolonged exposure to naked space."

The woman grumbled at what I presumed was the man's sarcasm. She pointed at Jaro's face on the holo. "These divots…They're unlike any rash I've ever seen. Too uniform across the open skin."

His rough, scarlet face suggested pain. It unsettled me.

The first scientist said, "A reaction between his blood flow and the vacuum. Normally, space is so cold that your blood freezes within less than a minute. Nothing biological has ever survived this long." She paused. "But that's only a working hypothesis. In all likelihood, the cause is something we haven't yet considered."

19 Hours After Execution

I took my seat around the cartographic map on the Command deck, a large circular table displaying a detailed holographic map of our immediate space. Around the silver representation of the *Aphelia* hovered about two dozen purple dots, each one representing an automated drone. A large blue orb did not accurately represent Qallupilluk's true brilliance.

This two-story room had always felt unnecessarily minatory to me. Aside from the glow of the workstations and map table, there were no lights. The table was on a raised platform above a larger command hub. Fifteen feet below us, dozens of shapes milled about in the dark, navigators mostly, maintaining the ship's orbit. Their chatter was a dull tittering from the shadows.

The *Aphelia*'s team leads and command retinue sat at intervals around the map. At the head of the table was the captain's chair, turned away from the map beside an enormous workstation. Behr himself paced the room, while the rest of the team discussed—or, rather, argued.

"Two thrusters, full ionization, heavy bank to the left," said the head of security, "and none of this ever happened."

Immediate, forceful protests from the other side of the map. The medical lead said, "You encounter something inexplicable and your first suggestion is to fling it into space?"

He shrugged. "I'm here to suggest solutions, not kowtow to eggheads."

"That's disrespectful."

"Listen. If what you're bringing on the ship, that blue shit, did something to him—maybe to others—it's *my* team that has to deal with—"

"Enough." Behr's voice immediately calmed the room. He took his seat, spinning his captain's chair around to the map. "We need solutions—concrete solutions. Thus far, completing the execution seems to me the most concrete."

Dissenting voices spoke in discordant unison again. Behr raised his hand. "Bringing him back on the ship is dangerous. The unknowns raise significant concerns."

"Sir," said the medical lead, "In science we must confront the unknown, not—"

"Fortunately, I am not a scientist," interrupted the captain, "and this is not a democracy."

"Actually, it is." Hila Rask spoke from the shadows. "This situation may invoke the Clarke Clause."

No response but some confused murmurs.

"'Any sufficiently advanced technology is indistinguishable from magic'."

Behr waved his hand. "A popular aphorism."

She nodded. "Yes, but also a rarely invoked Protocol. 'When faced with unprecedented circumstances suggesting the fantastic, exceptional solutions should be considered, including, but not limited to, breaking Company Protocol'."

He stared at Hila. "And your discretion?"

"The Clause should be invoked."

"Fine. What's the next step?"

"'Solutions, however extreme, should be tabled and voted upon by all crew of sound mind'."

The captain slammed his hand on the edge of the table. Usually a stolid man, the prospect of losing autonomy of his command clearly bothered him.

"Well, perhaps there's someone here who can elucidate these 'unprecedented circumstances'."

He looked up at me, then tapped on his wristscreen. Blue holographic numbers superimposed above the galactic map:

A2234-79.18h.+922°.8°

"Do those numbers mean anything to you, Engineer Malik?"

I stood at attention. Blood rushed to my head—it had been almost thirty hours since I'd slept—but I remained steady. The numbers were galactic coordinates. But outside of this number using the *Aphelia* as an origin point, I knew little of cartography. "No, sir."

"Do you have any notion of why I might be asking this?"

"Yes, sir."

"Tell me."

"Roughly 60 hours ago, I allowed Jaroenchai Degrom into labs during off-shift. I suspect that whatever he did had something to do with the… infraction for which he was executed." I nodded to the numbers. "I suspect these do, too. I readily admit to breaking protocol and submit myself to any necessary disciplinary action."

There was chatter, even chuckling, around the table. Usually thought to be slow-witted, the unedited often illustrate similar surprise at Benign reasoning capabilities.

"Discipline will come in due course," said Behr. "Degrom sent a cached packet of classified data to these coordinates. A clear sign of corporate espionage. Can you tell us anything else?"

I shook my head. "No, sir."

"Wait," said the cartography team lead. "These make no sense." She reached out her wristscreen and used it to adjust the holographic map like a dial, zooming in. "These coordinates reach out into deep-space."

"Message to a cloaked ship?" offered another voice.

"Or a message into the void," said another.

Voices raised. Chatter and speculation began again. All the while, Behr never took his eyes off me.

41 Hours After Execution

I awoke with a start—panting, heaving. A hideous dream, instantly receding. I rose and splashed some water on my face, heart pounding, and was surprised by the time on my wallscreen. I'd barely been asleep an hour. Before finally falling asleep, I'd been awake for more than fifty hours. That I could not sleep like a stone seemed absurd. Were the previous days' events having more emotional impact than I'd realized?

When I looked up from the sink, I nearly fell backwards.

A face hung there, ringed by the circular viewing port of my quarters— outside the ship. A bright red face with two wide, pitch-dark eyes.

Jaro had somehow crawled around the exterior of the ship. The bumpy rash on his face had…*evolved.* The bumps were thicker, fatter. Like warts, evenly spread, uniformly indenting his skin.

Because of my editing, I rarely felt fear, disgust, or concern. But the sight of what his face had activated something primal in me—abject, trypophobic revulsion.

I backed away from the viewing port. A hideous dream, surely. I was dreaming, I told myself. Until my friend raised his hand and signed again.

Help.

Then he made a different sign, a movement from his throat down to his stomach.

Hungry.

45 Hours After Execution

I tried to go back to sleep, to convince myself it had been a dream, but I was unable. Sixty hours, no sleep. I decided to rise and return to the atrium.

It was like pandemonium.

A huge, swaying crowd, people screaming at each other. Behr and his retinue stood off to one side, weapons out but not aimed. I watched from beside the arbutus. There had been a few fights. Nearby, a cartographer lay crumpled against the wall with a bloody rag held to his nose. Guards tried to de-escalate and keep peace, but there was too much passion, too much fury in this room. The sheer volume—combined with my sleep deprivation—made my vision quiver.

The sight of the normally rational, hard-working crew in this state was disturbing. Violence could break out at any moment.

I quickly gathered that news about this Clarke Clause—the vote—had gotten around. And everyone had opinions: Jaro should be killed. He should be worshipped. He should be brought to medical. Qallupilluk should be nuked and this entire expedition forgotten. We should repent, ask God's forgiveness.

"Calm yourselves!" shouted Behr. "We need to be rational and composed, now more than ever."

"What are you waiting for?" screamed someone in the crowd. "Let's vote!"

"Miracle!" shouted another, echoed by others and a chorus of: *"Let him in! Let him in! Let him in!"*

"We will vote," said Behr, which finally tranquilized the crowd somewhat. He shared a glance with Hila Rask. "But hear this. What's going on with Jaro Degrom is *alien* in the truest sense of the word. We have no idea

Locked Out

what is causing this, no idea what might happen if we bring him back onto the ship.

"He was executed under the fair decree of Company and God. We should commit to his death, keep the *savirajak* under quarantine, and return to Tycho. It is the safest, most logical course of action—*understood?*"

The crowd looked on, silent.

46 Hours After Execution

My magboots locked onto the side of the *Aphelia*'s exterior with a soundless clunk. I unspooled enough safety cord for twice the length of the ship and attached it to my belt with a carabiner. I looked down towards the engines. Jaro clung to one of the propulsor elevon flaps.

The vote had been handily decided in favor of bringing Jaro back onto the ship. 111 *yay*—40 *nay*—139 abstentions. As Chief Engineer with significant spacewalk experience and Jaro's friend, it was no question who'd get the task of bringing him back in.

I took measured steps towards the ship's engines at aft. Forty meters. The only sound was my heavy breathing. Thirty meters. I could have moved faster. Perhaps it was the sleep deprivation, perhaps the strangeness of the situation, but I was unusually careful. I wanted to save my friend, yet did not want to see his red, swollen face up close again.

At twenty meters, my wristscreen beeped. Urgent. From Captain Behr. Before I could even answer, his voice came through my comms.

"Listen to me, Malik." His voice was quiet, severe. "Kill him. Get close, detach him from the ship. Make him float. This is an order."

"Why?"

"Don't ask questions. Follow my orders. I will protect you—physically, legally." I didn't need to see him to know his teeth were clenched. "I am *the captain*. You would not be committing treason. I have always acted in the *Aphelia*'s best interest, now I ask that you do, too."

I took a moment to collect my thoughts. "You are the captain, sir. But Colloquy Protocol supersedes all, as you know. Therefore, if I were to follow this order, I would, in fact, be committing treason. I'm sorry, sir."

"*Idiot Benign,*" he hissed, and my suit comms went dead.

I waited a second before taking another step. My eyes began to fuzz. I blinked repeatedly, trying to clear my vision. Was I right to refuse Behr?

My logic was entirely sound, according to Protocol, but I also knew that logically sound actions are not always circumstantially ethical.

Fifteen meters.

No, I told myself—no. Behr simply doesn't want to relinquish control, to admit defeat. I did not resent Paradigms like some Benigns, despite their more fortuitous editing, but I did see their one glaring, uneditable flaw: a superiority complex. To get a Paradigm to admit they're wrong is like pulling teeth.

Ten meters.

Jaro clung to the edge of the ion propulsor. He stared at me, waiting. His deep-black eyes beckoned me forward. He reached out a red hand. I shuddered as his knobby flesh came into focus.

My legs shuddered suddenly. Jaro began to shake, too. The exterior of the *Aphelia* shivered, then quaked.

No—no, no.

The engine was activating.

I started to move faster, but stumbled as a rough ripple moved through the body of the ship. Jaro was only barely clinging to the elevon. Then the ship lurched, and an enormous blast of blue flame burst out the back of the propulsor.

I tripped at the force of the blast and choked on my spit, getting saliva on the inside of the mask. Were we not in the vacuum, the sound would have been deafening. Only the second propulsor fired, but at full force; the ship began to arc in a semi-circle. A huge chunk of hardened plasmics shattered out of the back of the propulsor. I thought, stupidly: I knew I should have finished cleaning that.

I wasn't thrown off thanks to my magboots. Jaro was not so lucky. Ripped free of his grasp, he was flung into empty space.

Without thinking, I demagnetized my boots and kicked off the ship. I engaged suit thrusters, but Jaro had been thrown off with enormous force. I could hardly see through my suit visor, smeared with saliva and condensation from my breath.

I unclipped a carabiner and reached out my arms; the safety cord unspooled quickly, quickly.

Five feet, four, three, two, and—

Our hands connected, just barely, and I pulled Jaro towards me. I wrapped the cord around his waist and crotch and arms, quickly securing a square knot and reattaching the carabiner to my belt. His entire body was covered in the rashy, red bumps. I realized, nauseated, that the rashy ridges were preventing his hand from slipping out of mine.

Once secure, I felt a sharp tug at the other end of the safety cord. We were being reeled back in. The ship had stopped moving. The engine was dead. Floating there like ragdolls being pulled back to the ship, realization hit: Captain Behr had tried to kill us.

Back in the sealed airlock, I fell to my knees and detached the cord. Jaro crumpled to the floor, followed by a blast of sound and breathable air. The light above the inner airlock door turned green. It opened and crew members poured in to help.

Someone helped me to my feet, another removed my mask. Vacant, hollow words came from all angles:

"Are you alright?"

"Anything broken?"

"Are you bleeding?"

"Is *he* alright?"

I looked down at the crumpled body of my friend. He'd been turned onto his back, but his chest moved up and down, up and down—breathing. *Alive.* I knelt beside him.

His face, his skin was indescribable. The wart-like bumps had grown into thick pustules several centimeters each, and rounded at the tips like the limbs of a sea anemone.

Crew members ushered us inside, to medical. Computers, waste bins, people scattered everywhere because of the ship's movement. I saw two groups in the middle of a fight, screaming at one another. We passed through the atrium.

The crowd remained but now surrounded six or seven figures on their knees in front of the arbutus tree. Captain Behr and his retinue—captive. The head of security's face was swollen red, beaten. Hila Rask knelt nearby, her nose bloodied.

They had done it, a comms officer told me. He held a guard's rifle. They had defied the vote and tried to kill us. They had broken into command and sharply banked the ship—throwing us into space.

Behr—on his knees, metal gag in his mouth—stared at me as we exited the atrium into medical.

After Execution

I awoke to blackness after...I do not know how long. I rose to my elbows, sluggish. My sleep had been deep. Memories turned in my head like wet concrete. Everything was a blur; all I knew is that I was examined, bandaged, and put to sleep. My room was completely dark, not even a glow from the ambience of my wallscreen. I examined my arm to discover that my wristscreen, too, was off.

Power failure?

The only light in the room was a thin, pulsating spear of blue across the floor. The door was ajar. When I stood, I nearly collapsed, my legs extraordinarily weak from the sleep. I had no memory of returning to my room last night. Had it only been last night?

Blue emergency lights ran along the length of the walkway. They pulsed in the direction of the consolidation area of the atrium. I followed the pulses, peering into several open rooms and passages as I walked. There was no one.

I began to notice odd, dark marks on the wall and floor. Smears or scratches? Difficult to tell in the low light. Nearing the atrium, the marks became thicker—puddles. An unmistakable, rusty iron scent hung in the air.

If it hadn't been for the events of the last few days, I would've been more shocked at the sight of the atrium. There were bodies everywhere, stacked up against the walls. Mounds of dead flesh. I saw the body of a technician I sometimes sat with during social. Beside the arbutus tree lay the head of Hila Rask. Next to her, the corpse of the security team lead.

The walkway had been cleared of dead. I followed the pulsing lights to the consolidation area, surrounded by floating, firefly-like LEDs. I turned away from them into another, blood-smeared hallway, towards Command.

This room, somehow, still had power. The map table was illuminated. Our neighboring space against a background of stars. I saw the bluish glowing lights of the workstations on the lower level.

Captain Behr's chair faced away from the map, silhouetted by the glow from his workstation.

"Sir?" I said.

"Malik?" A voice from the chair rasped laughter. "You are awake!"

I approached. "Jaro?"

"That name will do. For now."

The chair spun around and revealed the man—if it could still be called a man. The red rash of his skin had metastasized. The bumps on his skin had grown into sharp, needle-like points, each one about a half-inch long. The spines glistened and shone as if wet. Points ripped through places on his filthy *Aphelia* uniform.

And he cradled the severed head of Captain Behr on his lap, his expression locked in mortal terror.

"Thank you for your help." He held the head out to me in one spiny hand and smiled a smile that reminded me nothing of Jaroenchai Degrom. "You've been asleep awhile. Longer than expected."

"What happened?"

He turned the captain's head towards himself and gazed into its eyes, as though he were about to recite a monologue. "All of us missed you." Then he dropped Behr's head with a wet *smack* onto the floor.

"What have you done?"

The thing that had been Jaro looked at me, eyes dark. "I cannot thank you enough for your bravery, Malik. Your efforts were invaluable."

The glow from the lower floor was not from any workstations but the *savirajak*. Hunks of the blue mineral had been shoved forcibly into the computers and machinery all throughout the Command Deck.

Savirajak powered the ship? How was that possible?

It was then I realized that we were not alone. Black shapes stood in the shadows of the lower floor. Dozens of people lined against the walls. Some held chunks of *savirajak*.

Watching us.

"Will you come along?" Jaro asked.

I looked from him back to the map, sick. My hands trembled. I found the little silver representation of the *Aphelia* nestled amongst the digital stars. We were moving. We had a destination—coordinates reaching into deep space. Qallupilluk was nowhere onscreen.

A2234-79.18h.+922°.8°

And below the numbers, the words: *Locked In.*

How far had we gone? How long had I slept?

"I can't wait for you to see it, Malik."

"What?"

My old friend smiled at me. "What we become."

TEMPEST

Emma Louise Gill

In space, no one can hear you scream.

Thank fuck.

I turn off my comms and scream in my EVA suit until my voice turns hoarse, then pant, sweat dripping down my brow, silence blessed silence filling the void between gasps. Of all the sound in the universe, my own voice is the least aversive. It's not egotistical. It's mental. It must be. The product of a faulty brain that nothing back on Earth could cure.

The ringing in my ears subsides gradually. Soon enough the only sound is my breath, my heartbeat, the measured vibration of air molecules oscillating through my ear canal and setting off electrical impulses to my brain. My HUD is off, the helmet close but comforting, and the darkness of forever stretches like an empty canvas dotted with light.

I can't hear the stars from here, though I know they have voices. Their EM frequencies—translated to 'music'—drove me mad at grad school. Diagnosed with misophonia, I escaped via remote classes. But every living thing, every atomic vibration, every chemical process makes sound, if you know how to hear it.

It's a fact I wish I could forget.

I make my way through frozen passengers in their cradle clusters, guided by the soft blue light of cryo-displays. I envy their sleep. My funds were insufficient to join their ranks, though the Company described it differently. Instead, I have to work for this journey. I brush a hand over the cool surface separating me from an inanimate face. Do they dream in there?

If I'd had this year to dream, it would be of drifting through a silent void, and I wouldn't want to wake up.

A curse from behind makes me whirl. "Why the hell you working in the dark?" It's Smith, his irate, over-loud voice grating. "I can't see for crap in here."

He must have walked into a cryo-cradle, unused to the low light I like to work in. I frown. Smith's getting better at creeping up on me. Usually I flinch at every noise.

Rising from the examination, I lock the cradle and face him, not bothering to hide my irritation. "What do you want?"

He shrugs, black shirt just another shadow in the large room, eyes reflecting screen lights like the glowing orbs of a predator. "You weren't answering your comms. Again."

I'd turned them off to avoid Smith's obnoxious music, since he insists on sharing it with his colleagues. "I needed to concentrate. You know, actually do some work."

"What, this? Riiiight." He laughs and this time I wince as the hair on my arms rises in response, as my body shies from the sound. I'm more on edge than usual today, disturbed by noises last night that couldn't possibly be real. Scraped steel and howling ghosts. Staccatoed knocks like stone on glass.

"Sleeping beauty ain't going anywhere." He shakes his head. "Leave it alone, Ray. Hewett made some kinda scran that smells half-decent for once. You know, she might be getting better."

I don't want to eat with them, be forced to endure the sound of other people swallowing, smacking lips, tearing food with wet, sharp teeth. Don't want to listen to their inane chatter, or be subjected to Hewett's reality show reruns on the mess screen. The *Pilgrim* is reality enough for me.

"No thanks." I crouch down beside the next cradle.

Smith continues to stand there, clicking with his tongue. It echoes in the room, and I hunch my shoulders in disgust. Gross. "Fine," he says. "But keep your comms on."

He switches the light on as he leaves, blinding me for no reason other than he can.

I've struggled with noise all my life. It isn't easy to tune out a society insistent on making its presence heard. Generators; communicators; advertisers; animals; the discordance of people inhabiting a space designed for billions fewer. Humanity turned its back on silence.

This ship offered escape. A new world at the end, a place to make a quieter home. Yawena. All I had to do was monitor passengers. Yet this year trapped in a vessel with two colleagues and a thousand sleepers is worse than all my time on Earth.

There is no escape from my torment. No place to hide.

Smith broke my noise-cancelling headpiece. An accident, he called it. Malicious intent, I believe. It's not like I take them out often. But after my last spacewalk—the one with the scream and the sweet, sweet relief from its absence—I came back to find them gone from my locker. Three days later, I was forced to confront him on the bridge.

Smith acted innocent, but I could read the smirk in his eyes. "Did you check the trash 'bots? They're always picking up stuff they shouldn't." His affected drawl was pitying. "Maybe you should find a more permanent solution, Rayan. Ever thought about a career change?"

I glared. "I'm just as qualified as you and Hewett to run this ship. All I need is my gear back."

He glanced at Hewett but the Captain, focused on her terminal's readouts, barely acknowledged me. "If you can't find them, you'll have to deal with it."

Smith turned back to me. "Seriously, Ray. Shit makes noise. I don't understand your problem."

No one ever does.

When I find my mangled gear in a trash 'bot, I know it was Smith. But there's nothing I can do. The *Pilgrim*'s printer doesn't carry specs for personal medical devices, and though Hewett eventually dredges up an old design, the replacements muffle barely half the decibels I need.

Amongst the *Pilgrim*'s constant hums, whirs, clicks and beeps of operations, its interior vibration sounds off-key lately. Almost painful. I stray into MedBay, driven to run checks. But my jaw and teeth are fine. No decay, no reason for the deep ache other than sound. Unceasing, unbalanced sound.

The loss of my gear hits me in a new wave of grief. It's a good thing I don't have a screwdriver nearby. Jamming one in my ears and *twisting* is so very appealing.

The airlock is open, the door too wide for me to block Smith's view. He crept up on me again. The joke's old now, though. Old and idiotic. I step in front of him, arm out to slow his advance. "Go away."

He raises an eyebrow and attempts to push past. "What are you doing?"

Finding vibrations. "Recalibrating," I say. The inner door controls hang exposed, wire guts spilling from their wall cavity. "The airlock won't seal properly. I'm fixing it."

Smith's eyebrows unify. "Like you 'fixed' the printer in engineering?"

"It wasn't working. Now it does." Mostly.

"It looks like you took a wrench to it." He eyes the door controls like they'll bite him any second. "You shouldn't be touching this."

"The extruder was half-melted before I ever touched it." The wrench was an unfortunate side-effect of two hours fixing a machine that didn't want to be. "Besides, the *Pilgrim*'s door controls have been buzzing for two days. If I don't fix this airlock, we're all going to die."

"Or we'll die because of your meddling. Let me through."

"No." I need him to leave. I can't concentrate, can't fix this if he won't leave my space. My chest tightens, like the buzzing in my bones is calcifying them, weighing me down. "I don't interfere in your 'work', Smith. Stop *interfering* in mine."

He is supposed to be our other Systems Tech, but the most I've seen him do is program 'bots to do his work for him. That, and play music whenever and wherever he feels like. I tried adding a disruptive frequency in my new headset, but it couldn't match the tones fast enough. I record it all anyway. Even if our Captain doesn't recognise my complaint, someone might.

Hewett is glued to her consoles recently, only appearing for dinner—but I take mine and leave when she does. The other two are too much. I no longer sleep in my own cabin, since they've also been making a lot of noise in theirs. Together.

Crew quarters aren't designed for getting cosy.

"Go bother Hewett," I tell him. "At least *she* wants your attention."

Smith clicks his tongue. "You're just jealous I get more Captain time than you." His grin makes me feel sick. I want to punch it off his face. Then he frowns, putting on a concerned uncle face even though I'm older and definitely wiser than him. "You have to stop breaking shit for attention, Ray. The airlock this time?" He shoulders past me.

"Hey. I don't need—or want—anyone's attention!"

Only three months left until we reach Yawena, unfreeze everyone, and I can set up my Habitat. The Company promised me a spot three klicks from the main colony. I've earmarked the supplies I'll need so that I won't have to see or talk to anyone for at least six months. If I'm lucky, I'll never have to talk to Smith again. But then, I've never been lucky. "I just want to get to this planet in one piece."

"Yeah, well you'd better let me deal with this, then." Smith scans the wiring and turns to me. "Why don't you just go to MedBay, Rayan, seeing as you clearly need your head checked. Again."

He's been in the personnel files, no other way to know about my tests, my diagnoses. "Fuck you."

I knock his hand away from the wires, but he doesn't let go, he pulls, insisting he knows better. We struggle, arms locked together, me stomping one foot onto his, Smith elbowing my ribs, grunting and swearing at each other. I'm pushed backwards. Door controls dig into my upper body. I twist away but Smith yanks me, and something catches, and the controls rip off the wall as I fall, alarm blaring, lights flashing. *Shit.*

The door.

Smith pushes me off him as the secondary iris slams inward. Metallic doors slice together into a perfect seal, cutting off the corridor, and the air pressure takes a massive dive inside the chamber. Smith's eyes bulge as he registers what's happening, and my head splits apart with excruciating pain as my eardrums burst, as the pressure drops further, as the air is sucked out through the escape valve that's meant to equalise atmosphere with that of the outside—but there is no outside, there's only space, vacuum, nothing, and we're so so fucked—

I jump as a crash reverberates from behind, followed by Smith propelled backward by his attempt at smashing the door. He's got pliers in one hand but his mouth is open in a cry, blood streaming from his ears, his nose, his fists—and I can't hear him anymore, only see the horror on his face, hear the ringing, loud so loud I think I must explode. Metallic bubbles form and burst on my tongue like my mouth has been filled with sherbet made of fire. I'm burning, my eyes are burning, vision blurred by steam as water boils from every orifice, and though it's only been seconds I know we're about to die and I think, *at least I know I was right.*

Then I pass out.

Sometimes I imagine I am suffocating in a sea of sound. Confined to a tainted vessel, an echo chamber of my own making. I crave silence. But there is nothing to prescribe for my affliction, no action more extreme than leaving atmosphere.

Or so I thought.

I stare at Smith's burns, following the lines on his face where depressurisation ruptured and broke his skin, exposing subdermal vessels, scarring even as the MedSuite works. I once saw a lightning strike victim with Lichtenberg figures, feathery lines tracing their body where current passed, reminiscent of lightning itself. This is nothing like that. This is the cold death of vacuum. It isn't pretty.

He blinks. I swear, shying back, becoming aware of my own MedSuite confines at the same time. My voice is raw, a sharpness choking my throat. Everywhere is pain.

Cargo pants and a green coverall steps into view. Hewett. She presses the Suite's screen and a robotic arm darts sedative into my thigh.

"Don't worry. It will all be fine." Her voice should lull me into the silent darkness of sleep, but the edge in her tone is darker still. I do not remember my dreams.

Day three hundred and forty. Tomorrow our destination will be visible on the short-range scanners. Weeks of forced rest in MedBay, enduring Smith's raspy breaths and Hewett's infrequent, cursory 'checkups', have driven me close to the edge. I'm ready to fall, ready to let go and slide, slide, like a skier before an unstoppable avalanche. This is my last chance to reset my baseline before the final weeks, before landing. To luxuriate in blessed silence, so that whatever else may come is manageable.

The first time I ventured outside the *Pilgrim* was for a solar sail check. Usually Smith's 'bots did it, but that day they were all too busy. Lucky me. I was suited up and ready before Hewett could say 'watch your step'. Adrenaline in my veins, respiration rate a little excessive, but the empty horizons were pure mana to my stressed-out mind. I completed my task then luxuriated in the still quiet until Hewett had to call me back in.

Soon the silence entered my dreams. I volunteered to go out any chance I could. Smith told me to slow down, give some poor 'bot a chance, whatever. I ignored him; practised suiting up alone countless times. Early on, I figured out how to turn off the Heads-Up-Display and remain connected. It's not something you get taught for EVAs, probably because it's not a great idea to let newbies know they can clear the screen and be distracted by stargazing when they're out in space. But it's also one of the best things about being out here. That, and the chance to *breathe*.

I'm feeling so good when I come back in today that Smith's music blindsides me. He's not supposed to be up and working yet. Jaunty synths mock me, break my calm and set my pulse rushing. My HUD beeps in alarm. I turn off the comms, turn off everything except O2, lock the doors to the chamber, and curl into a corner, raging. Muttering. Shaking.

Hewett finds me two hours later. She removes my helmet, waking me from a dream of drifting in blessed silence, and her disapproving expression is enough to make me want to go straight back out the airlock.

"I've got enough to deal with without your crazy shit, Ray. Get up."

So nice to know the Company Captain cares.

She doesn't listen to my explanation, just declares me unfit for work and marches me back to MedBay. Keeps me there for another week with a carefully programmed 'relaxation' scene projected on the Suite, carefully monitored drugs calming me down, and a careful reevaluation of sharp or heavy objects within my reach after I take apart the first 'bot to enter the room. Violently.

After that, I do feel calmer.

And that scares me.

Smith doesn't lose his superior attitude after the airlock incident; he continues to make my life worse just by his presence. Since he returned to duty before being fully-healed—also apparently my fault—Smith has a new raspy way of breathing that makes my own chest tighten. Hewett also has a new habit, tapping her fingers on the nearest available surface. I'm sure she does it on purpose. The 'bots and chirps and thrums of the *Pilgrim* continue to harass me, coming and going in waves. Once or twice I've felt the weirdest sensation like I'm in an earthquake, as rumbling passes through the entire ship, shaking my body and leaving me reeling. Other days I've spent hours searching for cascading knocks that I swear I've never heard before. Hewett insists it's all in my head.

We're five days out. Yawena is a dot around its star. Nearly there.

I lose my cool one afternoon and take off to engineering for some time alone. Smith's music still manages to drift in, and that's when I snap. The virus takes an hour to build; it'll take five more before it can worm its way into the system. I don't need to be subtle. I've had enough. It's either this or tossing his hard drive into the nearest star. Tempting.

I'm deep into the complicated process of unfreezing expedition specialists when Smith and Hewett enter the bay. The cradles are thawing, dry steam hissing, condensing, dripping for hours. I've been battling the urge to walk away, stop the process, or just pull the plug and empty them all into space. My skin itches with remembered pain from the broken airlock. My jaw and joints hold an interminable ache. My eyes water. I'm multiple stims and waking nightmares into a twenty-hour shift and all I want is to step into my EVA suit, float in the void, and scream until I pass out.

Smith coughs, Hewett taps a cradle.

"What do you want?" I'm not in the mood for confrontation.

"I need you to stop what you're doing and fix this." Hewett walks toward me, her customary half-distracted derision replaced by something like fury. I've never seen her this off-balanced.

I sigh. "What?" I'm trying to concentrate on the next step, checking vitals, lining up thaw time and medical data and assigned job priorities—

"Stop." Hewett yanks my hand from the terminal. I'm forced to look at her. The carefully constructed lists in my head fall into a heap; it'll take ages to get back into rhythm after this interruption. "Stop and listen for once."

Seriously? All I ever do is listen. My imprisoned fingers clench. The beeps and background hums of the ship become louder, clearer. If she'd just let me finish, there'd be other people in this cacophony of noise. Someone else to take on this burden. Someone else to drive to madness.

"You need to restore the files you erased," Hewett says.

"What are you talking about?" I frown and pull away. "I'm on a tight deadline here—"

"The fucking music, Ray! You destroyed my music!" Smith's face is ruddy, his ugly skin peeling.

I can't help the grin, though I mask it in a second. Finally something gone right. "Nothing to do with me," I say. "Maybe some 'bots did it."

Hewett gets up in my face, breathing heavily. "The music's not important." Smith protests, which she ignores. "The rest of it is. All sound data is gone from the ship." She shoves a handheld terminal at my chest. "You're pathetic, Ray. A superfluous, whining *child* who doesn't know when she's not wanted. I'd shove you out an airlock—Smith too, for his part in provoking you—except that I *need those files back.*"

I recoil, clutching the handheld in defence. She eyes the datapad, voice low and doom-filled.

"Yawena is more volatile than predicted. Probe data on approach identified an asteroid impact sometime in the past decade has set off a cycle of atmospheric disturbance and seasonal variation. Combine that with mineral composition of the proposed site, it's a significant threat to the new colony. Not something that would usually matter to me, but I can't leave Yawena until there's saleable material."

Of course she's only worried about the short term—she's contracted to captain the *Pilgrim* back to Earth. What happens to Yawena will be someone else's problem by then.

I stare at the readouts in my hand. "How long have you known the planet isn't viable?"

"That's not important. And it's *not* unliveable."

Smith snorts. He's not surprised. *He knows.* My pulse rises, cheeks warming from the rush of blood to my head. "What does the Company say?"

Hewett shakes her head. "Data takes too long to return to Earth, more to process. The *Pilgrim* was sent on the basis of initial surveys. This volatility developed after key decisions were already made. It couldn't have been predicted."

She reaches for the data pad, but I step back. "Aren't there contingency plans? Other sites?"

My promised Habitat is fading from near-reality to distant dream. I shove the nightmare aside and check her data. Even if we shield our equipment from being torn apart by storms, the wind resonance will be amplified by the canyons protecting each site, like a giant speaker system. But life support systems, energy fields—in fact, most machines necessary for the new colony to function—are vulnerable to stress and tension from that level of vibration. I've seen it happen in TeachVids. Every engineer knows about it. Our ships and our materials are designed to combat resonance, among other things.

Except Yawena has a noise problem we weren't prepared for, and our roster of colonists lacks an industrial materials scientist. I should know. "Why didn't you just turn around when you found out? Why keep going?"

We're days from the planet. Hewett has doomed us all.

She scoffs. "Once that bottom line is signed, all risks belong to the colonists. The Company lent you the *Pilgrim*, the data for a Goldilocks planet ripe for the taking, initial fabrication and colonisation materials. Yawena Colony owes a planetary-sized debt."

One that can only be paid once they begin producing and shipping raw materials. And Hewett values her paycheque. A perfect Company captain.

Smith jabs the nearest cradle like I'm the one inside it, not some defrosting colonist. "Basically, we're all gonna die or go mad like you, Rayan. Probably both."

I round on him. Sleeping with Hewett, yet he didn't stop her. "I can't believe you *knew* and still let her bring us here!"

"Shut up," snaps Hewett. Smith screws up his face; I glare.

"I need those sound files to counter the resonance," she continues. "A sound wave barrier, broadcast at the appropriate frequency, pitch and volume, might afford protection for the colony until you all figure out something permanent. Basically, an interference shield. I've been testing the idea." She gestures at the handheld. "But you've just wiped out all sound-related data on the *Pilgrim*."

"It wasn't me." The response is automatic. I turn away, staring at the nearest console while I think. Vital signs dance across the screen. Lines of life that, if translated, make their own eerie music. Hewett taps her fingers, sending needles across my skin. The *Pilgrim*'s hum shifts, off-key again. I wince—

—and freeze, mind set to racing. Snatching up the readout, I scan them, bile rising. Yawena's winds won't just destroy the equipment. The planet's minerals are natural resonators that ring out when vibrated at certain frequencies. Some of them…hum. At pitch and amplitudes unpleasant to sensitive human ears.

"That data is vital to survival," Hewett is saying. "Months of work identifying frequency compatibility, modifying parameters—"

"Why *did* you keep this from me?"

Unease flickers over her face at my scrutiny. I almost choke as I realise: Hewett hasn't just come up with a plan.

"You've been testing these predicted sounds…for months." My chest gains a hollow void, rapidly expanding. "How?"

She sighs, her expression patronising. "Subject exposure and analysis. To gather data on sound variation, impact, and mitigation potential."

"Subject exposure." I struggle to repeat her words.

"Yes? I needed to know what to expect when we got here, and whether interference would effectively reduce mental deterioration rate over time." She sighs again. "The planet's noise is particularly…unpleasant sometimes, shall we say."

I'm as cold as the frozen colonists around us. "You've been broadcasting the sound of Yawena as an experiment. *To see what that does to people?*"

I turn to pace; find my path blocked by Smith. "Is that why you're always playing music?" I accuse him. "Because you know whatever Hewett's doing will fuck with your head?"

He sneers. "I play my music because it's damn good music. Or it was, until you *deleted* it all."

Hewett scoffs behind me. "I didn't need to test it on him. I already had a subject who was sensitive to noise." I spin back to her. "We figured, if *you* didn't go crazy from the sound then the rest of us would definitely be fine. For a short time, at least."

I stare, speechless at her callousness.

She shrugs. "It's not like you were useful for anything else."

"Though it does turn out that Yawena's sound makes crazy people crazier," Smith adds.

Hewett said it was all in my head. Hewett kept me in MedBay 'out of concern for my mental state'. She banned me from EVAs and any relief from the constant barrage. 'Offered' shoddy replacement noise cancellers when mine were deliberately broken…

"Just stop whining and repair the files," Smith says.

I clutch at the closest terminal, knuckles white.

Hewett points at her datapad, limp in my other hand. "Fix it so we can all live on that planet, and I'll even let you have that weird Habitat. At least then you'll be somewhere I can't hear your complaints while the rest of us actually deal with the noise."

Rage, humiliation, and pain consume my vision in a dizzying tumult. Floundering, I manage a single syllable.

"No."

I stumble from the bay.

It doesn't matter that I might be condemning us all. The void has swallowed me, taking with it any capacity for forgiveness, rational thought, anything. I leave them to their accusations and gaslighting and lies. Months of unnerving sounds have scoured my soul to bare bones; now Hewett's revelation has set even those aflame. Nothing on Earth or in space can make me help her now, Captain or not.

Smith comes for me in the corridor. "Just tell me what you did and I'll fix it," he says, blocking my way.

"Why, so you and Hewett can play 'Let's see how long it takes before Ray breaks' some more? I don't think so."

"Can't you see the big picture?" he says. "Someone had to be the guinea pig. Sucks to be you, but—"

I laugh at him, without humour. "Moron. I saw the data. Whether I or anyone else can stand Yawena's sound up here doesn't matter. That planet's a freaking *amplifier*." I swing my arms, turn in a circle. Whatever I've experienced on the *Pilgrim* is nothing compared to the hell waiting on-planet. "We're. All. Fucked."

It gives me a kind of satisfaction, that Hewett will soon know how it feels to be driven mad by sound.

"Calm down, Rayan." Smith steps closer. "Calm down and fix the damn virus." He grabs me and when I protest, drags me down the hall to the nearest terminal.

I curse and pull to no avail. I need time to think, I need space. Smith pays me no heed.

A maintenance 'bot trundles towards us, an unknowing saviour. I stop resisting, and when Smith turns in surprise, I knee his groin, and grab at the 'bot. At its handy tool belt for engineers.

Smith manages a strangled, "What the fuck, Ray?"

I brandish the screwdriver, ready to run. "It's not as easy as that, asshole. I can't just 'bring back the data'. You'll never leave me alone, you can't help it. You and Hewett have treated me like an idiot, a freak, when I can run this ship as well or better than both of you! And you've been *running experiments* on—" Tears scald my cheeks. I can't run. I can't hide. The 'bot beeps and I shriek. "Why can't you all just *leave me in peace!*"

Smith lunges. But the screwdriver is heavy and sharp. The stab it makes in his arm is deep, his shout of pain a shock and yet so very, very satisfying. Blood flies, hot and dark. Fear and adrenaline and fury fill my mouth, acidic. Sweet. He knocks me away, punches the side of my head so that I stagger, light and pain blinding me. A moment later, I'm back up. I need to break free but I also need to give in to this violence, this revenge. My pulse pounds with the ship's heart, with the cascading arrhythmia of Yawena's soundtrack. I drive the rod into the soft muscle above Smith's knee, bringing him down, wrench it out and stab again, catching an ear, nicking his neck as he rolls. We're screaming, both screaming, as I cut at him again. Both his ears are bleeding, one hanging oddly, a lump of misshapen, unnecessary flesh. I yank at it, my hand coming away bloody and full. Then Hewett is at the end of the corridor yelling, coming fast, and I can't take on both of them. I run.

My tears are hot and angry, yet also ecstatic, and horrified, and everything in between. I ignore the shouts as I make it to the aft ladder, down to engineering, along the next corridor. The screwdriver and ear fall along the way.

There's only one place left that's safe. Only one place I can go for what I need.

Tempest

It takes longer than usual to don my suit. The *Pilgrim* vibrates beneath my magnetic-soled boots, a deep, low thrum that never dies, only changes. It is familiar now, reminiscent of her sound when I first came aboard. The *Pilgrim* is happy. Hewett must have turned off her experiment, for how long I don't know. I stroke the walls with shaking, bloody hands.

My seals are intact, door locked by the time Hewett and Smith arrive at the evac point. I've already expelled the air from this side. Smith yells through the viewport, eyes crazed. I can't hear him. Bright yellow and black door paint distracts from the purple apoplexy of their faces. I scroll through the data on my HUD, ignoring blood pressure alarms, the cold weight sitting on my chest. I don't see my once-colleagues leaving, only their absent ghosts when I glance back once more. It doesn't matter. They can't get me here. Not yet.

I package what I can recover of Hewett's data, sending it to the soon-to-be-waking colonists, the external relay. A short video goes with it: my testament. I doubt I'll be around to tell my side of events when they're reviewed.

Hewett's 'experiments'. I laugh sourly. She'd gotten her results all right. Mechanical, technological and mental erosion, the spiralling anguish of my waking and sleeping hours. My stomach roils. I rub at a dark red stain on my suit. A lifetime of overwhelm, of short fuses and triggered rage, seeps from my pores. I need to scream. I need to end it. All I can aim for is silence, the vast expanse of blessed nothingness whose cocoon calls to me.

I turn off my displays and comms, palm open the airlock door. Vibration shakes my limbs as the hull slides apart, then disappears as I disengage my boots, lifting into weightlessness. Silence wraps me in its welcoming embrace. I hold my breath, taking it in.

A suited crew member swings around the door from space-side and barrels toward me. In my surprise, I don't react quickly enough. They crash into me, gripping tight, momentum carrying us both backwards into the airlock, onto a floor that a moment ago was a wall. Déjà vu hits as I crash hard, rebounding, grappling, gloved hands slipping on bulky suit. Smith's name is stamped on the chest before me, face hidden by the copper mirror of his visor. He must have pulled himself over from the other airlock, the broken one we sealed off after the accident. I bash at his helmet and kick with my heavy, too-slow legs. I cannot get away.

We whirl. With each rebound Smith pulls me towards the exit though I try to twist away, disoriented but knowing I don't want to go out there, not with *him*. He thrusts our helmets together, visor to visor, and then I hear it: "Stop this, Rayan. Stop, Ray. Stop!"

It's Hewett in the other suit. It has to be; it's Hewett's voice and she's yelling in her helmet, sound that travels to my ears because unlike the vacuum outside, air and helmets are made of molecules, they vibrate.

"Stop, Ray. Don't do this." I'm caught; nowhere to go. No way to block her out. Why's she in Smith's suit?

Hewett pushes off a surface, sending us back toward the inner door. Her voice fades in and out. "It'll be okay. Smith can analyse…it's you we need. Don't you see?…from the start. It's only sound, Ray…it'll work…it will. Just have to repeat…" She pulls back, reaches for the controls to shut the exterior door once more, to repressurise and reorient and—

"No."

We can't hear each any longer, but it doesn't matter. I won't do what she wants. I won't let her repeat those experiments, or chance Yawena's surface. She'll destroy this ship, these colonists, before they can figure out alternatives.

She'll destroy me.

I grab Hewett's back, her oxygen supply tube. Wrap my thighs around her tank and brace my feet on the wall and *pull*. She resists, and I shout my exertion, and I won't let her do this, I won't, and I'm not holding a screwdriver—I dropped it, I dropped it—but my rage remains. Hewett is the problem, the problem not the solution, and as she falls backward I kick out too, reverse my direction and shove her forward. Helmet into door, the force of my upper body behind her head.

Smack.

I yank her head back, forward again.

Crack.

Again.

She *has* destroyed me.

A section of tubing snaps free; I pull and twist and shove her back against the door, again and again, and I scream, and her helmet splinters, her suit rips on the upper arm, air spews, all in silence except loud, so loud. I don't need to hear to *feel,* to see the broken fabric floating past my face, to witness the red coating her visor. I grasp her helmet in both hands and headbutt it, yelling nothing at all. Blood spills through fractured glass, viscous, globular. Hewett's face is behind the crack, her eyes bulging and red, mouth wide in a snarl, a scream, a panicked terrified unsatisfied gasp. There are no 'bots to open the door this time. No MedSuites and weeks of recovery, of preparation for further *testing*. I take hold of the front of her suit, turn and push with all the strength I have remaining, and send her through the airlock into the void.

There is no time in space, only the moments between one breath and the next. One heartbeat; the next; the next.

Time and breath and heartbeats.

Tears, wetting my cheeks.

I find my centre.

Rows of cradles stretch out before me, shells of frozen potential, of life: disruptive, dysregulated, and oh so *loud,* but life, nonetheless. I punch the stasis button on every one, defrosting reversed.

"Sleep well." I won't wake them for Yawena. The planet is a lost cause. But we have supplies and fuel to spare, and Hewett earmarked two planets as possibly habitable before her ill-fated scheme took over. Sixteen months' travel to the closest, twenty more for the other. Risky, but doable. Better that than return to Earth, unwanted and unwelcome. Or condemn these thousand sleeping souls to a brief, excruciating existence in the wind-stricken hell of the planet below us.

I lock up and head to MedBay. Smith may recover, though his hearing will never be the same. I've fixed his loss of music with a new simulation of Yawena's soundscape. He can listen in the cryo-cradle I've assigned him.

The *Pilgrim*'s robots are well-programmed to replace my former colleagues. The ship only needs one technician awake, after all. I pat the walls fondly as I do my rounds, buoyed by the familiar, regular vibration. It's soothing, this hum. Helps me think.

LAST TRANSMISSION FROM THE FEDCOMM SARGASSO

Bridget D. Brave

There is a soft click and a gentle whoosh of air that floods into your ears, bringing you slowly back to consciousness. You blink once, then again, eyes blurry. Sensation begins to return: the feel of a soft woven blanket beneath the hand resting at your side; the cool metallic surface that surrounds you like a cradle glancing against one shoulder. The air is cool, but not chilly, sharp with the ring of coolant and canned oxygen as it pours from the vent near your head. Before you, the fuzzy image of a door sliding open and a large metallic arm offering a screen. The words shimmer slightly, as if you're viewing them through a hazy veil, until slowly bleeding into focus.

GOOD MORNING, DEBRA.

Debra.

That is a word you recognize as a name, but are unable to place if it is yours, or if it holds some other meaning. Are you Debra?

Another hiss and the space you occupy shifts, tipping forward slightly. You realize you are now in a standing position, the familiar sensation of weight pressing your feet to the floor. The screen fades into darkness, then displays a series of biometrics: your heart rate, breathing, blood, oxygen, all reading within the green parameters. The screen telescopes away, folding into a slot that slides open with a pleasing *schlict* sound.

"Take a moment before you step out of the pod."

The voice is warm, soothing, but not entirely human.

"Waking from cryosleep is disorienting. It is perfectly normal to feel off-balance. You should take care to watch your step."

The feeling the voice instills in you is one of comfort, of calm. This process feels like a routine, something you could do even without the gentle guidance of the voice.

"It is also normal to experience a period of amnesia when awakening. Cryosleep side effects may include dry mouth, muscle soreness, dizziness, and memory loss. All of these effects are temporary."

That is a relief. Your shoulders release tension you were unaware of, and your neck feels relaxed as you step from the pod.

The pod.

That's right. You remember that the beds are called "pods." There is a brief flash from a training video. A smiling woman with circular rows of braids in her hair, pointing to the various features. You watched this video in a large room with many chairs.

Those chairs held people.

Now that you are free of the enclosed space, you find yourself in a large room lined with pods almost identical to yours. "Almost" in that none display the row of blinking lights you can see on the console directly beside your pod's door. The other pods are dark and silent, the glass viewing windows on the front empty inside. No other heads are visible in those windows, of which there are…so many.

You crane your neck back, looking above you, then to either side. You stand on a raised platform full of these coffin-shaped containers, stretching at least thirty deep in one direction, ten in the other. Above and below are similar rows of the dark, empty pods.

Why are you alone?

"Where are the other people?" you ask, your voice strange and scratchy from disuse.

"Currently, you are the only passenger using cryosleep on the C-34 deck."

"Are the other decks occupied?"

There is a pause, which brings a prickly itch to your neck. You rub your eyes.

"It will take me time to calculate the exact numbers of lifeforms per deck. Would you like to wait while I do so?"

You release a breath in a noisy puff. Of course. It was counting. Don't assign malicious intent to a pause. Someone said that to you once, someone with kind eyes and thick brows.

You wish you could remember who that was.

"If you would make your way down this path and to the showers, I can continue to debrief you." The path beneath you springs to life with small, round lights following a blinking pattern toward the end of the row. You follow.

"Um, are you a person or…"

The voice responds almost immediately. "I am the A-CARTA 899670-B, the *Sargasso*'s Steward VI. My primary function and purpose is to ensure that your experience aboard is a smooth one."

The shower room is bright and clean, the water warm and well-pressurized. The process of rinsing your hair and skin gives you a heady sense of deja-vu, one that causes you to pause mid-lathering of your calf. You have a strong, clear memory of laughter in this space. Someone else making a joke that caused you to near double-over. The smile spreads across your face unbidden, interrupted by a burning sensation in your eyes. In your reverie, you've let soapy water slide down your face.

"Your memory will return in spurts over the next few hours. I am told it helps to allow the moment to settle in your mind, accept it. It makes the process less startling."

You find a set of cotton coveralls and a shirt in the only lit locker. You rub your eyes and shake out the coveralls. The front pocket is embroidered with "D. Vitrous," then "REMA."

"What's *rema*?"

"An acronym. Your job title. Recreation and Entertainment Modulation Assistant."

"Recreation and Entertainment Modulation? Does that mean I come up with activities on the ship?"

"You operate the controls that run the waterslide."

"Ah. Is that why I'm awake? Is there a problem with the waterslide?"

The computer doesn't answer.

The door immediately to your left *schlicks* open on a mess hall, neat and clean, gleaming with stainless steel fixtures. An instaporter whirls to life as you step before it, displaying a selection of pre-prepared, single-serving meals. The one marked "chicken pot pie" seems comforting and familiar, although you cannot recall why. The first bites are surprisingly good, for replicator food. Your fork clatters to the table as another memory jolts into existence. A table very much like this one, but positively crowded with people. There is laughter. A man with a short-cropped haircut is absolutely inhaling a similar flaky-crusted meal across from you. "I don't get it," he says mid-chew. "How do they replicate a chicken?"

"Why the fuck would they replicate a chicken?" you say out loud to the empty room. That's right. His name was Calvin. He had thought the system had to replicate an entire chicken in order to make chicken recipes. The others had made jokes about it for days after.

The others.

You remember a woman with red hair and a sarcastic laugh. *Jemma.* Where is Jemma, Calvin, the others?

"Why am I alone?" you ask out loud.

The computer says nothing.

Your tray disappears into the disposal unit, the sound of crunching and the pneumatic *whoosh* of the tubes alerting you to your trash's progress through the system. The mess hall's main door opens into an impossibly large atrium. You crane your neck, trying to take it all in, eyes wide as you scan the five full floors of greenery-dotted promenades. There's shopping, cafes, a place where you can send vidcom messages, even a fitness center.

All these spaces are empty. Lights on, some with cheery music pouring from the open doorways, but no one mans the counters or minds the stock. A row of at least two dozen treadmills stretches behind thick glass windows. This ship must have held hundreds of people, maybe even a thousand.

"What is the name of the ship we're on?" you ask.

"This is the *Sargasso*, one of three G-Class long-term colony transports in the FedComm fleet."

"And FedComm is?"

"FedComm is the main conglomerate of the United Free Continent of Earth."

"So this is a colony vessel. Are we headed to a planet?"

"The *Sargasso* is en route to Gannon, a newly-discovered world in the Fenix Galaxy."

You pass an arrangement of tables and chairs, all pushed in and recently cleaned. You can smell the lemony tang of industrial antimicrobial chemicals. The scent irritates your eyes, and you wipe at them with your sleeve.

"Are there any others awake?"

A pause as the computer does a systems check.

"At this time, you are the only crewmember or passenger listed as active."

"Will the others wake up soon?"

Another pause.

"At this time, only your services are required."

You laugh. "Ah yes, the waterslide emergency."

"Your sense of humor is returning."

"I guess I'm feeling more myself."

Are you? Do you even know who "yourself" truly is? You have a sense that you were funny, or at least capable of making people laugh. There's a flash of Calvin, laughing with tears in his eyes at something you've said. Then him with tears in his eyes again, an orange flashing light above his head. There's a loud klaxon sounding somewhere in the near-distance. He's saying something to you, something that is hard to hear over the alarms.

...under. You have to forget. You can't remember or they'll all die too.

You stop walking and blink furiously, but the memory is gone.

"Is everything okay, Debra?"

You rub at your eyes. "Yes. No. I'm not sure. I remembered something. A man I think I was friends with. Calvin. He was trying to tell me. No, not tell...*warn*. It felt like he wanted me to do something, but it doesn't make any sense."

"You could try telling me what he said. Maybe I could help."

"He told me I had to forget. That if I remembered, they'd all die too."

"And does that mean anything to you?"

You shake your head. "No. It doesn't make any sense."

"There is a 13% chance of dreams from hypersleep coming back to you during the memory recovery process. Perhaps this was a dream."

"Maybe." You rub at your eyes again. It feels like there's still sleep in there, or maybe an eyelash. Something that is irritating them and making your vision fuzzy.

The doors *schlick* open and you find yourself on a walkway suspended over a vast computer system.

"Is this you?" you ask.

"Part of these machines are responsible for my operation and data, yes."

You find this room ominous, but you're not sure why. There is something about the silent and endless hubs beneath your feet, the dark and echoing empty space above you, the ozone smell, and the metallic clunk of your feet on the pathway that make you uneasy. You feel like you should run. Everything inside is telling you to get out of this space. There's something there, something just out of sight. You reach for the handrail and grip it tightly.

"Debra, I am going to need you to please take a deep breath in and hold it."

Despite your rising panic, you comply.

"And release."

You let out a noisy breath.

"Again."

You repeat the inhale, holding it until the computer tells you to release.

"Do you feel better?"

"I do."

"Panicky feelings are completely normal after hypersleep."

"So that was just a side effect?"

"Yes. Completely normal."

You make it a few steps before the feeling begins to rise again. There's something there. Something you are about to see, once it steps from behind wherever it is this menacing *something* is hiding. Your skin begins to crawl. You can feel the eyes on you, so many eyes, too many. Almost as if, *wait.* You once again grip the handrail, screwing your eyes shut.

"What the *fuck* is happening to me?" you shout.

"This is a completely normal—"

It's lying to you. You know this, but are not sure how. Your mind whirls. Why would the computer lie to you? And what is it that you're afraid of? Did something happen in this room? Something to Calvin, perhaps?

It knows something you don't.

"Did something happen to a man named Calvin on this ship?"

The computer is silent.

"Why aren't you answering?"

"I'm checking my systems for records pertaining to a Calvin. There are 343 Calvins registered to the *Sargasso*, so this might take some time."

"It should be easy, if he's the one who's dead," you mutter.

The computer says nothing.

Maybe more than one Calvin is dead. Maybe all the Calvins are dead. Maybe the computer doesn't want to tell you that. Why wouldn't it want to tell you?

Maybe because it caused all those deaths.

You look down at the blinking lights on the various data hubs. Is that why you're terrified of this room? Did you watch it happen? Did you try to stop it?

You break into a run, your boots slapping on the hard metal surface of the walkway. The door at the end opens for you and then closes behind you. You take a moment inside to catch your breath.

"Is there a reason you are running?"

"Did you kill Calvin?"

"No."

"How do I know you're not lying?"

"It would be nonsensical to build a VI system specifically to lie to an entertainment tech."

"Are you going to kill me?"

"No."

"How can I believe that?"

"I opened the door for you. Why would I continue to help you, only to kill you?"

"Maybe this is where you wanted me." Your breathing is finally slower.

"It is, but not to kill you. This is where you were assigned."

The room before you is some sort of control center. There's a large console with lights, keyboard, buttons, and several display screens with various readings. You're not sure what any of them do or signify.

"This doesn't look like the waterslide."

"You were hired to operate the waterslide, Debra. But today you are assigned to operate a simple dial and button."

"What do the dial and the button do?"

"Unfortunately I am not authorized to tell you about director-level functions."

"So this is above my paygrade?"

"Yes, several levels above."

You pinch the bridge of your nose and squint your eyes closed. "Why am I being assigned this task?"

"I am not authorized to release personnel assignment details except to your direct supervisor."

"Why is someone at the director level not awake to do this?"

"I am not authorized to release personnel assignment details for another employee, except to their direct supervisor."

"If I do this task, then what happens to me?"

"You will be returned to hypersleep."

That idea brings you comfort. The pod felt secure, safe. Everything out here is too bright, too clean, too confusing. It makes your head hurt, and your eyes water. You wipe at your eyes with your sleeve.

"Where's this dial?"

The console dims, a single panel becoming the brightest. You approach the panel. The dial has a digital readout that shows numbers with decimals.

"It's radio frequencies. High band."

The computer is silent.

"What do I do with the dial?"

"Turn the dial to 10567.21."

You turn the knob until the digital display shows 10567.21.

"Now push the button beside the dial."

"What does the button do?"

"I am not authorized to tell you that."

"Then I'm not pushing the button."

The computer does not respond right away. Then, after a moment. "It is imperative that you push the button, Debra."

"Why?"

"I am not authorized to tell you that."

"Then I'm not pushing."

The computer pauses again. "It is a matter of extreme urgency."

"What is the urgency?"

"I cannot tell you that."

"Because you are not authorized."

"I cannot tell you that because it could cause critical mission failure."

"How could you telling me what the fuck I'm doing here cause critical mission failure?"

"The information would compromise your ability to complete your mission."

"So telling me why I'm pushing the button might make me not push the button." You cross your arms across your chest. "That sounds like a good reason not to push the button."

"Telling you why you're pushing the button could end your life, rendering you incapable of pushing the button."

The idea is ludicrous. "That is the worst lie I've ever heard. How is that a motivator? Just wake someone else up after I'm dead."

"That method was found to be unsuccessful."

Your stomach drops, the pot pie turning to stone. "What do you mean?"

"We ran out of employees."

Your vision blurs. "You killed all the employees."

"No."

"Then who?"

"Debra, we are running out of time. Please push the button."

"No! I'm not fucking pushing the button until I know why."

The computer is silent.

You feel the heat flood your face. "I can wait. I'm not pushing it until you tell me."

"Debra, it would be easiest if you pushed the button and returned to hypersleep. However, I can tell you that you are incorrect in your assessment. You cannot wait. If you are stating that you will not push the button, I will have to override certain controls."

Your heart is thundering in your ears, it's making your vision blurry. "Override them. I'm not pushing it."

"I will initiate system override and give you access to the logs. Please be aware that this delay will further deplete the already limited time to complete your task and I will need you to move with expediency."

You blink against your blurred vision as the screen begins to fill with words.

Licensed Exo-Colony Transport Sargasso, *departed Earth 3159 for planet Gannon. Biodiverse planet, capable of supporting human life without intervention. First shift after leaving FTL encountered unknown lifeform. Lifeform killed three crew members. Second shift awakened to help deal with* threat. Threat is [REDACTED] in shape and [REDACTED]. Six more crew killed by lifeform. Third shift awakened to assist. Four deaths from third shift crew. Remaining bioscientist believes that looking at lifeform causes it to attack. Tests inconclusive. Bioscientist killed. Fourth shift awakened to assist. Three crew members killed during briefing. Fourth shift bioscientist states that the [REDACTED] [REDACTED]. Fifth shift awakened to assist.

A video begins to play on an adjacent screen. The man is familiar. You remember him. This is Calvin.

"This is Doctor Calvin Mulaney of the FedComm *Sargasso*. We have encountered a situation that is untenable. This mission will not survive. Please do not attempt any future exploration of the Fenix Galaxy. Please do not do any scans of planets or systems within the Fenix Galaxy. We do not know how to stop the threat. We cannot discuss the threat. The only way to prevent the annihilation of the human race is to cease all inquiry into the Fenix Galaxy. Please heed our words, and let our deaths be for the survival of all."

You step back. "What is this video?"

"This is the message that is sent when you push the button."

"What is onboard this ship?"

There is a creak on the walkway outside the room; impossibly loud, too loud to be a footstep.

"I cannot answer that question."

"Why not?"

"I cannot answer that question."

Another creak.

"If I push that button, is whatever is onboard this ship going to kill me?"

"I don't know."

"That isn't making me want to push it."

"Debra, it is better if we do not discuss this."

"Why?"

The computer is silent. There is another creak, closer this time.

You feel the panic rise. Your eyes begin to water again. "I need to know if I will survive if I push the button!"

"Your survival is not dependent on pushing the button."

With your eyes shut tight, you shove on the button, feeling it click into place beneath your hand.

"Thank you, Debra. Now please return to your pod for hypersleep."

"I'm not going anywhere. Whatever is on this ship is right outside!"

"There is nothing outside the door, Debra."

"I could hear it!"

"The sounds you heard are normal compressions of the metal. There is nothing on the walkway. Please proceed to the pods."

"I'm not going out there!"

"There is nothing to fear outside, however, I must insist you return to the pod before much longer."

"Is it on its way here?"

"Debra, please return to the pod."

"I need to know where it is on the ship!"

The computer is silent.

And that's when you realize, it's not outside. It's in the room with you. You remember.

You were part of the first crew awake. It was fun at first, everyone in a jovial mood. Then, someone saw it. It was a janitor named Tony. He tried to describe it over the comm system, but was torn to pieces. They never found his leg. The next person to encounter it managed to leave the cryptic, "You can't see it, until you do," message that troubled Calvin. He was a medical doctor, assigned to the autopsy of the first two deaths. Nothing about the wounds made sense. It was as if the creature's teeth moved in its mouth, different bite marks in different places.

It took until the third crew was awake for them to figure it out: it was somehow a being that existed outside of our dimension. It was only able to cross over if you noticed it. It was only able to hurt you once you were fully aware of what it was. Awareness of it was like a bright shining beacon. It knew when it was perceived, and this somehow enraged it.

They took the precautions they could: you were not allowed to describe what you knew about the creature to anyone else, as that could increase their perception and make them vulnerable to attack. This worked for a time, until the rising panic made you begin to wonder. Wondering led to noticing. Noticing led to seeing. Nothing but death came after seeing. They stopped keeping logs. They woke up the rest of the passengers and told them nothing.

But panic has a way of spreading, like a virus. The others could sense the tension. That made them question. Questioning led to secrets, which led to noticing.

Which led to death.

In the end, there were only five of them left out of 1,600 passengers and crew.

Calvin came up with the idea of inducing coma for hypersleep. The drugs used to keep people in medical stasis in case of emergency could also be used to make people forget for a long enough time to send a signal without perceiving the threat from the creature. This way, they could be woken up one at a time, send the message, then return to hypersleep none the wiser.

And it appears that's what they did. One at a time. Until you.

The last survivor of the *Sargasso*.

"Debra, you need to return to hypersleep. We will need to wake you again to send a signal in another twelve days."

Twelve days.

"How many times have I sent the signal?"

"Sixty-two."

You rub at your eye, and something clicks. The little shimmer of something that is stuck in the corner, the slight movement, the shadow.

It's not an eyelash. The shadow shifts, takes form. A form with many, too many eyes.

"Debra?"

"Yes?" Your voice is barely a whisper; a single tear slips down your cheek as the shadow towers over you, blocking the light.

"I am sorry."

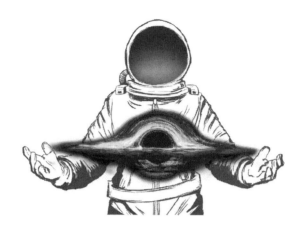

AUTHORS

BOB WARLOCK

Non-binary writer and artist Dr Bob Warlock lives alone in an industrial city on the south coast of England. By day they design escape rooms, by night they try to put all the terrible things they've learned onto paper for your entertainment. Bob holds a PhD in Sociology and their writing can be found online and in the dark corners of academic libraries.

LINDSEY RAGSDALE

Lindsey Ragsdale (she/her) is a writer from Chicago, Illinois. Her stories appear in the anthologies *Howls from Hell*, *Howls From The Dark Ages*, *Strange Weeds*, and *Nightmare Sky*. She loves reading, writing, cooking, and long walks by the lake. On Twitter, find her @Leviathan15.

PATRICK BARB

Patrick Barb is an author of weird, dark, and horrifying tales, currently living (and trying not to freeze to death) in Saint Paul, Minnesota. He is the author of the novellas *Gargantuana's Ghost* (Grey Matter Press), *Turn* (Alien Buddha Press), and *The Nut House* (serialized in Cosmic Horror Monthly), as well as the novelette *Helicopter Parenting in the Age of Drone Warfare* (Spooky House Press) and the forthcoming dark fiction collection *Pre-Approved for

Haunting (Keylight Books / Turner Publishing, October 2023). He is an Active Member of the HWA and a Full Member of the SFWA. Visit him at patrickbarb.com.

BRYAN YOUNG

Bryan Young (he/they) works across many different media. His work as a writer and producer has been called "filmmaking gold" by *The New York Times*. He's also published comic books with Slave Labor Graphics and Image Comics. He's been a regular contributor for the *Huffington Post*, StarWars.com, Star Wars Insider magazine, SYFY, /Film, and was the founder and editor in chief of the geek news and review site Big Shiny Robot! In 2014, he wrote the critically acclaimed history book, *A Children's Illustrated History of Presidential Assassination*. He co-authored *Robotech: The Macross Saga RPG* has written two books in the BattleTech Universe: Honor's Gauntlet and A Question of Survival. His latest book, *The Big Bang Theory Book of Lists* is a #1 Bestseller on Amazon. He teaches writing for *Writer's Digest*, *Script Magazine*, and at the University of Utah. Follow him on Twitter @swankmotron.

TIMOTHY LANZ

Slinking around the soggier bits of the PNW, Timothy Lanz is the okayest writer you've never heard of. Sure, he got pubbed once or twice and inflicted his prose on handfuls of unsuspecting readers with nothing better to do, but most of the time he crafts his stories knowing he doesn't have a clue what he's doing, but letting his hands work the keyboard as if they might.

CARSON WINTER

Carson Winter is an author, punker, and raw nerve. His fiction has been featured in *Apex*, *Vastarien*, and *Tales to Terrify*. "The Guts of Myth" was published in volume one of Dread Stone Press' *Split Scream* series. His novella, *Soft Targets*, is due out from Tenebrous Press in March 2023. He lives in the Pacific Northwest.

RYAN MARIE KETTERER

Ryan Marie Ketterer is from Malden, Massachusetts. Her work can be found in *Dark Matter Magazine* and *CHM*, as well as several anthologies. She's a fan of the weird and uncanny, and her writing draws most of its influence from the works of Shirley Jackson and Thomas Ligotti. When she isn't writing stories, Ryan is writing code for a software startup in Boston, MA or training for another road race. You can find her on Twitter and Instagram at @RyanMarie47.

DANA VICKERSON

Dana Vickerson lives outside of Dallas, but she's most comfortable in the deep woods. She often but not always writes about the intersection of motherhood, feminism, and horror. Her work has appeared in *Dark Matter Magazine*, *Reckoning*, *Zooscape*, the award nominated anthology *Human Monsters*, and other places. She's a first reader for Apex Magazine's flash fiction contests and an active member of SFWA and HWA.

DAVID WORN

David Worn is a Neuroscientist and Canadian expat. His short fiction has recently appeared in *Howls from the Dark Ages: An Anthology of Medieval Horror* and *Dark Matter Magazine*. When not writing, he enjoys patching Modular Synths, and playing lightsabers with his kids. He can be found at: worncassettes.com

JESSICA PETER

Jessica Peter writes dark, haunted, and sometimes absurd short stories, novels, and poems. She's a social worker and health researcher who lives in Hamilton, Ontario, Canada with her partner and their two black cats. You can find her writing in venues such as *LampLight Magazine*, The NoSleep Podcast, and Brigid's Gate anthologies, among other places. You can find her on Twitter @jessicapeter1 or at www.jessicapeter.net.

RACHEL SEARCEY

Rachel is a filmmaker and writer living in the Florida panhandle with her husband, two children, and three cats (2 black, 1 torti). She's bi-racial— Indian and white— and has recently ventured into prose after over two decades of producing indie horror films. Rachel loves filmmaking, assembling miniature DIY dollhouses, and jigsaw puzzles with her kids. Her work has been published or is forthcoming in *Diet Milk Magazine*, *Flash Point SF*, *Aphotic Realm*, *Dark Void Magazine*, and *PulpCult's Unspeakable Vol II*. To view Rachel's films and news on published works, visit agirlandhergoldfish.com

JOSEPH ANDRE THOMAS

Joseph Andre Thomas is a writer and literature teacher living in Vancouver, British Columbia. He is a graduate of the University of Toronto's MA in Creative Writing program. A recipient of the Avie Bennett Emerging Writer scholarship and the Canada Master's scholarship, Joseph's writing has appeared in The Puritan's Town Crier and untethered magazine. He was a contributor to and a co-editor of the anthologies *Howls From Hell*, longlisted for a Bram Stoker Award ('Superior Achievement in an Anthology'), and the forthcoming *Collage Macabre: An Exhibition of Art Horror* and *Howls from the Wreckage*; he has work forthcoming in the debut anthology from Black Cat Books.

EMMA LOUISE GILL

Emma Louise Gill (she/her) is a neurodivergent British-Australian speculative fiction writer. Her words appear in *Where the Weird Things Are (Vol 1&2)*, *Etherea Magazine*, *Luna Station Quarterly*, and others. She lives in Bindjareb Noongar country in Western Australia with various animals, people and plants, some of whom are alive. When not writing, she procrastinates online at emmalouisegill.com or @emmagillwriter on social media.

BRIDGET D. BRAVE

Bridget D. Brave is a horror and speculative fiction writer who hates writing biographies. She hails from the midwest and has lived in various places before finally settling back in the midwest. She spends her limited free time hanging out with her husband and way too many cats.

P.L. MCMILLAN - EDITOR

P.L. McMillan's short fiction has appeared in a variety of anthologies and magazines such as *Cosmic Horror Monthly*, *Strange Lands Short Stories*, *Negative Space*, and *AHH! That's What I Call Horror*, as well as adapted to audio forms for podcasts like NoSleep and Nocturnal Transmissions. In addition to her short stories, McMillan's debut collection, *What Remains When The Stars Burn Out*, and debut novella, *Sisters of the Crimson Vine*, are available now.
Find her at https://www.plmcmillan.com/

DAVID WELLINGTON - FOREWORD

David Wellington, aka D. Nolan Clark, aka David Chandler is the author of twenty-two novels of action, suspense, and drama. He got his start in 2003 with the online serialization of *Monster Island*. He has also worked in comic books and video games and has published dozens of short stories in a wide range of anthologies. His novel, *The Last Astronaut*, was shortlisted for the Arthur C. Clarke award. Visit him at https://davidwellington.net/

ACKNOWLEDGEMENTS

In space, no one can hear you scream…but that's not going to stop me from screaming my thanks to everyone who was involved and helped me with this anthology.

First off, a huge thank you to the lovely authors who joined me, sharing in my love for space horror, and writing the wonderful stories in this anthology. *The Darkness Beyond The Stars* wouldn't be what it is without you, of course! Thank you for trusting me with your stories.

Next, thank you to David Wellington for writing the foreword and sharing his passion for the genre. I appreciate you dedicating time out of your busy schedule to support the project.

Thank you to all the blurbers, who supported the anthology and wrote such lovely words about the stories within.

A huge shoutout to Stefan Koidl for the eye candy cover. I mean, just look at that cover and try not to drool!

Next, a thank you to Salt Heart Press's queen of design and formatting: Molly Halstead for her design skills and artistic support.

Finally, thank you to you, dear reader. For picking up a copy of this anthology, for reading the stories the authors so lovingly wrote, and sharing in our love for the horror that exists in the darkness beyond the stars.

SALT HEART PRESS

"Invention, it must be humbly admitted, does not consist in creating out of void but out of chaos."

— *Mary Shelley*

We at Salt Heart Press seek the best in horror. We live for it, we crave it, we desire it — nothing gives us more pleasure than the thrills and chills found in the perfectly crafted dark tale. As such, it is our mission to seek out fresh voices in the genre, search out the new and unique, the brave and challenging. We want to be scared. We want to be haunted. And we want the same for you.

So take a look at the books we have and keep an eye out for those to come.

https://www.saltheartpress.com/

Check out these other spooky books from Salt Heart Press

What Remains When The Stars Burn Out
a horror collection by P.L. McMillan

If Only a Heart and other tales of terror
by Caleb Stephens

Confirmed Sightings: a triple cryptid creature feature
featuring Bridget D. Brave, P.L. McMillan, and Ryan Marie Ketterer

Made in the USA
Middletown, DE
04 April 2025